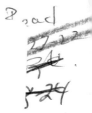

A SCANDALOUS
DECEPTION

LYNN MESSINA

potatoworks press
greenwich village

CHAPTER ONE

Beatrice Hyde-Clare owed her change in status in her uncle's household to a singular fiction invented to coax confidences out of an Incomparable during a weeklong house party at a country estate in the Lake District. Hoping to discover information about the young lady's blighted love affair with a gentleman of inferior social standing, she'd created for herself a blighted love affair with a gentleman of inferior social standing. She gave him a name, a vocation, a steadfastly disapproving father, and a scar that ran all the way from his right temple to his left nostril.

Her family, shocked to discover that the veteran of six unsuccessful seasons had not only a history but a torrid one at that, began to plot her return to the Marriage Mart. Their expectations were still low, of course, but if they anticipated a poorer quality of shopper, perhaps this time they might achieve their goal of finding a buyer.

Amused by their attitude, Bea would not have minded their renewed focus on her future if they had been content to leave her torrid past in the past. Alas, her aunt was determined to bring it into the present—something she felt confident she could achieve, for a scar that cut across a man's entire visage was a noteworthy feature.

"Naturally, I can sympathize with the challenge of locating one clerk among the droves who work in the

Chancery courts and Lincoln's Inn and the Old Bailey," Aunt Vera said with gracious concession. "But how many of these men can have angry marks on their faces?" She turned to her niece with her brows pulled tightly together, as if trying to read a sentence that was written in very small print. "You say it runs across his eye in a slash?"

Bea smothered a sigh, for she had answered this question at least a dozen times since they had come to London the week before. Their return to the capital in anticipation of the new season marked the beginning of the hunt for Mr. Davies, a development she had not anticipated, for why would her family be interested in an erstwhile beau of hers. The inability to conceive of their fascination was a failure of imagination on her part, she realized now— although, to be fair, she had never meant for them to hear the story. She'd invented it solely for the benefit of Miss Otley, who, she now knew, was incapable of keeping a secret. "Yes, from his right temple to his left nostril."

"So it is several inches long," Aunt Vera said, looking around the table as if seeking confirmation from everyone present that a line that connected those two points on a face would be of the proposed length.

"I'm not sure I would say *several,*" Bea hedged cautiously, for she had no idea the precise number of inches encompassed by that terrain. During her conversation with Miss Otley in the Lake District, she had been pulling physical characteristics out of thin air, not measuring them with a ruler. "Perhaps a few."

Her aunt accepted the qualification with equanimity. "Very well. How many clerks among the droves who work in the Chancery courts and Lincoln's Inn and the Old Bailey can have a scar on their face that is a few inches long? There may be five or six, certainly, but the number cannot reach as high as the double digits."

Bea wondered what her aunt thought a law clerk did to believe so many in the profession would have acquired such an extravagant disfigurement.

"But surely his name is all the information we need to locate him," Flora said, her hazel eyes opened wide with confusion.

At this practical observation, her brother, Russell, who shared his hazel-eyed sister's handsome looks, with auburn hair pleasantly disheveled à la Brutus, nodded at once and observed that "Theodore Davies" had a distinctive ring to it. Clearly, their father must be doing something wrong to have not discovered his whereabouts by now.

Bea found his agreement to be a particularly alarming development, for her cousins generally liked to bicker about everything, regardless of how apparent the facts, and if they'd reached consensus on a point so glaringly obvious neither one could poke a hole in the other's argument, then clearly the truth must be known to all of them.

Her shoulders tense with dread, Bea waited for Uncle Horace to raise up to his full height of five feet ten inches, narrow his heavy-lidded eyes and declare Mr. Theodore Davies to be a phantasm of his depraved niece's imagination.

It was cowardly, she knew, but she tilted her head down and stared at her plate of kippers rather than confront the contempt that was sure to be gleaming in her uncle's eyes.

And yet no startling revelation was forthcoming. Instead, Uncle Horace sighed with frustration, assured his son he was doing the best he could and promised his family he would continue to make inquiries.

It was, for all who sat at the breakfast table, a dispiriting way to start the day, but most particularly for Aunt Vera, who could not help but feel this mysterious gentleman, unknown to them prior to their September stay in the Lake District four months before, was the key to her niece's happiness.

By "happiness," of course, she meant her betrothal, marriage and removal from the Hyde-Clare household, a position the girl had assumed at the age of five, when her parents drowned in a tragic boating accident.

Although her aunt's eagerness to see her gone was hardly flattering, Bea could not take offense, for she knew how much her presence vexed her aunt. Newly married and three months away from setting up her own nursery, Vera Hyde-Clare, née Harkness, had not anticipated having to care for the child of her husband's older brother, whom she had met just once and fleetingly at that. Unfamiliar with the details of her husband's resentments, Vera knew only that they were longstanding and deep, which was more than enough for her to adopt them.

Years ago, after that first inauspicious season, she had resigned herself to the inevitability of Bea's enduring presence, for the girl wasn't lively enough or interesting enough or pretty enough or wealthy enough or clever enough to attract a suitor.

And now suddenly, as if out of nowhere, there was a countervailing narrative to the one she had told herself for almost a decade. Her niece had found love! Yes, she had found it with a meager law clerk well beneath her station whom they would never invite to share their table, but it was still an accomplishment of which nobody had believed her capable. The affair had ended on a desperately sad note for Bea, with the love of her life marrying another and settling into blissful domesticity in Cheapside with their children.

Aunt Vera, however, refused to be daunted by the tragic ending, for if mutual love had blossomed once with a law clerk, it could blossom again with another.

Although she personally could not comprehend what an eligible young man might find to admire in her niece, she knew the ways of the heart often defied logic. That Mr. Davies had succumbed to Bea's paltry charms proved incontrovertibly that love was irrational. Now she was convinced that if she could simply locate and study the law clerk, she would be able to decipher the elements that had attracted him to Bea and made Bea attractive to him in return. All she needed to see her niece permanently settled in her own establishment was more information about the type of man who appealed to her.

Obviously, this plan was ridiculous, and Bea could not believe that her uncle had fallen in line with it or that her cousins continued to support it. Whatever strange impulses moved the human heart, they certainly could not be distilled down to a few easily identifiable character traits to be effortlessly reproduced and molded into a reliable facsimile of the original. If Mr. Theodore Davies had been an actual flesh-and-blood man, not merely a devious calculation to elicit confidences from Miss Otley, then surely there would be something ineffably unique about him.

Bea knew better than to try to explain these self-evident truths to her aunt, for if the heart could be implacable in its desires, it was positively compliant in its open-mindedness when compared with the woman who had raised her.

To be fair, it wasn't only Aunt Vera's perception of Bea that had altered with the revelation of a secret beau; her cousins looked at her differently as well. Twenty-year-old Flora, who was days away from the start of her second season, thought it was remarkably dashing of her cousin to initiate a romance with a man wholly unknown to her. She found it difficult enough to create a meaningful connection with a gentleman with whom she had an acquaintance or two in common, so the prospect of Bea striking up a conversation with a handsome and intriguing stranger confounded her. In her wildest imaginings, she would never have thought her cousin had the pluck. She'd certainly never demonstrated it in the ballroom or the drawing room.

Russell, likewise, had assumed Bea was too dull and plodding to ever engage in any behavior the *ton* would deem scandalous. That she had succeeding in pulling off an entire courtship behind his parents' backs encouraged him to wonder what feats of stealthiness he himself might aspire to, and he repeatedly asked for instructions on how to evade his parents' notice. Obtaining a membership to Gentleman Jackson's Salon was explicitly forbidden for the twenty-two-year-old, but if Bea could manage an entire affair, then he should be able to contrive a training session or two.

For years, Bea had sought a more intimate relationship with her cousins, for they were the closest she would ever come to siblings, but the tenor of their interest made her distinctly uncomfortable. As the older relative, she had hoped they would look to her for guidance and advice, not tips for how to tell convincing lies and get away with secretive deeds.

By all accounts, her seemingly harmless little lie designed to inspire an honest confession had turned in a considerable problem, and Bea wasn't quite sure how to handle it. Having earned her family's respect, she was reluctant to lose it, and yet the circumstance was untenable. Uncle Horace could not keep sending out letters inquiring after a man with a three-inch scar on his face, and she could not maintain the pretense that he might eventually find him. Every day, the weight of her falsehood grew heavier and heavier.

What made the situation particularly painful for her to bear was the fact that she had actually done something deserving of their respect during their visit to the Lake District. There, at Lakeview House, when not lying to Incomparables, she had pieced together the truth behind the mysterious death of Mr. Otley.

Yes, it was true.

One of the house guests at Lord and Lady Skeffington's elegant house party had gotten his skull bashed in with a candlestick, and Bea had discovered the information necessary to identify the killer.

It was, she thought, a striking achievement.

Although her aunt was impressed by her niece's deductive skills—and, it must be said, genuinely relieved she had come to no harm in her pursuit of the truth—she was more horrified by her astuteness and daring.

No one had imagined under that placid exterior, so

docile and eager to conform to the requirements of her family, was an agile mind that could quickly knit together disparate pieces of information. She had a well-documented curiosity about the world, to be sure, for her head was frequently buried in books about faraway lands and obscure historical figures, but the importation of knowledge did not mean the exportation of wisdom.

When had Bea become so clever?

No matter how many times Aunt Vera put that question to her family—her husband, her children, even her niece—nobody had a satisfying answer.

What was especially distressing about her niece's unexpected intelligence was how liberal she was in its demonstration. Any other Hyde-Clare in the presence of an esteemed personage such as the Duke of Kesgrave, who had been a fellow guest in the Lake District, would hold her tongue in appropriate awe, but not Bea. She addressed him directly and challenged him openly and even taunted him with teasing remarks that implied she considered herself his equal.

The audacity was insupportable and no doubt unprecedented in all of his grace's two and thirty years, and the only thing Aunt Vera could think of to explain the change in her niece's behavior was exposure to the brutally slain corpse of Thomas Otley.

How thoughtless of the spice trader to provoke his murderer into bashing him on the head in the library of the elegant Jacobean manor house, where any young lady with a sleep difficulty might discover his battered body oozing blood everywhere!

If only Beatrice could have been persuaded to start reading *The Vicar of Wakefield*, which she had brought with her on the trip, rather than wandering the corridors at night, then she would never have begun investigating the death of Mr. Otley or interrogating fellow house guests or stealing into gentlemen's rooms to inspect their belongings or provoking dukes.

Aunt Vera was terrified of what her niece's newly discovered brazenness might portend for the family's success in the coming season. True, the girl had been her familiar quiet self in the intervening four months, filling the hours with her usual occupations of reading in the library and taking long walks in the countryside. But Bexhill Downs' society was sedate and dull, with few luminaries and certainly no dukes, and there was nothing to provoke a newly emboldened spinster to express her unnatural opinions.

Now that they had returned to London, however, they would be awash in opportunities, and it seemed inevitable that the chit would do something truly mortifying that would harm Flora's chances of finding a husband or injure Horace's standing at his club or deny them all vouchers for Almack's.

The Duke of Kesgrave, in particular, seemed to incite Bea's impertinence, and although Vera had gratefully latched on to his promise to call on the family in London when it was originally proffered at the end of their stay in Cumbria, for a visit from such an esteemed personage would be a coup for the pleasantly self-effacing Hyde-Clares, she hoped now that he would withhold his influence. His affect on her niece was far too dangerous.

It was little wonder, then, Bea thought with amusement, her aunt had been so grateful to learn of the existence of Mr. Davies and his ennobling scar, for he was a ray of hope just when the situation seemed impossibly dark. If her niece liked serious-minded men of the law, then they would find her a serious-minded man of the law.

In light of this discovery, Aunt Vera considered Bea's unmarried state to be partly her own fault, for she had never made her low expectations for her niece clear. If only she had thought to explain to the girl when she was still fresh from the schoolroom that they knew her to be of a shy and retiring nature and would happily consider all comers, regardless of how unconventional their upbringing.

The Hyde-Clares' standards, though inviolate for their

own children, were entirely open to negotiation for the plain-faced orphan in their midst.

Alas, Aunt Vera had not spoken so candidly with Bea, and all she could do now was apologize for the oversight and pledge not to make the mistake again. She would find her niece a lowly law clerk before the season was halfway through.

Or maybe even a quarter.

As absurd as her aunt's intentions were, Bea sympathized with her plight, for the change in her conduct unsettled her too. If she had spent her life conforming to her family's requirements, it was only because she didn't know she had a choice. When she'd arrived at her aunt and uncle's London town house as a young girl, sad and lonely and petrified of what her new life would be like, she had found little comfort or softness in her relations. After a pair of frigid hugs, she was handed off to the butler, who put her in the care of the housekeeper, who kept her company until a governess could be found. At every stop along the way she was told to be good, she was told to be grateful, she was told to be quiet and respectful and biddable. She was told to cause no problems or she would be sent to live with a family in the village, who would consign her to the scullery for the rest of her days.

Beatrice believed it, every word, and let the fear dictate almost every aspect of her behavior for the next twenty years until the moment she found herself standing in a crowded drawing room about the announce the name of a brutal killer.

It was the most outré thing a Hyde-Clare had ever done, and her family did not renounce her.

Her actions were not entirely without consequences, of course, for in the months since the house party she had been forced to endure one interminable lecture after another on how a proper young lady comported herself, including what she should do when confronted with a dead body (apologize for intruding, leave quietly and find a servant to handle the matter more fully), as if that abnormal occurrence were likely to happen on a regular basis. The rambling sessions were long, severe and tedious, but for a girl who had expected to be cast out for making a single wrong move, there was something comforting in her aunt's steadfast determination to lecture her into submission. Indeed, it was a more convincing display of her affection than the hug she had given her in the Skeffingtons' field after Bea had fought her way out of a dilapidated shed in which she had been trapped.

That her relatives seemed to hold some genuine affection for her was a revelation to Bea, and she did not know if being freed from the shackles of fear would alter her behavior in any significant way in London. She rather thought it would not, for, despite the newfound sense of security, she was still the same dowdy nonentity she had always been. Marked by features so unassuming her uncle once described them as apologetic—apologetic chin, apologetic nose, apologetic lips that pressed tightly together when something made her uncomfortable—she had never failed to blend into any setting. With her brown eyes, narrow brows and limp hair of an indeterminate color, she was as inconspicuous in the drawing room as in the ballroom, a circumstance that drove her aunt to distraction, as she'd hoped to unload the girl onto another family before it was time to launch her daughter into society.

If history was any indication, Beatrice Hyde-Clare would meet the coming season with the same sort of baffled disinterest with which she had met the previous six.

And yet there was still her interaction with the Duke of Kesgrave to consider, for it demonstrated the other side of the coin: An intelligent woman who didn't hesitate to look a challenger in the eye and question his decisions and tweak his ego when the opportunity presented itself.

Poor Aunt Vera!

The older woman was not equipped to contend with uncertainty, for she liked everything to be in its place, especially inconveniently orphaned nieces. That was why, Bea believed, she would not easily give up on her hope of leg-shackling her to the first law clerk with an interesting blemish to cross their path. Indeed, the young man—and, to be fair, he didn't *have* to be young, per se—could be from any profession so long as he had the resources to maintain a wife and family.

Or perhaps just a wife.

Really, all he needed was a cottage to bring her home to.

And of course a hovel would do in a pinch, as there was no reason to be too fine in one's notions.

Bea didn't doubt that her aunt would cheerfully marry her off to an impoverished villager if it would free her relations from their obligation.

No, she thought in amusement, Aunt Vera and Uncle Horace would never consign her to the scullery. But they were happy to let her husband do it.

Although she understood her aunt's concerns about her behavior, Bea felt they were a little overblown, for they failed to take into account the very great peculiarity of the circumstance in which she'd found herself at Lakeview Hall. In general, one did not stumble over the murdered corpse of one's fellow guest at a house party, and one certainly did not often find oneself forced to stand silently by while a constable ruled the obviously irregular death a suicide at the Duke of Kesgrave's urging. Those two events were highly unusual, and if she had not stared across the slain body of Mr. Otley at Kesgrave, she doubted she would have ever said a word to him at all. Rather than hurling insults at him directly, she would have contended herself with fantasizing about tossing selections from the various evening meals—fish patties with olive paste, stuffed tomatoes, veal cutlets, poached eggs, fillets of salmon, meringues with preserves—at his condescending head.

Bea reminded herself of this fact daily, for some part of her could not wait for the moment when she met Kesgrave again and challenged him on some new frontier. It was an absurd expectation, of course, for the circumspection of the drawing room bore little resemblance to the audacity of the murder scene. Restored to the milieu where she felt most uncomfortable, she would no doubt lapse into her usual silence.

Likewise, Kesgrave would not be the same. At Lakeview Hall, the society had been limited to the Skeffingtons' guests, a small assortment that in no way represented the usual company the Duke of Kesgrave kept. If he had favored Bea with his interest, it was only because they shared a single purpose and there were few distractions to claim his attention. In London, however, a man like Kesgrave, who had every advantage of wealth, status and disposition, did not lack for offers or diversions. Unlike her aunt, who worried that he might actually pay them a call, Bea knew the duke had already forgotten his promise, which had been issued only out of a sense of politeness, and doubted he would even recall her name if they happened to meet in the park or at a party.

Although she prided herself on being a pragmatic young lady, Bea found this thought to be upsetting in a way she couldn't properly articulate. It was not, she firmly believed, because she had formed a tendre for the duke. Without question, there was much about him to set even the most withered spinster's heart to flutter, but she was far too sensible to develop a hopeless passion for someone quite so above her touch. If he were a little less extravagant in his perfection—if, for example, his nose encompassed more of his face or his rank dropped a few notches to earl—she might have been susceptible to his charms.

No, the problem cut deeper than mere infatuation with an unattainable lord, a situation, she was convinced, she could have handled with equanimity and grace, for she was far too sensible to allow herself to succumb to any sort of romantic despair. Rather, she feared her distress had its roots in the unexpected amiability of the enterprise, the sense of camaraderie that had sprung up between them as they sat quietly by the fire in her room discussing suspects in Mr. Otley's murder. In those moments, she'd felt known by the duke in a way she hadn't been by anyone else, and it made her sad and unsettled to realize how quickly he would cease to know her.

Annoyed with the gloomy turn her thoughts had taken, Bea sat up straighter in her chair and decided she needed a distraction. She was thinking of Kesgrave now only because they would be attending the first ball of the season in a few days and her anxiety about it had increased in equal measure with her excitement.

"Flora could make a drawing of him," her aunt said as Dawson removed her empty plate from the table.

Bea's cousin paused as she lifted her cup of chocolate and furrowed her brow with curiosity at her mother. "I could?"

Aunt Vera nodded vigorously. "You're a skilled artist."

"Thank you, Mama," Flora said. "I feel that I've improved greatly in the past couple of months, and I'm grateful to you and Papa for hiring such an excellent tutor."

"I say, Flora, cut line," Russell insisted with a disgusted look at his sister. "You don't have to polish the apple so assiduously."

Offended by the implication that her words were intended to curry her parents' favor, Flora insisted she wasn't polishing anything. "I'm merely expressing appreciation for my drawing instruction just as you would for your boxing lessons."

Russell's plump lips tightened as he was reminded of a sore point, as his parents refused to condone his interest in pugilism. "I don't have boxing lessons."

"Yes, that's right," Flora said with a wide smile.

Russell seethed silently.

"You could make a drawing of Mr. Davies," Aunt Vera explained, ignoring now, as she always did, her children's bickering. "It would be based on Bea's description of him."

"Oh, no," Bea said, so startled by the idea she spoke the words aloud.

Flora's eyes lit up at the suggestion. "I could do that," she said before turning to her cousin and offering her assurance. "Truly, all you'd have to do is tell me the shape of things. His chin, for example, is it sharp or round? Then I could sketch something and you tell me how close I am to the original."

Beatrice could not imagine anything more horrible. "I really don't think—"

"Capital notion, Vera," Uncle Horace said as he looked at his wife over the newspaper. "I don't know why we didn't think of it sooner."

Her aunt preened under the compliment and turned to her niece. "There's no reason to be anxious, my dear. I'm sure you'll be able to reproduce his appearance down to the very last hair on his head. You're very good with details," she added with an accusatory note in her tone.

Aunt Vera had not quite been able to forgive her niece for having such a fine grasp on the particulars that she figured out the precise circumstance of Mr. Otley's death. If Bea were a little more scatterbrained like a proper female, then Vera would still be friends with her old classmates from Mrs. Crawford's School for Girls and her daughter might be engaged to the son of a baron.

In seeking justice for the spice trader, Bea had served her aunt a great unfairness.

"We can start after breakfast," Flora said. "Let's use the front parlor, as the light is better in there."

Bea smiled weakly as she tried to produce a picture of Mr. Theodore Davies in her head. All she saw was an angry red scar running across his face and cutting his right eye in half. It was the only thing she could visualize because it was the only feature she could recall bestowing on him. Other than the disfiguring mark, the Teddy of her memory was a jumble of vague character traits: funny, kind, intelligent.

Obviously, she could make up anything she wanted, as there was no standard against which her description would be compared. But it felt oddly terrifying to have no constraints at all. What if she wound up describing a monster?

Or, worse, someone they all knew?

As apprehensive as the drawing session made her, it was nothing compared with her agitation over how the picture would be used. Would Uncle Horace bring it down to a printshop and request copies that he could include in his letters of inquiry? Would he post it in barrister offices in Chancery Lane? Would he print it in the dailies?

Bea felt her cheeks turn unbearably hot as she contemplated the advertisement her aunt would run seeking information about the law clerk. To see his name in the newspaper under the picture that she described would be utterly—

The newspaper!

Bea bobbled the teacup in her hand as she realized the newspaper offered a way out of the contretemps she'd unwittingly created. Of course it did! All she had to do was place a death notice in the *London Daily Gazette*. Uncle Horace, who made a proper perusal of the paper every morning, would read it and share the unfortunate discovery with his wife. Aunt Vera would be desperately disappointed for a couple of days, then rally when she realized there was nothing to be done. Death came for us all in the end.

Encouraged considerably by her plan, Bea agreed cheerfully to meet Flora in the front parlor in a half hour and excused herself from the table. She had scarcely eaten anything, but she was too eager to compose the notice to linger over kippers. She did, however, refill her teacup and carry it with her back to her room.

Although she had little experience writing obituaries, she knew to keep the notice brief and to the point. "On Monday the 27th, in this city, Mr. Theodore Davies, youngest son of Mr. Harold Davies and devoted husband. His manners were most gentle, his affections ardent, his thoughtfulness was not to be surpassed, and he lived and died as became a humble Christian."

She read it through three times, confirmed the punctuation and spelling, and slid it into an envelope to mail to the newspaper. Just as she was about to seal the envelope, she realized some sort of remuneration would also have to be included, for the newspaper would not run the paragraph for free.

How much did it cost to report the fabricated death of a fictional law clerk?

Bea had no idea and realized the only way she could find out was to deliver the notice herself. Doing so meant going out alone in London, something she had never done, and she felt a momentary twinge of fear at the possible outcomes of such a bold adventure. The metropolis had always felt like a welcoming place to her, but she had never been abroad without the protection of her family or the company of her maid.

Lone females, she had been meant to understand from Aunt Vera, did not fare as well.

Although she knew her aunt was not a fount of considered opinions, Bea felt some wariness was appropriate, even in the bright light of day, and she inspected her wardrobe for the least interesting item she owned. Given the drabness of her options, it was surprisingly difficult to make the decision and, after some thought, she settled on the gray walking dress she had worn in mourning for her maternal grandfather five years before. It was an unadorned and unremarkable garment, practical in its purpose, much like herself, and she felt confident it would draw little, if any, attention.

With the notice written and her outfit selected, she could see no further reason to put off the inevitable and returned to the ground floor. Flora was waiting for her in the parlor, her charcoals and sketch pad laid out on the end table. She looked up eagerly when her cousin entered, seeming to relish the assignment—either for the challenge of capturing the appearance of an unknown stranger or finding out more about him from a firsthand source. All the information the family had gathered was courtesy of Miss Otley, as Bea had refused to discuss the matter personally with any of them, including her aunt. She claimed it was too painful.

"Let's begin," Flora said, asking first about the shape of Mr. Davies's face. Was it round, oval or square or was it more interestingly complex like a heart?

Bea closed her eyes, thought a moment and decided he had a heart-shaped face because it seemed the most challenging one to draw.

Delighted, Flora nodded and moved onto the law clerk's nose.

"It had a long bridge," Bea said, examining the bust of one of their relatives on the pedestal next to the window, with his aquiline appendage.

"Good," Flora said in encouragement. "Now tell me about the width of the bridge. Is it very narrow? Does it have any bumps or dips?"

Bea thought for a moment and identified its width as medium narrow, which sounded nonsensical to her, but Flora nodded in comprehension. "And there was a bump about halfway down."

After an hour, Flora sighed as she dropped her charcoal onto the table and announced they'd had a very good first session. She held up the sketch to reveal a firm-lipped gentleman with kind eyes, a pointy chin and an almost featherlike scar skirting his features. He looked nothing like the image in her head and yet he seemed disconcertingly familiar.

Taking her silence as approval, Flora announced that they would refine the details tomorrow. "We are close. I can tell from the look on your face."

Uncertain what her expression actually revealed, Bea nodded and thanked her cousin for making the drawing. "Your mother is right. You're a skilled artist," she observed—not only because it was true but also because she felt horrible about wasting her cousin's time. The story of her thwarted love for Mr. Davies was the first and only coldly calculated lie she had ever told in her life, and it had spiraled so wildly out of control, she wouldn't be surprised if Prinny strode into the front parlor to ask for a description of him.

It was, she thought, a salutary lesson in the destructive uncertainty of falsehoods. All you knew about a lie was where it would start, never where it would end. That kind of insecurity was not for her.

Having determined never to lie again, Bea immediately defied her own resolution by feigning light-headedness and excusing herself to go rest until she felt more the thing.

"Oh, you poor dear," Flora said with a sympathetic moue. "This must be so trying for you. To be entirely honest, I'm not sure why Mama is so focused on Mr. Davies. Her theory that we can learn more about you from the man you loved than from twenty years of living with you strikes me as somewhat flawed. To be fair, however, none of us suspected you were conducting a secret love affair with an unsuitable young man for months, so it's possible she is right and we don't know you at all."

This observation was at once thoroughly accurate and widely off the mark, and Bea could come up with no clever response that didn't make her feel even more ridiculous. Rather than say anything at all, she dipped her head in acknowledgment and left the room. Returning to her bedchamber, she immediately changed into the gray walking dress. Then she selected a poke bonnet in an equally subdued color, and tying the ribbons under her chin, confirmed that it hid her face almost entirely from every angle except directly head on. Next she considered how much funds she would need to cover the cost of transportation and the obituary. Having no idea how much either would be, she took four shillings, closed her reticule and immediately opened it again to add one more coin.

Cautiously, she stepped out of the room into the empty hallway, proceeded to the staircase and lightly skipped down the steps. Pausing briefly to confirm she was still alone, she considered the relative benefits of scurrying quickly or walking sedately. She settled on the latter and tensed sharply a few feet from the front door when Dawn suddenly stepped out of the drawing room, fully expecting to be exposed. The footman, however, brushed past her as if she were not there and disappeared into the dining room.

Once outside, Bea felt another wave of uncertainty, for she had been so consumed with the goal of exiting the house, she had not considered what to do after she'd attained it. Waving down a hack directly in front of her house would be the height of folly, she thought, and walked to the north end of the square to the busier thoroughfare. There, she hailed a cab and directed the driver to the offices of the *London Daily Gazette*. Traffic was thick in the early afternoon and seemed to grow heavier as they drew closer to the Strand, but she arrived without incident and alighted onto the crowded sidewalk in front of the office. One thirty-two was a tall brick building, narrow and simple, with grid windows, and as she stepped inside, she was taken aback by the pervasive calm that filled the room. Given the competitiveness of the newspaper business and the hyperbolic headlines used by broadsheets to grab readers' attention, she'd expected a frenzied environment, with editors yelling at reporters and reporters yelling at typesetters and typesetters yelling at printing presses and printing presses grinding loudly as their gears turned. Instead, she encountered a dozen industriously minded men working quietly at their desks in a low-ceilinged room.

Reluctant to interrupt, she stood awkwardly on the threshold for a moment, and moved forward only when the front door opened behind her and a man called loudly, "Advertising!"

Although the voiced boomed through the subdued

space, nobody looked up except for a dark-haired man in spectacles. He nodded at the newcomer and indicated with a gesture that he should step forward.

Appreciating the effectiveness of the approach, Bea shouted, "Death notice!"

To her surprise, it produced the desired effect, with the relevant editor raising his arm, if not his head. Bea walked across the floor and waited for him to acknowledge her presence, which he did with an outstretched hand. Not immediately understanding, she began to explain that she'd like to publish an obituary in the next day's paper but broke off when he wiggled his fingers. She took the notice out of her reticule and handed it to him.

He read it quickly, confirmed it would run tomorrow and barked out an amount.

Bea handed him the shillings, paused a moment to make sure he needed nothing else from her and thanked him for his assistance.

The whole exchange was neat, quick and efficient, and Bea, congratulating herself on how easily she had resolved the difficult matter of Mr. Theodore Davies and his troublesome scar, strode purposefully to the entrance. She was only a few feet away—possibly three, most likely two—when a gentleman in a pristine *coup au vent* haircut and an immaculate Oriental knot stumbled through the door, stepped into the office, opened his mouth to speak and, failing to articulate a single word, promptly dropped at her feet.

Protruding from his back, its jade handle glistening with jewels, was a knife.

CHAPTER TWO

Although she considered herself to be a generally kindhearted and compassionate human being, Bea's first thought as she stared at the supine gentleman on the floor of 132 Strand was of herself.

She did not ponder the remarkable unlikeliness that a shocking death would cross her path for a second time in less than five months, nor wonder what cursed star she'd had been born under that she continued to be afflicted with freshly made corpses. No, her mind darted at once to her family and what conclusions they might draw if they discovered she had been in the offices of the *London Daily Gazette* on the very same day the death notice for her former lover had been placed in the paper. Would her uncle take the two disparate pieces of information and draw a line between them, effectively connecting the dots?

Yes, as Beatrice stood there, watching the blood seep into the fibers of the dandy's burgundy superfine coat, all she could think was that her aunt must never know Mr. Davies was a fiction.

"Step back, miss, step back," someone told her. The voice was stern, authoritative and a little impatient, as if annoyed with her for blocking his view of the crime.

It was, she discovered, the dark-haired man who sat closest to the door. He pushed past her, dropped to his knees to examine the victim, pressed his fingers to the throat and affirmed what Bea already felt to be true. "We've got a clay pot! Clay pot in the doorway," he yelled to his colleagues in the newsroom. "Guv'nor's as dead as my Grandaunt Martha."

Again, he told her to step back, but she was too stunned to move. The newspaperman grabbed the knife by its handle, a delicately carved jade horse's head swathed in rubies and bedecked with elegant pearl flowers, and wrenched it out of the man's back.

Bea gasped in horror.

Other men, more than she had imagined were in the building, crowded the scene as they also told her to move away, gently shoving her, one by one, farther and farther back until all she could see was the top of the dead gentleman's head.

The room was filled with chatter now, as the reporters argued over how to proceed and whom to call and what to write about the dramatic event that had unfolded in their very own entranceway.

What a veritable stroke of luck, one of the men said.

A call went out to turn him over, from whom Bea couldn't tell, and two reporters rolled the dead man onto his back so they could inspect his face.

Curious, Bea pressed closer, squeezing her way between the reporters until she had a clear view of the victim's face. It was a rather handsome visage, with its straight nose, dimpled chin and well-formed lips. His dark hair was brushed forward in the dashing style and artfully arranged to look as if he had just ridden his horse in from the moor. His clothes, impeccably tailored and so well fitting they seemed as if to have been sewn on, gave the contrasting impression that he sat all day in the bow window of White's providing an amiable site for passersby.

He was not an amiable sight now, Bea thought, shuddering with cold horror as she contemplated the lifeless expression on his face.

Mr. Otley had spared her the unnerving view by dying facedown and remaining facedown during her entire examination of him. Naturally, Kesgrave deserved the credit for that, for he was the one who had the good sense not to move the body from its original position. Knowing nothing about the pursuit of murderers, he had intuited the usefulness of not disturbing the scene itself until all possible information could be gathered.

"Goddamn it," bellowed a man in beaver as he glared down at the victim. "Who turned him over? Who did this?"

The room fell silent for a moment as the men registered the harsh disapproval, then exploded in commotion as several perpetrators were identified and disavowed.

"I have one rule about the care and upkeep of the office, gentlemen. One rule," the man said angrily. "No blood. It was instituted after Miller broke Adam's nose over the Courtauld affair, but it applies as much to stabbing victims as to untrustworthy colleagues who steal your sources."

An offended reporter—presumably Adams—insisted that he had merely borrowed the source and the information gathered during the loan pertained to a story wholly unrelated to Lady Courtauld's stolen diamond necklace, while another lamented his failure to sufficiently damage his associate's appendage. "It was only severely bruised," Miller grumbled.

The bickering reporters were ignored as the man in the beaver hat sought to impose order on the chaos by discovering what gears had already been set in motion.

Was someone outside interviewing witnesses?

Yes, Johns and Bryant.

Had a doctor been sent for?

Green ran to get old man Turner.

And the Runners?

Peterson, sir.

As the voices whirled around her, Bea slowly took several steps backward, determined to call no attention to herself as she charted her exit from the busy newspaper office. It would not be easy, as the entry was crowded with a dozen reporters and getting to the door would require sliding past all of them unnoticed. In their rush to examine the oddity of a dead body in their very own office, they had forgotten about her, but sooner or later they would remember the woman at whose feet their victim had fallen.

All too easily Bea could imagine the effusive article juxtaposing the brutal ugliness of the dandy's slaying with the delicate fragility of its female witness.

Although the prospect of being subjected to such mortifying prose made her escape a vital necessity, the fact that the article could unintentionally reveal the truth about her own elaborate story gave the matter particular urgency. Even if the newspaper elided her presence or failed to include her name in its report, she would still be hopelessly entangled in the investigation, for it seemed impossible to her that one could be interrogated by the Bow Street Runners for witnessing a murder and no word of the event get back to one's family.

Clearly, this affair would garner the interest of the *ton*, for everything about the victim indicated nobility, wealth and breeding. The cut of his coat alone unequivocally stated that he was Someone of Note, and although not a single word about the matter had been written yet, she could imagine the reams of newspaper pages it would consume.

A nine days' wonder would be succinct in comparison.

The man in the beaver hat, who revealed himself to be the chief editor when, frustrated by his inability to silence the cacophony, he yelled, "Goddamn it, I'm the chief editor and you will listen to me," claimed everyone's attention with his outburst. A dozen pairs of eyes flew to the speaker, and Bea, grateful for the distraction, walked swiftly behind their backs and slipped gently out the door.

Her relief at stealing away unseen was short-lived, for the throng of pedestrians on the sidewalk had coalesced into another crowd outside the *London Daily Gazette*'s door, as word of the murder had quickly spread. Several newspapers called the Strand home, and reporters from neighboring buildings—the *British Press* to the right, the *Morning Chronicle* to the left—clamored for a glimpse of the victim, some claiming to be witnesses in hopes of gaining information from Bryant and Johns.

"I saw everything," insisted a man in a brown coat with sewn patches and side whiskers in need of trimming. "It was a knife, wasn't it? With a long and slender handle? The sly cove stabbed him in the shoulder and ran away. Let me inside. I saw the whole thing."

Bea tilted her head down and, hoping to blend in with the crowd, began to mutter about death and murder. "In the middle of the day...shocking...shocking... Is no one safe?"

Even when she was well clear of the throng, she continued to mumble, as the words seemed to take on the air of a magic incantation, protecting her from harm or discovery.

She stopped only when she had secured a hack and was safely on her way back to Portman Square. With her head pressed against the worn fabric of the coach seat, she tried to make sense of what had just happened. She understood the basics, of course, which was to say that a man's life had been ended when an enemy drove a knife between his shoulder blades into his heart. And she realized there was a story behind that act, an entire world of hatred and betrayal and seething resentment, either at the man or for the man or near the man or around the man. Even if the thrust had been issued in complete anonymity, even if neither victim nor villain had ever seen each other before, the event was the product of myriad unaccountable decisions blossoming and festering into action.

Even so, Bea couldn't quite elude the conviction that the murder had somehow been contrived for her benefit to demonstrate the dangers of lying.

Naturally, she knew such thinking was not only absurd but also revealed an egotism that was as puffed up as it was unsupported. In the whole of her six and twenty years, fate had done nothing to make its interest in her known and she very much doubted it would start now in such a ruthless fashion. The dandy's death had no more to do with her than the chief editor's favorite flavor of snuff, and in considering her place in the universe she was reminded rather forcefully that she didn't have one.

If she did merit consideration from providence, then she would not have had to sneak off to the offices of the *London Daily Gazette* to place a death notice for a fictitious beau.

But as firm as her comprehension of the truth was, she continued to feel a niggling sense of unease that somehow the gentleman in the newspaper office had died to atone for her sins.

"You are the most inane creature," she said as she climbed down from the hack and paid the fare to the driver.

Slipping into the house was as easy as slipping out, and although her aunt was standing in the hallway examining the salver for invitations, she barely acknowledged Bea as the girl walked past. It certainly did not occur to her to wonder if her niece had been outside, and if so, where she had gone without a maid in tow.

Flora, as well, seemed to be under the impression that her cousin had been present for the whole afternoon, for when Bea appeared in the drawing room for tea—in a jonquil walking gown, of course, not her mourning weeds—she addressed her as if they were already in the middle of a discussion.

"You're right, of course. There's no reason to worry about it before it happens," Flora said with amiability. "The Otleys are most likely not even in London, and if they are, they would certainly not be accepting callers. I cannot say if one is supposed to mourn for the full year a man whose immoral character brought about his own brutal death, but four months cannot be long enough. It's indecently short, and it's well-known that piling one wrong on top of another does not create a proper situation."

Given that the conversation had started without her,

Bea was confident it could continue in the same vein and nodded absently at this observation.

A few minutes later her aunt entered the room to simultaneously bemoan the discouraging lack of festive opportunities for the week and preen over an invite to go to the opera with Lady Marsham in a few days' time.

"She's Amersham's aunt, a real highflier. Not quite the type Hyde-Clares usually consort with, but we don't want to give offense to the earl," Aunt Vera said, pouring herself a cup of tea. "He was so lovely to us after that unpleasantness in the Lake District, and I would enjoy seeing him again. Flora, you might want to consider encouraging his interest. His fortune is secure, and I think you would enjoy the privileges of being a countess."

"Yes, of course, Mama," Flora said with little enthusiasm.

Bea could hardly blame her for her lack of eagerness, as Lord Amersham had done nothing to endear himself to the Hyde-Clares during their stay at Lakeview Hall other than be of noble blood. A gentleman of only four and twenty, he displayed none of the maturity one would want in a husband, preferring to spend all his time with Mr. Skeffington, another young man rapidly approaching his majority and yet gaining no maturity.

To change the subject, Flora raised the issue of the Otleys, for now that they were back in town, they could no longer ignore their obligation.

Aunt Vera darted a baleful look at Bea, for she considered the dreadfulness of the situation to be her niece's fault. If she hadn't staged that dramatic scene in the Skeffingtons' drawing room during which several disagreeable details emerged about Mr. and Mrs. Otley's inappropriate relationships, then nothing awful would have happened during their stay—well, nothing *more* awful than Mr. Otley losing his life to an unfortunate blow from a candlestick. If ignorance had prevailed, they could have visited Mrs. Otley and her daughter with all the feigned delight of the best social calls.

But Bea had deprived them of that pleasure with her insistence on the truth.

Although there were several things she could say in her defense, Bea kept her lips firmly shut and her expression bland. It did not matter to her aunt that the esteemed Duke of Kesgrave had also been determined to discover who had killed the spice trader.

"I'm not sure we have to settle the matter yet, my dear, as we don't know if the Otleys are in London," Aunt Vera said.

Flora smiled with approval and announced she thought the exact same thing. The two women, in perfect accord, switched to another, more pressing topic and debated the exact number of pairs of gloves they would need to confront the season with aplomb. After they had discussed it to their satisfaction, they consulted Bea, who, despite being present for the entire exchange, had no opinion on that matter.

When both women gaped at her in disappointment, she selected a number at random—eight—which caused them to laugh with genuine amusement.

By any measure, it was an entirely ordinary afternoon in Portman Square, but far from taking comfort in the small mundanities of her life, Bea felt agitated by them, for they served only to throw the extraordinary events of the day into high relief. At nine-thirty, she retired to her bedchamber because she was exhausted from apprehension and restless with anticipation and didn't know how to handle either one without calling attention to herself.

Although the clock in her bedroom marked the time with the same evenhanded tick as always, tonight each second seemed to boom more loudly than the next—as if, she thought, counting down to some dire moment.

The revelation that Mr. Davies had passed out of this world wasn't that shocking, and yet she could not stop herself from imagining how her aunt would react. She kept picturing Aunt Vera divining the truth from her expression and casting her out once and for all, furious that she'd lied not just her family but also to all of London.

Even as she created these dismal scenes, Bea ordered herself to stop, for she could not believe she was so self-absorbed she couldn't spare a single thought for the man who had died at her feet just that afternoon.

She found her indifference particularly disturbing in light of how ardently she had pursued justice for Mr. Otley. From the moment she had stepped free of the bookshelves and saw his lifeless form in the moonlight, she had been determined to discover the truth. As the Duke of Kesgrave made repeated efforts to shoo her away, she came up with excuse after excuse to linger. She feigned missish helplessness in order to examine his boots up close to confirm that the dark patch near his heel was mud. (In fact, it was not.)

Surely, this unknown gentleman deserved the same respect.

And yet even as she chastised herself for her failing, she knew the two situations varied wildly. At Lakeview Hall, she was the only one who cared to discover the truth about what happened to Mr. Otley. Ultimately, she learned Kesgrave was also investigating his death, but that information was not immediately available to her.

In the matter of the murdered dandy, however, there was almost a surfeit of concern, for the *Gazette* reporters, who felt a proprietary sort of entitlement to the dead man, had been determined to keep the rivalrous newspapermen craning their necks at the door away from their corpse. In addition to those parties, the Bow Street Runners had been called to handle the proceedings in an official capacity.

The victim was clearly not languishing for want of attention.

And what if, standing there in the entry of the newspaper office, she had resolved to solve the mystery of the poor man's death? How would she begin to discover that information? Would she start with the *London Daily Gazette*?

Was the newspaper central to the stabbing or merely incidental? Had the dandy been in the process of seeking out the office when he met his end or had he stumbled in in hopes of getting help and perhaps saving himself?

It was impossible to tell from the evidence.

The newspaper, she didn't doubt, would quickly identify the victim, but she didn't need an article to know quality when it dropped dead at her feet. The victim was a gentleman of wealth and breeding, and to discover who wished him harm would require interviews with the *ton*, a truly terrifying prospect for a woman who had stammered her way through six seasons. Even the most harmless inquiry about her health brought on nonsensical stuttering and a flush of embarrassment. It was madness to believe she would have the composure to ask members of the beau monde intrusive questions about their movements and relationships now. How would she even frame her sudden and unexpected interest in their lives? "Bear with me, please, as I am in pursuit of a killer."

In every way that mattered, the events of the *London Daily Gazette* murder differed from the events of the Lakeview Hall murder, and Bea was welcome to consider herself free of any further obligation.

She could devote all her energies to worrying about how her family would receive the news of Mr. Davies's sudden and unexpected death with an entirely clear conscience.

Naturally, such an occupation appealed little to her, and she picked up the biography of George Stepney she had been reading the night before. She'd found the early chapters of the poet and ambassador's life surprisingly engrossing, with its humble beginnings that nary hinted at the greatness to come, but now the story wasn't holding her interest. One precocious scholar at Cambridge's Trinity College was just like any other precocious scholar at Trinity.

Her cynical assessment wasn't fair to Mr. Stepney, and it certainly wasn't fair to his biographer, whose writing style she had admired only the day before.

No, the problem was she was too distracted by the scene at the newspaper office to focus on the words, for now that she had given herself permission not to think about the dead man, her mind could consider nothing else.

"You are a perverse creature," she said softly, returning to the book with renewed determination. But it was no use. No matter how she tried, she could not erase the image of the murdered dandy with the bejeweled jade knife jutting out of his back. How perfectly in line the instrument was with his aesthetic, she thought now in the quiet of her bedchamber. If consulted prior to his stabbing on the weapon he would most like for the deed, she felt certain he would have chosen just such an artifact from one of the display cases in the British Museum.

She smiled as she imagined the care and deliberation with which he would approach the selection, considering, as he examined the museum's assortment of ancient knives from all over the world, which one would best complement his burgundy greatcoat and enhance the overall picture of beautiful youth mercilessly cut down in its prime.

It had been almost three years since her visit to the museum, but she knew its collection of knives to be extensive, with many lovely examples from India, China and Africa. Craftsmanship varied depending on the time period of construction, as some examples had been forged more than two millennia ago in primitive fires. Others were exquisitely made implements, with glittering jewels meant to dazzle the eye, she recalled, picturing a particularly stunning piece that had held her attention for several minutes. Its handle had also been carved from jade and had graceful latticework on the bottom of the hilt.

Was it latticework?

No, it was more swirly, more like a flourish than an actual design. Indeed, as she closed her eyes to focus her mind more strongly, she realized the elegant design resembled a horse's bridle.

That's right, she thought. The hilt had been carved into the shape of a horse just like—

Heart pounding, Bea sat up straight and even though she knew it was ridiculous to think the two knives were the same, she couldn't quite convince herself that her conclusion was entirely outlandish. Her memory was dim, certainly, but they looked so similar.

She would get no rest until she confirmed it.

At once, she began planning a trip to the British Museum for the following day. She would have to go alone, of course, for showing undue interest in its knife collection would alarm her family. They would also be disturbed when she insisted on speaking to a librarian about one knife in particular—especially, as she expected, the dagger in question would no longer be in the collection.

But how to arrange a solo visit?

In many respects, it should be easy, as her family displayed little interest in the artifacts of the British civilization—or, indeed, any civilization. Her aunt had visited the venerated institution only once and had begrudged every moment of the experience, which had been undertaken at the request of her elderly aunt, Lady Wattingford. Desiring to see the Townley collection of classical sculptures before she died, her ladyship had insisted her niece take her, and Vera, finding her offspring impervious to the demands of familial obligation, dragooned Bea in their stead. Although Bea was no more fond of the irascible Lady Wattingford than her cousins, she'd enjoyed the outing immensely, especially when she managed to slip away for a half hour to discover the museum on her own.

The challenge, of course, would be in convincing them to allow her to go with only her maid in tow. Her aunt would be scandalized.

Or would she, Bea thought.

In the last few weeks, Aunt Vera had taken pains to make it clear that the standards to which she held her own daughter did not apply to her niece. She would object vociferously to Flora undertaking such an excursion but most likely would have no strong feelings about Bea doing so. After all, she was little known among the *ton,* so it was doubtful anyone would recognize her and object. In addition, the Hyde-Clares were particularly ill-suited to the requirements of solace, something Bea had learned firsthand when her parents died and discovered again when Lady Wattingford finally cocked up her toes after years of threatening to expire. Her aunt and uncle were so embarrassed by death, they avoided each other's gaze for almost two months in the wake of her ladyship's passing. Given their discomfort, they would probably be grateful for the thoughtful way she removed herself from their presence in the wake of Mr. Davies's unexpected death. Eager to be spared the awkwardness of her grief, they would happily wave her off and tell her not to return until the museum closed.

A greater concern was the knife itself, Bea thought, for she knew how incredibly implausible her deduction was. More probably, she was misremembering the design of the other one. Far from being a horse's head carved out of jade, it would almost certainly turn out to be a hawk's head molded in bronze that had been tinted slightly green by the air.

And yet as much as she told herself to be reasonable in her expectation, she could not quite squelch her excitement. Earlier, she had professed disinterest in the dandy's murder, and as sincere as it had been, she knew it was based partly on an inability to imagine a purpose to her interest. The circumstances of his death had simply made it too difficult for her to investigate.

But now she had a piece of information she could probe on her own without anyone's permission, and she discovered, to her horror and delight, that she couldn't wait to get started. Had the British Museum been open at that hour, she would have put on her pelisse, marched out of the house and hailed a hack to Russell Street.

Alas, the beloved institution did not open again until ten the next morning and she had to content herself with pacing her bedchamber while she alternately assured herself that it was and wasn't the same knife.

Truly, she didn't know which actuality she wanted to prevail. If it wasn't the same implement, then her involvement in the murder would be at an end, which, although disappointing, would no doubt be for the best. The dead man in the *London Daily Gazette* offices had nothing to do with her, and inserting herself into the mystery would be as foolhardy as it was foolish, for she had naught to gain but the ready ridicule of her family and society. She could even see the caricature by Mr. Rowlandson of her dressed in the uniform of the Bow Street Runners with a caption that mocked her as a new recruit.

Her interference, if exposed, could earn her the attention that six seasons had failed to secure, a horrifying prospect.

But, oh, how she longed to interfere!

The discovery that Beatrice Hyde-Clare was clever hadn't just struck her relatives as a disconcerting revelation; it had also struck the girl herself as one. Although life had given her many opportunities to display her intelligence, it had not done so in a format within which she felt comfortable. Trading bon mots with eligible partis in glittering ballrooms required a level of clarity she was too easily flustered to attain. Struggling for a witty reply, she would settle for a belatedly plodding one, which would flatten the conversation and dampen a suitor's interest in continuing it. Knowing how badly she'd bumbled the response would make her overly aware of herself, which had the inevitable effect of further undermining her confidence and deadening her mind. Entirely undone, she would stare dumbly and wait for the moment to pass.

Naturally, knowledge of the unavoidable outcome further degraded Bea's ability to answer cleverly and her stock in society dropped as quickly as her faith in herself. Six seasons of self-conscious stupidity had even blunted her ability to discourse in private, and rather than embarrass herself further, she had surrendered to silence. Her discomfort was so acute, she would have failed to take even if a mean-spirited heiress hadn't emerged early in her first season to scathingly call her a drab thing.

And then suddenly, finally, providence provided her with the ideal setting to display her intelligence— incongruously, the scene of a murder—and she comported herself so favorably she managed to impress the Duke of Kesgrave with her acuity. Based on nothing but her insistence that she had figured out who the murderer was, he had gathered the entire company in the Skeffingtons' drawing room, fetched a Runner from town and given her the floor to unmask the villain.

Bea was humbled by his belief in her, yes, but more than that she was emboldened, and now that another opportunity to test her detection skills had presented itself, she was eager to see how she would perform.

Indeed, there was something thrilling in the uncertainty because for so many years her failure had been assured.

Having settled the matter, Bea picked up the Stepney biography, climbed into bed and turned to the page describing an exchange with a particularly challenging tutor. With the vague concerns that had been fluttering on the edge of consciousness now fully lodged in her mind, she knew she could finish the chapter on Trinity and perhaps the next one as well.

Indeed, two hours later, Stepney had not only entered the diplomatic service but was en route to Brandenburg.   Pleased with her progress, Bea yawned, returned the book to the night table and blew out the candle. She fell asleep almost as soon as she put her head down on the pillow.

CHAPTER THREE

The next morning, Bea awoke with invigoration and eagerness and immediately summoned her maid to help her don a walking dress.

"We're going to the British Museum today, Annie," she said cheerfully while the dark-haired girl pulled a light-blue gown out of the wardrobe. "And that is not the royal *we,* as Prinny might use, nor is it a reference to me and my family. By *we,* I mean you and I, Annie. Do be ready to leave at eleven."

This statement, uncustomarily bold and wholly without precedent, startled the servant, who paused to tilt her head to the side before promising to be ready at the prescribed time.

Bea smiled happily. "Delightful."

Her mood remained buoyant fifteen minutes later when she entered her breakfast room, for she could not wait to have her suspicions confirmed. She could even picture the moment she stepped into the room with the extensive knife collection and saw the empty space where the jade dagger should have been. Evincing surprise, she would locate the nearest librarian and interrogate him on its strange disappearance.

In this sanguine mood, she greeted her family, who were still gathered around the table, even her uncle.

"Good morning," she said brightly.

Aunt Vera muttered something incomprehensible in response and looked at her husband with a fierce frown. Catching her disapproval out of the corner of his eye, Uncle Horace acknowledged her displeasure by raising the newspaper slightly higher. His wife harrumphed.

Although this interplay was unusual for Aunt Vera, who typically allowed her husband to read the newspaper at the table unaccosted, Bea paid it no heed as she listened to Dawson describe the breakfast options. At the mention of food, her stomach growled furiously, which she tried to cover up with an unduly eager request for eggs. Then she glanced around the table to see if she needed to apologize for the rudeness. Her aunt's cross expression remained focused on her husband, whose interest in the newspaper was more studied than genuine, as his eyes remained steady and did not move across the page. Russell's gaze was fixed firmly on his plate, which was empty, and he didn't look up when Dawson asked if he wanted another serving of eggs. Flora was likewise distracted, examining the lace that edged the sleeve of her morning gown.

The intense concentration was unusual for the breakfast room, but it did not detract from Bea's positive mood and, observing the sun shining through the window, said, "My goodness, it's a lovely day."

Nobody spoke.

As the statement could not have been any more benign or banal, the deafening silence it elicited was entirely out of the ordinary. Undaunted, Bea asked her aunt what her plans were for the day, suggesting that a stimulating walk through the park might be in order for the brisk but sunny February day.

Aunt Vera looked down at the table and muttered something about calling on her sister.

Bea nodded and looked at her cousin. "What about

you, Russell? Perhaps a ride on Rotten Row while the weather is so lovely or maybe along the heath?"

He, too, kept his gaze averted as he mumbled, "Yes, perhaps. Thank you."

Untroubled by their strange behavior, Bea said brightly, "I have made plans myself and encourage you all to consider joining—"

"No, dear, stop," Flora said gently, reaching across the table to grasp her cousin's hand in her own, her eyes full of pity. Then she turned angrily to her father. "For goodness' sake, Papa, we agreed you would be the one to tell her."

Uncle Horace coughed awkwardly and raised the *London Daily Gazette* even higher, so that his chin now stuck out below the bottom of the newspaper.

Flora scoffed in disgust, turned to her cousin and announced with simple straightforwardness that Teddy was dead.

Bea blinked, uncomprehending. "Who?"

Aunt Vera whimpered in distress as Flora said with tragic understanding, as if not at all surprised by her cousin's inability to grasp the truth, for it was too consequential, "Theodore Davies, darling, the love of your life. He has died."

"Oh, goodness, yes, Teddy!" Bea said loudly.

How could she forget something so hugely significant as the death notice she herself had placed less than twenty-four hours before?

Naturally, her family attributed her reaction to shock at the tragic news. Flora rushed over to embrace her, Russell patted the air in the general vicinity of her hand, Aunt Vera mewled again, and Uncle Horace said, "I trust you will not let this development undermine your intention to find a husband. Onward and upward, right, my dear?"

Given that the dead man, as far as any one of them knew, had a wife and two children, Bea didn't think this was a particularly insensitive remark, but Flora chastised her father for his lack of tact and Russell glared at him disapprovingly as he said, "There, there," to his cousin.

As a concession to her aunt, who seemed genuinely distressed by the death of Mr. Davies, Bea assured her uncle he was correct. "Indeed, yes, sir. I am more resolved than ever to find a husband"—she peered beneath her lashes at Aunt Vera to see how she was receiving these remarks—"as a tribute to Teddy, may he rest in peace."

The answer was taken very well indeed, for her aunt perked up immediately and expressed her approval for the sentiment, which she considered to be everything a dead lost love would long to hear. "As you observed, it's a lovely day. Perhaps later we can take a drive to Lincoln's Inn and inspect prospects."

Flora looked at her mother in horror. "My cousin has just suffered a very shocking loss and cannot realize what she says. Even though she knew logically she had no chance of happiness with Mr. Davies, I'm sure she nurtured hope in some small corner of her heart that he would abandon his wife and children for her sake and they would live together in shame and mortification in some hovel on the edge of a slum. A bright, beautiful dream has died today and we must be patient with her as she tries to figure out how to mourn. To that end, we must all keep her company in the drawing room and be on hand if she needs anything."

Bea could not say which horrified her more: Flora's vision of her future in which she lived in dishonorable squalor or her plan for her present. The lowered expectations and dismal compromises of the former indicated a truly despairing view of spinsterhood while the latter would constrain her movements and prevent her from visiting the museum.

"No!" she said more forcefully than she'd intended and then tried to soften her response with a sad smile. "I cannot accept your disrupting your plans on my behalf."

"You must not distress yourself, darling," Flora insisted softly. "We had nothing scheduled that cannot be put off to another day. Isn't that right, Mama?"

Aunt Vera glowered at her daughter for several seconds before agreeing. "Yes, yes, of course, my dear. Nothing at all. Just my sister, Susan, who I see regularly so she doesn't count as a particular plan, although we *had* arranged it last week when we got the invitation to the Leland ball. She requires my help in selecting the right outfit for your cousin Julia to wear to her first London party. But that is a mere bagatelle in comparison to Bea's distressing news," she said, her voice trailing off slightly as she looked at her daughter, as if seeking confirmation of her statement. When Flora remained stony-faced, she continued as if it had never been in doubt. "Of course that can be rescheduled for tomorrow. There's still plenty of time to make sure Julia is appropriately attired. Obviously, I am delighted to keep Bea company all day long in the drawing room, just sitting with her silently, hour after hour, never taking any fresh air despite the amiability of the weather, if that's what she requires. She is my niece, and I am here to support her in whatever way it's deemed necessary. If she *needs* to honor him by meeting other men of his profession, then I'm happy to do that too," she added hopefully before darting a fleeting look at the girl in question. "You have only to tell us what you require, Bea. I trust it goes without saying that it's your well-being that matters most to me."

But the particular emphasis she put on the word *your* made it clear to everyone in the room, even Dawson, that it was her own well-being that concerned her more. Bea smothered a smile at her aunt's enduring self-interest and gently announced she would rather pass a quiet day alone in her room than impose her company on others.

Flora cried out at the use of the word *impose,* insisting that they were all eager to have an opportunity to provide her with comfort during this time of tragedy. Uncle Horace coughed, as it to excuse himself from his daughter's aggressive inclusiveness, and Russell looked down and mumbled something about meeting a friend at the Serpentine at noon. Aunt Vera glanced out the window and observed wistfully that the day was indeed lovely.

Bea smothered a smile at their awkwardness and wondered how despondent she would be if Mr. Davies had indeed been the love of her life. Would she be devastated at the loss of a quietly nurtured fantasy, as Flora implied—although, hopefully, not one quite so miserable—or would she be sensible about it and feel only a fleeting sadness at the absence of his goodness from the world?

Regardless of the direction her grief would have taken, her family would have provided little comfort. Even Flora's attempts, which were as sincere as they were kindhearted, felt designed to make an anguished griever even more despairing.

"I hope you will not adopt mourning colors, for they are quite unflattering and you are already so deathly pale," Aunt Vera said, sounding a practical note. Immediately, she found herself the target of her daughter's disapproving stare. "I'm thinking only of Bea's spirits, as one's mood can be powerfully influenced by one's clothes, especially when one's choices make one look as if she had died last Saturday and nobody noticed. There's no need to glare at me, Flora. I'm speaking in scientific terms, as my dear friend Mrs. Ralston has made a study of it. If you are critical of the conclusions, you must take it up with her."

Given that it would be highly inappropriate for Bea to don widow's weeds for a man to whom she had no material connection, she agreed immediately to her aunt's suggestion.

"And you must not feel compelled to socialize before you are ready. If you would prefer not to attend the Leland ball, I would of course support you," Aunt Vera added on an optimistic note. "It had never been my intention to make you feel as if you must interact with the *ton*."

Bea thoroughly appreciated her aunt's machinations, for she had not thought the woman shrewd enough to manipulate a tragedy to further her own agenda. "I will certainly keep that in mind," she said placatingly. In truth, however, she had no intention of missing her first opportunity to observe the Duke of Kesgrave in his natural setting.

Delighted that good sense had prevailed, Aunt Vera expressed her pleasure at both her niece's willingness to be reasonable and the positive impact Mr. Davies death was having on their lives, stopping just short of wishing the unfortunate event had occurred sooner.

As difficult as it was not to laugh, Bea kept her expression downcast throughout the rest of the meal and waited with increasing impatience for her uncle to leave. She wanted desperately to get her hands on his copy of the *London Daily Gazette* to see what the paper reported about yesterday's shocking event. Uncle Horace made no mention of the incident, but his reticence was only to be expected, as murdered dandies were not fitting conversation for the breakfast table.

Usually, her uncle left around ten to meet with his steward, Mr. Wright, to discuss estate business, which he handled earnestly and sincerely, and Bea kept one eye on the clock, counting the minutes. Today, however, he decided to linger over tea with his family, displaying, Bea feared, proper avuncular concern for her emotional frailty after the terrible news of the morning. It was, she thought, a considerate gesture, full of a sweetness she never expected from him, and it required all her strength not to huff impatiently at him and say, "Yes, yes, sir, you've done your duty and may go now. I'm perfectly fine."

When he finally stood up to leave, his wife remonstrated him for deserting his niece in her time of need, and Bea, unable to restrain herself, smiled at him brightly and discreetly shook her head. Grateful, he nodded in return and all but ran out of the room.

Bea picked up the paper, but before she could read a single word, Flora enveloped her in a hug and said, "You poor dear, of course you want to see it for yourself. Here, let me show you. It's the first notice after the wedding announcements, which is, I think, a benign placement."

Smothering a sigh, she thanked her cousin for her

consideration and followed her finger to the small box containing the text that she herself had written only the day before. She professed herself so moved by the lovely write-up, she required a moment alone with the paper to collect herself.

"Of course, darling, take all the time you need," Flora said.

Bea took the newspaper to her bedchamber, closed the door and eagerly scanned the first page for a story on the murder: shipping news…theater advertisements…navy office report…Parliament debates…

Ah, there it was: "Slain Lord."

Under the brief headline, it continued.

"Robert Hanson Crestwell, Earl of Fazeley and Baron Crestwell, was found dead at 132 Strand yesterday at 1:42 p.m. He had been stabbed in the back with a fourteen-inch jade dagger whilst on the sidewalk and staggered into these newspaper offices, where he fell to the floor and died. Diligent canvassing of the area revealed no witnesses to the event and provided no suspects. A woman of indiscriminate appearance and age who had visited these offices to place a death notice in the paper and at whose feet the victim fell left the premises before she could be interviewed. It is unknown if she is connected to the incident and is being sought for questioning by the authorities.

"Lord Fazeley was a prominent member of Society and an arbiter of style and wit who rejected Mr. Brummell's preference for elegant simplicity and led the revival of ornate complexity. His highest accomplishment in that arena was the creation of the Fazeley Flow, a knot so difficult to tie it is said to require one valet, two footmen and a broomstick to achieve.

Based on several comments his lordship had made in recent months, it was generally believed that he was writing a memoir of his experiences among the *ton,* speculation he tried to smother by steadfastly denying the book whenever the question was put directly to him. Many members of the beau monde hoped his denial to be true, for Lord Fazeley was thought to be in possession of many interesting stories about his friends and associates.

"Investigators are looking into his death, which they believe to be murder."

Bea read the notice three times and could scarcely credit the information, for the Earl of Fazeley had been pointed out to her last season by Flora during a rout at Mrs. Ralston's house and on that occasion she'd been struck by his air of invincibility. He held himself with such daunting aloofness, as if he couldn't bear to look at his fellow humans, for they were an endless source of disappointment and distaste. She also remembered an afternoon walk in Hyde Park not many days later when her aunt suddenly found herself in his path, her feet seemingly rooted to the spot in terror of earning his disapproval. A goldfinch fluttered its wings, drawing his lordship's attention with its loveliness, and in that brief moment of distraction, Uncle Horace pulled his wife aside, as if out of the way of a rampaging horse.

She imagined her aunt was not alone in fearing his attention, for he was famous for issuing finely worded proclamations of impatience and disgust that frequently left targets too stunned to reply, a state commonly referred to as "being fazed." His lordship's high expectations and low tolerance for his fellows did not bode well for the investigation. The more terror a victim inspired in the individuals around him, the more people who wished him harm, a group that would only expand if the rumor about a memoir was true. Nobody relished the exposure of private information, but did someone fear it enough to murder him?

The answer, of course, lay in the pages of the manuscript if it actually existed.

How, then, to discover if the story about the memoir was true?

She was considering the problem when Flora peeked her head into the room to ask if she may enter now.

Unused to such deference, Bea started in surprised

and then promptly said yes. She was eager to go to the museum, but it was still early enough in the day to indulge her cousin's need to provide comfort. She was, in fact, deeply touched to discover how much Flora cared, and Bea submitted to her ministrations for as long as she could manage. She even made a desperate effort to squeeze out a few tears as a show of respect, but her proficiency in producing them on demand was sadly lacking. Her exertions were so finely wrought, however, that her cousin mistook them for grief.

As affecting as Flora's concern was, its excessive and cloying pity, as if the sad little fantasy she'd envisioned for her cousin had been her only chance at happiness, agitated Bea. Even though she'd resigned herself to her diminished prospects years ago, she felt an almost unbearable heaviness descend as Flora tried to raise her spirits.

Finally, she feigned surprise at how late it was—a little after eleven—and professed herself in desperate need of a little nap. "You don't mind, do you?"

Flora jumped to her feet at once. "Of course I do not!" she said. "You must be exhausted. Do get some rest, and I will come back in a few hours with tea and cakes. How does that sound?"

Although she had no idea how long her mission to the British Museum would take, Bea quickly calculated the length of the drive both there and back and decided she was likely to have returned by three. "That sounds wonderful, thank you," she said, managing a wan smile.

Flora drew her cousin's drapes, fluffed her pillows and left the room with a concerned frown. Grateful to be alone, Bea pulled the bell tug and waited impatiently for her maid to appear.

As the news of her tragedy had reached belowstairs, Annie was taken aback to discover their excursion to the museum was still in the offing. Perceiving her surprise, Bea realized she needed to somehow win her maid's loyalty, for there was no way to stop her from telling everyone belowstairs the details of their outing. Slowly but surely that information would find its way to the drawing room.

"I cannot bear to remain here, shut up with nothing but my thoughts," Bea said with a miserable tremor in her voice. For a woman who had resolved only the day before to never tell a lie again, she was honing her prevarication skills with alarming efficiency. "Flora wants me to rest, but I need something to keep myself occupied so that I may avoid despair. To that end, I think it's better that we stay the course and go to the museum. There's a particular item I'm interested in gathering information about. Teddy would want me to, I think."

"Of course, miss, of course," she said, her brow clearing as she offered sincere condolences on what she described as Bea's Great Disappointment.

'Twas hardly encouraging to discover the unflattering portrait the staff held of her, but Bea managed to nod somberly without flinching. Then she suggested they move swiftly through the house, lest Flora discover her intention and intercept them on the way to the front door. Her legs were longer than the petite maid's, and Annie had to run to keep up with her. Outside, she announced they would get a hack, as she didn't want to court her aunt's disapproval by requesting the carriage.

"She wouldn't be as understanding about my need for occupation as you have been," Bea said, hoping to reinforce her maid's allegiance with flattery.

Annie nodded at once. "Of course, miss."

At the corner of their street, Bea, who considered herself an old hand now at public conveyances, efficiently hailed a hack. Annie eyed the driver warily as Bea climbed in. Although she was reasonably confident they would arrive at the British Museum without incident, her maid's caution made her anxious and she was relieved when they pulled up to the building.

Finally, she thought, as if she had been waiting days, not hours.

Entering Montagu House a little after noon, she was delighted to see it was bustling with visitors, as she didn't want her interest in the knife collection to stand out. Annie, who was only a year or two younger than Flora, gaped in awe at the stately entrance hall.

Observing the wonder in her eyes, Bea recalled her first visit to the museum and insisted the young maid take a couple of hours to enjoy the museum on her own. "Truly, there are so many spectacular things to see such as Egyptian mummies and Grecian statues. I'm going to look at some dreary old weapons."

After a brief moment of uncertainty in which curiosity warred with obligation, Annie agreed to the arrangement, and Bea crossed the floor to the grand staircase. Antiquities were one flight up, and she climbed the steps with an almost irrepressible sense of excitement. Even if the knife did not prove significant in revealing who had stabbed Lord Fazeley—although she was, of course, convinced it would—she was grateful to have a purpose. It was so rare for a young woman of her status to have a mission at all, let alone one of genuine importance.

She was disappointed almost at once, for the seemingly random hodgepodge of artifacts in the antiquities rooms did not match her memory of them at all. Rather than an impressive assortment of knives and weaponry, she found Egyptian coins, Roman pottery and Greek medals. She hadn't imagined the collection, had she?

Of course not. She was merely looking in the wrong place.

The next room contained vases and urns, and the one after that was filled with votive statues from various ancient religions. But then she stepped into a hallway with a sign that read "Sir Walter Heatherton's collection," and she remembered that the knives had been part of a bequest from the Scottish diplomat.

Relieved, she smiled and examined the display cases lining the wall for the precise one she remembered. No, not muskets…or crossbows…or whips. Swords was getting closer…

There it was!

Bea raced to the case with two dozen knives and pressed her nose close to get a look at the dagger. It was exactly as she remembered, which was to say, identical to the one that had struck down Lord Fazeley.

Look at those pearl flowers, she thought, bending forward to more carefully examine the delicate handiwork, which she had seen only from a distance the day before. They were beautiful.

She was so thrilled to have found her quarry exactly where she'd expected it to be—all right, so maybe a few rooms to the left—that it took her a full minute to realize the disappointing truth: If the dagger was here, then it couldn't be there.

Obviously, this wasn't the knife that had been driven into the Earl of Fazeley's back.

Determined not to despair, she considered the possibility that the one used to murder his lordship was a copy. Or, she thought, her excitement rising again, perhaps this implement was the copy, which the villain had left behind when he'd secreted the original out of the museum.

Alight with possibilities, however implausible, she read the placard next to the dagger, which described it as an eighteenth-century ceremonial knife from Jaipur, India, with a jeweled jade handle and identified it as one half of a pair made for the raja of Amer.

Bea gasped. One half of a pair! That meant it had a twin.

Of course, she thought. An unexpected but delightful third option.

Now all she had to do was discover who owned the second one and she would know the identity of the killer.

She spun around and looked for a librarian to whom to put the question. Finding none, she strode through the other rooms, past votives, vases and coins, until she spotted

one at the top of the grand staircase under a trio of giraffes. He was explaining the process of mounting animals
for preservation and display to a pair of gray-haired gentlemen who could not have been any more fascinated.

If she hadn't been so impatient to discuss her own
consuming passion, Bea felt certain she would have been
just as interested in how the wire bodies were constructed.
As it was, it was all she could do not to advise the men to
seek out a book that would allow them to savor the arcane
details at their leisure.

Finally, the librarian arrived at the end of his narrative. "And what you see before you, these tall majestic animals from a faraway continent, are the result."

Bea wanted to cheer.

While the gentlemen turned their attention to the
mounted rhinoceros that shared the pen, Bea approached
the librarian, who was tall and thin like the giraffes about
which he'd rhapsodized. He was a few years older than Uncle Horace's fifty and wore brown trousers that were a little
too wide in the waist. "Excuse me, sir, I was hoping you
could tell me more about the ceremonial knife from Jaipur."

His eyes flickered in surprise as he said, "It's a gorgeous piece, simply gorgeous. Made in the eighteenth century for the raja of Amer. It has a nephrite handle with
rubies, pearls and emeralds. The blade is forged of steel
and is fourteen inches long. It's one of the highlights of Sir
Walter Heatherton's collection. The only item to surpass it
is the Mahmud dagger from earlier in the century. It's a
gorgeous piece, simply gorgeous, with a lush floral pattern
depicted in brilliantly colored enamel. The craftsmanship is
dazzling to behold. The work was actually signed by the
artist, which makes it even more precious and rare. Come,
I will show it to you."

Beatrice followed him through the series of rooms,
debating whether to announce her lack of interest in the
Mahmud knife. She was eager to discuss the object that had
value to her but knew nothing could be gained by offend-

ing the librarian. If he wanted to share his excitement about a particular piece, she'd rein in her impatience long enough to appease him. Perhaps her enthusiasm might make him more inclined to provide the information she sought.

Twenty minutes later, she was forced to reassess her plan, for it was apparent that Mr. Goddard could spend the rest of his day—nay, week—enumerating all the ways the Mahmud dagger was precious and the Tiger sword was special and the sarissa from Macedonia was a marvel of ingenuity. He spoke at length about each one and gave no consideration to anything but his own zealousness.

Afraid the museum would close before she had a chance to speak again, she interrupted his dissertation on a Persian scimitar with a gold hilt. "Your knowledge is quite remarkable, Mr. Goddard, and I must own I'm quite in awe of all the details you've managed to commit to memory. I fear I would get them all muddled up if I tried. As impressed as I am, I would beg you to return your attention to my original query, which was about the knife from Jaipur."

"Ah, yes," he said, his nose jumping slightly in disapproval. "Eighteenth century steel blade made for the raja of Amer. Its handle is nephrite with rubies, pearls and emeralds. Gorgeous piece. One of our best."

No, Bea thought, we are not playing that game again. But rather than protest the repetition and grumble about how much of her time he had wasted, she smiled sweetly and said, "Yes, sir, that's precisely the one. How clever you are to know exactly what I mean. The placard says it's one of a pair."

"Indeed, yes," he said as they walked over to the display case to admire the weapon. "They were made for Jai Singh II in honor of his fortieth year as ruler. He was by my own, as well as by many scholars', accounting a most enlightened ruler, and some consider him to be the most enlightened ruler of India, even to this day. He was succeeded by his son Ishwari Sigh, who, sadly, lacked his father's wisdom and did not last long, taking his own life after only seven years at the helm. He was in turn succeeded—"

Before he proceeded through the entire line of Indian rajas, she interrupted with an apology. "It occurs to me, Mr. Goddard, that I could happily spend the rest of the day listening to you discuss the remarkable artifacts found in this room. In fact, I can imagine nothing more pleasurable. But what about all the other people who want to know about the science of mounting animals or the history of the votive figurines in that very interesting-looking gallery we passed through to arrive at the Heatherton collection? All those poor people languishing in ignorance! I simply cannot reconcile the thought or allow myself to bear the responsibility. So please, Mr. Goddard, for the sake of my conscience, do let me squeeze in one more quick question before you return to your very important duty of educating the masses."

The librarian accepted her comments with equanimity and remarked on the difficulty of sufficiently sharing one's vast knowledge. "It's the cross I must bear, I fear."

"And you bear it so gracefully, as well, if I may be permitted to observe," she said, suddenly aware of how the exchange would appear to Aunt Vera, who would unhesitatingly conclude she had set her cap for the bald-headed gentleman with the gap-toothed smile. He was, she imagined, precisely the sort of suitor for which her aunt believed she should aim—someone near to the bottom if not flanking the line. "Now, as I was saying, the placard describes the knife as being one half of a pair. Do you know where its mate is?"

He smiled confidently and assured her he did. "The information is in Sir Walter's original notes, and the British Museum would never be so irresponsible as to lose the original notes of one our greatest benefactors."

"Of course you would not," Bea said with a sincerely amiable smile. "I never doubted you for a moment. Would you be so kind as to supply me with that information? I'm working on a very important project and can't proceed to the next step without it."

Mr. Goddard said no.

Inside she gaped at the audacity, for she had listened to him drone on for half an hour and surely that deserved some reward, but outwardly she smiled more brightly than ever. "I understand it might be a minor break with custom to provide that information to the public, but we've had such a lovely chat and gotten to know each other so well. I promise you, Mr. Goddard, I will put the information to good use."

His expression changed only slightly—a quiver of an eyebrow, a flare of a nostril—but it was more than enough to convey his disgust. "Although I very much doubt that, miss, what you do with the information is not under discussion. The archives are for serious patrons only."

"I *am* a serious patron," she said hotly.

"You are female."

Bea felt the color in her cheeks rise as she glared at the pompous librarian with his sneering disdain. How dare he disqualify her based on his paltry and arbitrary opinion of her sex! "Now, listen here, you preening windbag, I insist you present me to your superior at once so I may lodge a complaint about your small-minded understanding of the world as well as your inability to notice when your tedious displays of knowledge are quickly putting your visitors to sleep."

"What Miss Hyde-Clare means to say," insisted a familiar male voice behind her, "is that she understands you have the challenging duty of regulating access to the archives, for they are in great demand, and she's confident that upon reconsideration, you will realize she *is* a serious patron and provide her with the information she seeks."

At this ingratiating and inaccurate speech, Bea spun on her heels and found herself staring into the amused blue eyes of Damien Matlock, Duke of Kesgrave.

CHAPTER FOUR

The thrill Bea had felt upon hearing the smooth condescension of the Duke of Kesgrave's voice could not be easily described, for she barely comprehended it herself. She was at once nonplussed to discover him peering over her shoulder with a look of faint amusement and entirely unsurprised by his presence. It was inconceivable that he had just happened to know exactly where to look for her, and yet the fact that he had managed to find her was perfectly in keeping with his air of unshakeable competence, which upon occasion feel like omniscience. She was excited to be once again in his orbit while genuinely peeved that he would insert himself so calmly into hers.

What was immediately clear to her, however, as she contemplated his handsome face—deep blue eyes offsetting a square jaw and sculpted nose—was that she had neither sought nor appreciated his attempt to appease the librarian on her behalf. "On the contrary," she said darkly, "I meant to say that Mr. Goddard is an insufferable prig with an overly developed sense of his own importance. But I was too polite to utter such words."

The duke kept his expression placid as he dipped his blond curls and called her a brat under his breath before addressing the other man. "Very well. What *I* meant to say, then, is I understand, Mr. Goddard, that you have the challenging duty of regulating access to the archives, for they are in great demand, and I hope you will grant *me* permission without doubting my level of seriousness as a patron."

Mr. Goddard was so impressed with the commanding nature of the request, he literally jumped to do Kesgrave's bidding, his feet lifting several inches off the floor. "Yes, yes, of course, my...lord," he said, his tone rising at the end as he tried to guess the newcomer's status.

"Your grace," Kesgrave corrected.

"Ah, yes, your *grace*," the librarian said with satisfaction, as if the duke's presence had been arranged for his pleasure alone. Then he darted a miffed look at Bea, whose unwelcome company diminished the singularity of the honor. "If you will come with me, I will arrange access to the archive immediately."

"How very kind you are, Mr. Goddard," Bea said archly, transforming her moue of annoyance into an overly gracious smile. Then, as he led them through the familiar rooms to the grand staircase, she entertained him with a seemingly endless list of facts about Sir Walter's life. She started with his childhood in Jamaica, which a well-placed placard had described, and ended with his death in a volcanic eruption three years before, an almost universally known tidbit, as it was such a strange and conspicuous way to die. She imagined nothing she said was unfamiliar to the librarian, which was rather the point of her long monologue, for now he knew what it was like to be subjected to unsought information.

When they arrived at the room reserved for researchers, Mr. Goddard requested that they sign the guest book and invited them to take a seat at one of the unoccupied tables. Kesgrave deferred to her with a look, and Bea selected a pedestal table with green leather chairs next to the window. As she sat down, she glanced around the room, with its rich woods and frescoed ceiling, and examined its other occupants. There were four in total, all men and all appearing to be no more or less serious a patron than she.

"You haven't asked how I found you," Kesgrave said as he leaned back in the chair.

"No," Bea agreed.

"You aren't curious?"

As she was only human, Bea was extremely interested in learning how he had contrived to appear on the first floor of Montague House at the very moment she required a figure of authority to smooth her way, but she refused to give him the satisfaction of revealing it. "Not particularly."

His lips twitched at the firmness of her tone. "I'm going to tell you regardless."

"Well, naturally, you cannot resist the opportunity to show off," she said.

Far from offering offense, her rude observation amused him further. "It would be futile to fight my true nature."

"No doubt it's a very impressive tale," she observed with as much condescension as she could muster. "Perhaps you should wait until Mr. Goddard returns, for I think he would be a more appreciative audience."

"Speaking of our librarian friend, you have yet to express your gratitude to me," Kesgrave said provokingly.

Bea tilted her head and asked him for what she should be grateful.

"Access to Sir Walter's papers," he explained, "for you would still be berating that poor fellow had I not arrived when I did."

Although she objected to his characterization of that caddish bore as a "poor" anything, Bea knew this to be true, and in a bid not to utter the words, she decided to flatter his ego. "Your impressive tale?"

"Your heartfelt thanks?" he said with the same air of expectation.

Bea stared at him silently, determined not to look away before he did, and felt an inexplicable flush of pleasure. The setting bore no resemblance to the fireside at

Lakeview Hall, where they'd traded thoughts on suspects in the brutal murder of Mr. Otley, but she felt the same sense of camaraderie. As unwise as it was, she welcomed the feeling and she paused to wonder if he did too.

No, she realized, taken aback by the foolishness of the thought. Kesgrave had dozens of opportunities each day to establish an intellectual connection with his peers. Brooks', gaming hells, the House of Lords—the possibilities for a gentleman to find stimulation were endless.

"Here we are," Mr. Goddard said, placing a stack of papers wrapped with a dark blue ribbon in the center of the table and effectively bringing their impasse to an end. "All the material we have on the Singh dagger, as requested by his grace, the Duke of Kesgrave."

"Toady," she muttered, causing the duke to grin.

Impervious, the librarian added with aggressive obsequiousness, "Do let me know if there's anything else I or one of my colleagues may supply to further assist you in your business, your grace."

"Thank you, Mr. Goddard," Kesgrave said solemnly. "I will not soon forget your kindness."

The librarian seemed to glow with delight as he backed away from the table, reluctant to remove his eyes from such a gracious and serious patron.

"Your Lady Bountiful is exquisite," Bea said satirically.

Despite her aim, the barb did not hit its mark. "Indeed. On my next visit, I'll wear my coronet."

As she had in the Lake District, Bea found herself taken aback by the arrogant duke's willingness to laugh at himself. His manner was so high-handed, his condescension so complete, she kept expecting him to exist in a place beyond humor and frivolity. With every calculated provocation, she expected to draw forth the supercilious nobleman who had stood opposite her in the darkened library at Lakeview Hall, the corpse of Mr. Otley cooling between them, and insisted he could not be a suspect in the gentleman's murder because he was a duke. To any number of

things she'd said, he would be well within his rights to issue a stinging set-down and stride away in disgust.

And yet he didn't.

Bea found it as troubling as it was bewildering.

"It was the notice," he said as Bea reached for the
papers Mr. Goddard had delivered.

"Excuse me?" she asked, looking up from the ribbon,
which required little attention to untie.

"The method by which I found you here," he explained. "I saw the death notice in the *London Daily Gazette*
for an unfortunate young man named Theodore Davies
and knew it at once as your work."

Bea, who had, only a little while ago, believed she
could be no more surprised by anything than his sudden
appearance in Heatherton Hall, gaped in shock at him
now. In what possible way could she have revealed her
authorship in those few benign lines?

Kesgrave was clever enough not to acknowledge her
astonishment, which, naturally, caused her to feel it all the
more keenly. "As Miss Otley made sure everyone in the
manor heard your tragic tale of thwarted love, I knew in an
instant who must have placed the notice," he said simply.

As he explained, Bea wondered if she should be flattered by his insight or insulted by his assumption. What
did it say about her that he'd known at once that her beau
could only be an elaborate fiction?

"I had meant to congratulate you," he continued, "on
creating such a useful story—Miss Otley seemed particularly moved by your young clerk's dramatic scar—but
events intruded and I never had the chance. Indeed, we
had no opportunity to speak privately before you left Lakeview Hall, a development that I deeply regret. Do let me
congratulate you now, even as I offer my condolences. I
feel compelled to ask, however, if it was entirely necessary
to treat him so cruelly? Having served his purpose as a
man of straw, could he not be allowed to pass the rest of
his days in domestic bliss in St. Giles?"

"It was Cheapside," she said, blushing slightly, for whether or not he intended it, she felt the implied criticism: that she had been compelled to take revenge on a man who, real or invented, had found happiness with another woman.

"Ah, yes," he said, "comfortably set among the merchants."

"Mr. Davies's existence had become untenable, as my aunt was determined to meet him in an attempt to discover more information about me," she explained. "As a story, Aunt Vera had found him a little too useful. So I wrote the notice and placed it in the paper my uncle reads every morning."

"And while you were there, Fazeley suffered a fatal knife attack and fell at your feet," he said.

This time she was not surprised by Kesgrave's astuteness. "Opened his mouth as if to speak and then dropped like a brick."

He was quiet for a moment and then said gravely, "That must have been horrible for you. Otley's death was brutal enough for a young lady to endure, and to have to go through it again seems remarkably unfair."

"I agree," she said, "and yet I am here at the British Museum, extending the horror by trying to locate the owner of the knife. So clearly fate has a small idea of what it is doing."

The duke nodded. "I had wondered what you were up to, for I came to your house earlier to offer my respects on your loss and observed your leaving with a maid. Rather than derail your activity, I chose to follow."

Again, she marveled at the frivolity—not that he'd indulged in a wild-goose chase out of a sense of playfulness, for she did not believe he was motivated by an impish spirit. No, it was rather that he, with all his accomplishments, felt compelled to show off his cleverness. Impressing her with his deductive powers regarding Mr. Davies's unfortunate demise paled in comparison to appearing in Heatherton Hall as if by magical incantation to impress her with his revelations.

"Come now, your grace," she said with a cynical smile, "I can't believe you don't have something better to do with your day."

As if he'd wondered the same thing, he said with a bemused smile, "Neither can I."

It was the confusion in his tone—just enough to convey sincerity—that threw her own thoughts into disarray, and she looked down at the pages she'd freed from the ribbon. "I cannot know how much of my conversation with Mr. Goddard you heard, but the knife in the collection here, this knife, which hails from Jaipur in India, has a twin. I believe that twin was used to kill Lord Fazeley. I did not get a close-up view of the weapon, but its design was unmistakable, even at a distance of six or seven feet. This means that if we find out the name of the man who owns the twin, we will find out the name of the man who murdered the earl," she explained, then immediately flushed at her presumption. Despite how it might feel to her, they were not at Lakeview Hall and this was not a redux of their investigation into Mr. Otley's death. "That is to say, *I* will find the name of the killer. I am, of course, grateful for your helping in arranging access to the archive. I trust you won't feel obligated to remain beyond your interest. My maid accompanied me so the proprieties have been observed."

"I see your game, Miss Hyde-Clare, and it will not work," he announced as he took a document from the top of the pile.

"My game?" she asked, drawing her brows together in perplexity.

"You're trying to hoard your mystery," he explained, "but I will not be fobbed off by displays of false courtesy. Lord Fazeley's death is a matter of public consumption, not your private possession. I know this because I read about it in the *London Daily Gazette* this morning."

By implying that she could feel a sense of ownership to a dead man, he was being deliberately absurd in an attempt to provoke a response and she resolved not to accommodate him. If the Duke of Kesgrave wanted to spend his day sifting through dreary documents in the research room of the British Museum just to goad her temper, who was she to object?

As the hour wore on, however, she began to wonder if her understanding of his motives was less than complete, for he quietly perused page after page without complaint. The apparent earnestness of his interest forced her to reconsider her assumption, and in the end she was compelled to admit that he'd remained for a purpose other than to tweak her ego.

Why, she thought, would a gentleman of wealth, breeding and status who had every avenue of entertainment open to him choose to waste an afternoon reading letters to and from auction house clerks and antiquities dealers? The correspondence did have a few bright spots, such as the mix-up over a knife thought to be from the tomb of an Egyptian king but in fact belonging to the archeologist's local guide. But the vast majority of the letters were filled with the minor details of amassing a collection as far-reaching and impressive as Sir Walter's. Every step he'd taken to obtain the Singh dagger was provided in alarming specificity, and Bea wondered if the art of acquisition was his true love, not ownership itself.

Surely, Kesgrave found the documents as tiresome as she did.

But no, she thought, peering over the top of a letter at the duke and noting genuine fascination on his handsome face. She shouldn't have been surprised, for this was, after all, the very same man who had sat across from her in the dining room at Lakeview Hall and listed the name of every ship that had fought in the Battle of the Nile in order of appearance. He relished details and minutiae and ardent displays of arcana and pedantry.

She could easily picture the dinner party at which he would thoughtfully and painstakingly enlighten his fellow guests on the challenges of acquiring a pair of eighteenth-century daggers from a raga's former steward. How engrossed everyone at the table would appear! How intrigued! Nobody would grimace or interrupt or suggest that perhaps they turn the discussion to something everyone could participate in, such as Joseph Grimaldi's performance in *High-Mettled Racer*. No, they'd sit demurely, smile politely and privately imagine throwing scalloped oysters at his smug head. And they would do it because he was a duke and their fascination was owed him as much as their respect.

And that, she realized with sudden insight, was why he'd remained behind to study the documents in the reading room. The Duke of Kesgrave held himself in too high esteem to readily accept the blow she'd dealt to his consequence by figuring out who murdered Mr. Otley before him. That event, most likely unprecedented in his existence, had created a deficit in his self-worth, which he was determined to restore by discovering the identity of Fazeley's killer.

His intention to redeem himself explained why he had paid a visit to Portman Square that morning, as his claim of wanting to offer condolences on the death of Mr. Davies had sounded highly suspect when he'd issued it. Once again, all one had to do was consider his position in society and the opportunities available to him to recognize the truth. Tweaking the ego of one unimportant spinster had never been his objective. This matter was about vanity, yes, but not hers.

No wonder he had avoided her so assiduously at Lakeview Hall! From the moment she had announced to him she knew who the murderer was, he had evaded her presence, disappearing on an errand or bracketing himself in Skeffington's study with his lordship. She'd expected him to arrange a tête-à-tête to discuss the matter either before or after she revealed the identity of the culprit and was both disappointed and confused when he hadn't. But of course that made sense now, for in outwitting him she had pricked his ego and he felt no obligation to gratify hers.

And so the calculated condolence call to discover what information he could about Lord Fazeley's demise from the woman who, according to the *London Daily Gazette*, had witnessed it.

Bea did not begrudge him his interest, as she herself could not smother her own, but she did resent his motivation and believed it was an act of cruelty to draw her aunt into the affair. What an excruciating visit that would have been for poor Aunt Vera, torn between delight at having the illustrious Duke of Kesgrave in her humble drawing room nibbling on stale tea cakes from the day before and horror that he knew the depth of her family's shame, allowing a gently bred young lady to mourn the death of a penniless law clerk from Cheapside.

It was wrong, of course, to smile at her aunt's suffering, real or imagined, and yet she couldn't quite suppress her amusement.

"You found something?" Kesgrave asked suddenly.

Shook from her reverie, Bea tilted her head as she furrowed her brow in confusion. "Excuse me?"

"Have you found something that will point in the direction of the second dagger?" he asked. "You were looking at me and smiling, so I thought you might have something useful to share."

As embarrassed as she was to have been caught staring, she refused to give into the discomfiture and kept her light-brown eyes steadily trained on his vibrantly blue ones. "No, not yet," she said, then added as a distraction, "I was merely thinking how much the level of detail in these letters must appeal to you."

He knew he was being teased and yet answered sincerely. "As a collector myself, although nowhere on the scale of Sir Walter, I'm impressed with his ability to retain a dealer's goodwill while making an insultingly low offer. It's a skill I lack, as I always jump several steps ahead in a negotiation by starting with a fair offer, which provides me with fewer opportunities to counter. My agents despair of me."

The honest admission, like so much about Kesgrave, disconcerted her, and she glanced down at the letter in her hand. "I'm sure Mr. Goddard will be pleased by your admiration of Sir Walter. You must tell him that when he returns."

"Admit to the esteemed librarian that I'm unable to gain the upper hand in negotiations with auction house clerks?" he asked with exaggerated horror. "Relaying such trivialities will convince him I'm not a serious patron."

"You are a duke," she pointed out, as if that was all one needed to know to be convinced of anything.

He dipped his head in acknowledgment. "True."

Bea said nothing further as she returned to sorting through the archive: a letter from Mr. Bonham at the auction house, a report on the condition of the daggers, a bill for the cost of shipping the items from India, another letter from Mr. Bonham, a note announcing receipt of the daggers.

She was just beginning to think the project was hopeless when the duke said, "Lady Abercrombie."

"Lady Abercrombie?" she asked.

"He gave the second dagger to Lady Abercrombie in 1812, when he acquired them. He held on to one and gave her the other," he explained.

At once, she pictured the raven-haired beauty who had taken a string of lovers after her husband was killed on the Peninsula during the campaign's first year. The lady had recently passed the threshold of fifty and, if Bea was remembering it correctly, had a son only a year or two younger than Russell.

Although a knife struck her as an uncommon courting gift, she reminded herself it was beautifully carved and bedecked with jewels. It was also a rare collector's item and most likely worth more than the usual diamond bracelet.

"Did they have an affair? I never heard their names

linked, but I'm at best an indifferent gossip. It's not as interesting when you don't know the people."

"I believe they had a brief relationship," Kesgrave said thoughtfully. "Tilly is not one for constancy."

"Tilly?" she asked sharply. "Do you know her, your grace?"

"I do, yes," he said with a simplicity Bea found oddly unnerving. "Almost everyone does. She is a true social butterfly, amiable and outgoing. In general, she likes everyone and everyone likes her. You will like her too."

"Will I?" she said quietly as Kesgrave began to return the papers to a neat stack. She didn't know which surprised her more: his assumption that she was soon to meet the famous widow or that he was thoughtful enough to straighten up the table before they departed.

"Obviously, anything is possible, but I think it's highly implausible Tilly stabbed Fazeley," he explained as he arranged the documents in size order, with the largest ones on the bottom. "It's more likely she gave the knife to the person who did."

"It becomes less implausible if Lady Abercrombie was to be a chapter in Fazeley's book," she pointed out. "As you observed, she is not known for her constancy. Certainly, there is much opportunity to provide fodder."

He shook his head. "Tilly? No, she's too brazen to keep secrets. Everything she does is out in the open."

Bea, who felt a curious urge to scream every time Kesgrave said the other woman's name, found it hard to believe that a lady notorious for taking a string of lovers had no skeletons hiding in her cupboard. She did not mention that, however, because it was clear from the way he spoke of her—warmly, fondly, with affection—that the duke held her in high esteem. Naturally, she could not help but wonder if he did not number among her suitors.

"Furthermore," he added when she didn't respond, "I think Fazeley's talk of a memoir was all a hum to puff himself up. He did not have enough interest in anything to write a full sentence about it, let alone an entire book. Rather, he enjoyed having a cudgel with which to intimidate other people."

"But if those people believe it's real," she said, "one of them might have acted out of concern. The memoir's actual existence is incidental to one's perception of it."

He agreed with her point while taking a moment to reassert his conviction that Tilly had nothing to do with it. "But of course we will put the question to her with no further delay."

Hearing him say her name in that doting way yet again, Bea gnashed her teeth together in an effort to stay silent. She could not conceive what bothered her so much about his attitude, for it was no business of hers whose string he had chosen to adorn. Even at the height of her optimism, during those giddy first days of her first season, when she had believed there was something endearing about her freckles and the way her eyes twinkled with amusement, she would never have looked so high as the Duke of Kesgrave. A baronet, perhaps, or the son of a prosperous landowner. Aunt Vera, who worried that even those modest goals were too lofty, thought a second or third son would do better, someone whose prospects were already limited by a misfortune of birth.

Nobody, not even her late parents, whose judgment had most assuredly been corrupted by love, imagined anything so soaring for Beatrice Hyde-Clare as a duke.

And now here she was, a rolled-up spinster at the advanced age of six and twenty, her days of optimism long behind her and her spirit resigned to the ineffable reality of life. Not once in her drab existence had she railed at the fate providence had seen fit to assign her and then she heard the blasted Duke of Kesgrave say the name Tilly with tender affection.

Suddenly and all at once, she felt an urge to object.

'Twas pure foolishness, of course, and she was almost inclined to seek refuge in her grief, for what woman deep in the throes of mourning a lost love could be relied upon to be sensible. If only Mr. Davies had managed to avoid that speeding mail coach or had properly chewed that joint of mutton before trying to swallow or learned to swim before jumping into that pond to retrieve his hat, Miss Hyde-Clare would not be in danger of developing a tendre for the unattainable duke.

She was, of course, far too levelheaded to allow herself the pleasure of attributing a real feeling to an artificial emotion even in jest. But the idea itself, the fact that it existed in even some small way as a possibility, made her smile, for her lively mind appreciated any scheme that had absurdity at its core. Immediately, she felt her gloom lift and with it her perspective. Her developing anything for Kesgrave other than a deeper sense of contempt for his condescension was laughable. It actually caused her to chortle.

Ah, there it was again—her appreciation for a scheme with absurdity at its core.

Her frame of mind improved, Bea reached for the ribbon to help secure the orderly stack and turned her attention to the duke's last statement. What had it been? Something about putting the question to Sir Walter's former mistress with no further delay.

And she was reasonably sure he had used the pronoun *we*.

Startled, she looked at him and said, "Both of us?"

"Are you not as curious to know what happened to the dagger as I?"

"Yes, of course I am," she responded at once, "but going right now…it's unexpected and I'm…"

At a loss, she trailed off.

"In mourning?" he asked, lips curving into a smile.

Baffled, she thought. Bewildered. Confused by the invitation and willingness to share his access to the dazzling widow. If they were engaged in a race to see who could be more clever in figuring out the murderer this time around, then why surrender his advantage? For her, the chase for the dagger ended right there, in the research room of the British Museum. She could not call on Lady Abercrombie, identify herself as an interloper and boldly ask about a knife her dead lover had given her. Similarly, she couldn't dress in her darkest colors, skulk around the lady's town house until she gained entry into the residence and poke through her things looking for information about the weapon.

She did not have the courage for either one of those activities.

With his entrée to every drawing room in the kingdom, he would have won handily this time. Why, then, would he seek her company?

Truly, it was a puzzle, and perhaps the only way to make sense of it was to reevaluate her earlier assumption. Maybe he *did* seek an appreciative audience, for a duke who sparkled unobserved did not sparkle at all. She'd assumed he was determined to prove something to himself by identifying Fazeley's killer, but as she pondered the unlikeliness of his invitation, she considered the possibility that he did indeed feel compelled to prove something to *her*. After all, she was the one who had gained the upper hand by outwitting him in the Lake District, and as the Duke of Kesgrave, he had privileged access to his own perfection. He did not require corroborating evidence to be in awe of it. But Miss Beatrice Hyde-Clare, with her acute perception and her contempt for his importance, needed persuading.

It surprised her that a man of Kesgrave's temperament would care about her opinion at all, for she must appear like an ant to him, something so small as to pass almost unnoticed. It wasn't merely that her standing in society was so much less than his; it was also the fact that she'd failed to perform appropriately for her own class. The only creature of less importance among the beau monde was the elderly female, a form she would take sooner or later.

She wondered if that in itself was the problem, for it must be very galling for a duke to find himself down a point against a plain-faced nonentity. In the regular order of things, he should not even have been required to notice her existence, and yet there she was, eternally present, a niggling concern buzzing in his ear, more fly than ant.

Did she truly believe Kesgrave could be so miserly in his generosity that he would begrudge an aging spinster her small moment of triumph? Bea did not know. What she did know was what she had always known: the yawning disparity of their situations. The duke already had so much. Did he really need this too?

But perhaps she was being uncharitable in her understanding of his motives. She had seen for herself his need to establish order, the way he felt obligated to correct mistakes no matter how minor or irrelevant to the point under discussion. His desire to reassert himself might simply be an extension of that compulsion: She had upset the natural order of the world, and he could not rest until his dominance was restored.

Ultimately, it didn't matter what motive impelled his offer to introduce her to Lady Abercrombie. The fact of the matter was she had run into a large impediment to her investigation into the dagger, and the Duke of Kesgrave had provided her with a way around it. She could stand on principle and decline, of course, but that would mean depriving herself of something she enjoyed. And she could not avoid the truth any longer: She thoroughly enjoyed the challenge of trying to identify a villain. It was thrilling to have a purpose to one's day and invigorating to know one had something useful to add to the world. Usefulness beyond fetching a pair of scissors for her aunt or cousin was an entirely new sensation for Bea, and she was unwilling to give it up so easily.

"I *am* in mourning, your grace," Bea said after a long interval, "and indeed at this very moment I am tucked up in my bedchamber weeping inconsolably into my pillow."

"How long do you expect that to last?" he asked as they rose from their chairs. He picked up the stack of documents and carried it to the clerk who sat at the desk in front of the door to the archive.

"It's difficult to say because one's moods can be so changeable, but I wouldn't be surprised if the tears start to subside a few hours before the Lelands' ball," she said, nodding at the young man, who was too in awe of the duke to notice the gesture, much less return it.

Kesgrave's lips twitched in amusement, but he shook his head. "Having met your aunt, I would advise you to taper your tears sometime today, or she will insist you are too grief-stricken to attend the event."

"She has already played that card," Bea said. "In all actuality, she has probably discovered by now that I'm not in my room, for Flora has been quite devoted in her concern for me, equally lovely and smothering. She will be horrified to learn that I went to the museum today."

"And your visit to Lady Abercrombie?" he asked curiously. "How will you account for that?"

It was a good question, and Bea cursed the demands of propriety, which obligated her to tote a servant behind her every time she stepped outside. If she were alone, there would be no way for her aunt to discover how she'd passed the day. Of course, Bea could always ask Annie not to mention their diversion to Grosvenor Square, but she had no idea how such a request would affect the young maid. Perhaps knowing the information was delicate would make her more inclined to share it.

Elevating it to an order would no doubt make spreading the tale irresistible.

Very well, Bea thought. She would let the strangeness of the visit stand for itself. "I won't try to account for it. It will merely be further proof of a mental deterioration sparked by an unfortunate proximity to Mr. Otley's bloodied corpse. Perceiving a striking difference in my behavior since our sojourn to the Lake District, Aunt Vera has been alarmed for months."

"Has there been a striking difference?" he asked.

Even as she marveled at the inappropriate frankness of her conversation, she answered him honestly by saying yes. She even added that her aunt's understanding of the events wasn't too wide off the mark, as discovering Mr. Otley's dead body on the floor of the Skeffingtons' library had indeed shifted something inside her.

As candidly as she spoke, however, she did not tell him the entire truth. She did not reveal that the change had everything to do with him. She did not explain that it had begun the moment she'd stepped free from the row of bookshelves and saw him standing over the lifeless figure of the spice trader. Any fear she had felt at the persona he affected, the imperious and imposing duke simmering with disdain, was violently supplanted by terror of his person: the lithe, powerful man capable of snuffing the life out of her.

It was impossible to cower in self-conscious regard when you believed you were about to die.

It was also impossible, she'd discovered in the minutes and hours and days that followed, to revive the awe you once felt. Having confronted Kesgrave in the dead of night and suffering no ill effects, she could not resist challenging him in the bright light of day—in the drawing room, at the dinner table, in the privacy of his own room, which she had stolen into to demand answers to his inexplicable behavior.

Yes, something ineffable had altered in that moment when she discovered Mr. Otley's corpse, and because it had, she did not feel the least bit discomfited at the prospect of being in a carriage with him. What would have been a form of torture during her first six seasons struck her now as a pleasant diversion, and during the ride to Lady Abercrombie's establishment in Grosvenor Square, she chatted easily and unrestrainedly about her aunt's concerns for her mental acuity and funeral arrangements for poor Mr. Davies and whether the term "fazed" to describe a stunned silence in response to a cutting set-down would continue to prosper in the absence of the man who embodied it. Indeed, she was far more unsettled by the baffled look Annie had given her when she'd appeared in the entry hall of the museum in the company of the duke and continued to give her during the whole of the drive to Grosvenor Square.

CHAPTER FIVE

Although Beatrice had met few women who counted a pet lion cub among their possessions, she felt positive she would find them all just as objectionable as Lady Abercrombie.

"Go on, please, there's no reason to be afraid," the widow insisted, her red lips curved into an amiable smile. "He's a darling, I assure you, and delights in being held. Here, you must."

Bea stared at the squirming mass of golden fur no larger than the mouser who slept under the table in the kitchens at Welldale House. It was adorable, to be sure, with its fluffy ears and large paws, and her desire to cuddle the endearing creature was equal to her horror at finding it in a London drawing room. And what a drawing room it was—a fantasia in the Chinese style to rival the pavilion at Brighton: lotus-shaped chandeliers, gilded serpents coiling around the coved ceiling, a bamboo canopy, trompe l'oeil wallpaper with dragons, dolphins, birds and flowers.

Verily, the room was bursting with so much color and curios she didn't know where to look.

No, that wasn't true, for the woman at the center of the room holding out a lion cub demanded attention. She was indeed as beautiful as reports had indicated—

brooding eyes offset by a pert nose, heart-shaped face with fulsome lips, glossy black curls piled on the top of her head and tumbling down in calculated disarray. Her gown was just as eye-catching: elegant, colorful, revealing.

Sweeping into the room a few minutes earlier, she had apologized for the informality of her ensemble. It was only her impatience to see Kesgrave that had kept her from retreating to her dressing room to prepare properly for her guests.

She offered the statement with a sheepish smile, as if charmed by her own irrepressible idiosyncrasy, but Bea recognized the claim for the disingenuous nonsense it was. Lady Abercrombie was already a study in perfection, and to pretend she could ascend further by way of formality was to imply the lily could be gilded.

Obviously, she lived in constant expectation of receiving visitors, a state that was not unusual for a woman of her standing. No doubt her extravagant drawing room saw a steady stream of callers. Bea did not begrudge her that, for she wasn't so small-minded as to take exception to another woman's popularity. No, her complaint ran deeper and fixated on the pretense, the determination to make her life's work invisible so that the perfection for which she'd labored for hours appeared effortless. It distressed Bea to see how hollow she was.

Why else take a wild creature to your bosom and show it off as a rare and wonderful novelty? The baby cub had done nothing to deserve the cruel treatment other than be born in the wrong place. If it were on the African plain where it belonged, it wouldn't be unique at all.

As these thoughts ran through Bea's head, Lady Abercrombie pressed the lion into her arms and smiled with approval as he licked his new host's elbow.

"You see that?" she said. "Henry is a lamb. As gentle as can be. I take him for a walk every morning in the square and he doesn't even chase the birds."

Bea readily acknowledged that the cuddly little cub

was placid and sweet and that holding him was an uncommon delight. But how she felt about the animal had never been the point, for its comfort was more important than her fleeting pleasure, and she could not help but wonder what would happen when he gained a few hundred pounds, grew into his paws and learned how to rip flesh from bone with his mighty teeth. Would Lady Abercrombie consign him to a cage in the corner of the room or deliver him as a gift to the Royal Menagerie at the Tower? Both fates seemed desperately sad to her.

"You named him after your dead husband?" Kesgrave asked, amused.

Satisfied with how well Bea and her pet were getting along, her ladyship sat in an armchair upholstered in red silk and said, "I name all my pets after my dead husband because I'm so accustomed to saying his name in a tone of fond exasperation and baffled tolerance. Do you think Henry would have minded?"

The duke graciously said that he didn't believe her husband would have minded anything she did.

Bea cringed at the unctuous reply, but their hostess was much gratified by it and reminded him of the time she had poured a glass of muscatel on Henry's box of prize snuff by accident. Kesgrave laughed with appropriate humor, and encouraged by his response, Lady Abercrombie launched into another story that was ostensibly about her clumsiness but was really about how charming she was. After relating a few more anecdotes in the same vein, she switched the subject to the Earl of Fazeley's death, which caused Bea to sit up straighter in her chair in expectation of hearing something interesting. Alas, the widow merely avowed shock at his lordship's stabbing and pronounced herself astonished that the gentleman appeared actually to have died in the encounter. "Naturally, when I first heard of the attack, I assumed it was a spectacle arranged by the earl to draw more attention to himself. As you know, he adored being the object of speculation."

Although Beatrice agreed with this summation of the earl's character, it was rather strange hearing it come from a woman who was sitting in the middle of an Oriental-style fantasia with her pet lion cub only a few feet away.

Perhaps, Bea thought, it was merely a case of like recognizing like.

"I wouldn't be surprised if he'd arranged the whole thing himself," she said, "and something went dreadfully amiss in the execution."

If the duke disagreed with this assessment, he did not say so, but rather chastised Lady Abercrombie for her cynicism in a tone so playful it rather sounded like a compliment. Then he asked about mutual friends he expected to see at the Lelands' upcoming ball, which was the first of the season.

Although the conversation was banal and provided Kesgrave with few opportunities to demonstrate his superior understanding, he was wholly engaged in the enterprise and responded eagerly to all her comments.

Watching the duke interact with the lovely widow was a revelatory experience, for Bea had never before seen such an expert display of ingratiating enthusiasm or determination to entertain.

Only a little while ago, she'd thought she would never feel intimidated by the Duke of Kesgrave ever again, and yet she felt the fear crawl over her as she observed his performance. This, she realized with growing dread, was who he really was—this creature of the drawing room, this man who deferred on every point and offered compliments both effusive and unnecessary. With no compunction at all, he sat in the middle of that ostentatious grotesquerie and flirted enthusiastically with a woman who seemed to have no more control of her décolletage than she did the poor African animal she shamelessly adopted to make herself appear more interesting.

Bea could not blame him, of course, for being like all the other men she had met during her seasons—the ones whose approval she'd never earned, the ones whose attention she'd never caught. If the discovery caused a pang, it was only because she'd thought Kesgrave was different, for that was how he'd appeared at Lakeview Hall—as if he was so far above the regular order of the *ton* he wouldn't be able to see it even if he bent down to look. But now she realized that it was merely that the company at Lakeview had been so far below it.

As their tête-à-tête wore on, Bea opened her mouth at least two dozen times to announce that they were there to discuss the Jaipur dagger. In her head, she made the statement with a majestic indifference to their absorption, as if blithely unaware that they had been talking to each other. In reality, however, she was too timid to speak. What she feared most was not that they would glare at her in displeasure at the interruption but that they would not notice her at all. Sitting there with, of all things, a napping lion cub on her lap, she was wholly unseen. It was like every ball she had ever gone to.

And then suddenly she looked up and they were both staring at her with an air of expectation. What had she missed?

"I was just telling Tilly about the dagger," Kesgrave explained.

Startled by the development, Bea said, "Thank you."

It was an inane thing to say, and she regretted it the moment the words were out of her mouth. What did she have to be grateful for?

The duke must have also thought it was an idiotic comment, for he tilted his head at her and furrowed his brow. "I explained how you wanted to acquire the knife for your uncle as a birthday present, for he has long admired its twin at the British Museum, and that I agreed to assist you as a favor to my father, who was a great friend of your own father."

Given that they had not discussed any sort of ruse in the carriage—how could they, with Annie only a few inches away—Bea was taken aback by this information and wondered why he had not informed her of his plan earlier. Did he not think it was relevant?

Aware that she had let the silence stretch a little bit too long again, she said, "Yes, of course. And that is why I'm so grateful. I would have no hope of acquiring such a prize piece without his grace's help. I'm afraid I have few resources when it comes to things like antiquities and weaponry."

Lady Abercrombie accepted this information with an affable nod, for it was, Bea noted wryly, very easy to believe she was a woman without resources. "And you say you are a Hyde-Clare?"

"I *am* a Hyde-Clare," she said with needlessly pointed emphasis. Of course her ladyship wasn't trying to imply that she wasn't actually a member of the family she claimed as her own.

The other woman nodded thoughtfully for several long moments as she considered the information. "Your father was Richard, then, and your mother was Clara."

Of all the things Bea expected to happen during this interview, meeting someone who had known her parents was not on the list. "Yes, that's correct."

Her ladyship sighed. "I remember when they died. Such a tragic accident and a shock, too, for your father was an excellent yachtsman."

Bea had never heard anything about her father's boating skill before, and she leaned forward in her chair, disrupting the sleeping lion, who rubbed its paw against its nose before settling down again. "Was he?"

"Oh, yes, the finest. He was quite the Corinthian, your father," she said with breathless admiration.

"The dagger," Kesgrave said with a hint of impatience.

Although Bea longed to remind him of the fifteen minutes he'd just spent talking about the Earl of Fenwich's weekend party two summers ago, she contented herself with a scowl.

"I'm still not entirely clear on which dagger you mean," Lady Abercrombie said.

Bea found that difficult to believe and wondered what her ladyship was trying to hide with her evasive answer. "How many daggers did Sir Walter give you?"

Her hostess let out a throaty laugh and said, "A great many," in a way that made Bea feel out of step and unworldly.

"Tilly," Kesgrave said warningly.

"It's the truth, Damien. I swear it to you," she said, her eyes twinkling with mirth. "Every time I turned around, there was Sir Walter with another dagger. They were like flowers to him. Arrive late to the opera? Here's a jeweled dagger for your troubles. Have a particularly satisfying outing? Take this jeweled dagger as a token of my appreciation."

Although Bea did not quite comprehend the undercurrent to the conversation or its cause, she certainly understood the meaning of a satisfying outing. Determined to brazen out the awkwardness she felt, she said, "We are looking for one with a jade handle carved in the shape of a horse."

"Ah, you mean Henry," Lady Abercrombie said.

"Do you name all the tokens of appreciation from your lovers after your dead husband or just the ones with animal figurines?" Kesgrave asked dryly.

"Just the ones that are fourteen inches long," she said, tilting her eyes down in a coy expression.

With no effort at all, Bea could picture her at the vanity practicing the look in the mirror until she established the ideal angle for maximum coquettishness. It had probably taken her several hours, and Bea again felt disgusted at the artifice. She knew it was unfair to judge her, for the *ton* demanded pretense. Any woman hoping to succeed had to affect any number of poses and opinions and learn to shrug off slights as if they hadn't been uttered.

Needless to say, Bea had never mastered any of these skills. Thanks to her great timidity, she was as unartful as she was inarticulate in company, and the more matrons of society she met—Lady Abercrombie, Lady Skeffington, Mrs. Otley—the more grateful she was for her inadequacies.

If the duke was impressed with the widow's display, he gave no indication as Bea asked where Henry was now.

"That is the question, isn't it?" she asked thoughtfully. "I'm afraid I'm not at liberty to say at the moment, as it would reveal information that isn't yet public."

Bea considered this statement to be rather definitive, but Kesgrave saw it as an opening gambit in a negotiation and immediately began cajoling her ladyship to divulge the name. He talked of their long history and their shared affection and her cruelty in forcing him to break a promise he'd made to his father to help the orphaned child of his dear friend. Although the compact had been a practical invention devised only a few minutes before, he defended it as ardently as if it had predated the agreement between King John and the rebel faction that resulted in the Magna Carta.

He complimented her complexion and praised her wit and pointed out how skillfully she reduced men like him to mere desperate applicants for her attention.

This last comment made Lady Abercrombie laugh with genuine amusement, and she said, "You are reduced to nothing."

It was, Bea thought, the first display of intelligence she had seen in the woman, for her observation was accurate in both its meanings. With his coaxing attempts coldly calculated, Kesgrave remained firmly in control and had not been reduced to anything. And yet the effort alone, with its cold calculation, made him something smaller.

Her ladyship, either bored of the game herself or worried that the Duke of Kesgrave would lose interest in it first, admitted that she had given the knife to Lord Duncan.

"Lord Duncan?" Kesgrave repeated in surprise.

Perceiving him shocked, Lady Abercrombie preened. "He is a friend of my son's—George, you know, who is my youngest. He spent the Christmas holidays with us at Derenfield Park, and it only seemed right that I give him a present in gratitude for his delightful company."

As the tenor of that delight was clear even to Bea, she

understood the duke's response and her ladyship's intention in eliciting it. What escaped her comprehension, however, was why the other woman had implied earlier that the information would soon be widely known. "You said *yet* before."

Her ladyship, her eyes challenging Kesgrave to disapprove of her daring to tryst with a significantly younger man, spared only the briefest glance at Beatrice. "Excuse me?"

"Before, when I asked to whom you had given the dagger, you said the information was not public yet," she explained. "Why did you say *yet*? Are you and Lord Duncan preparing an announcement? Is there a future to your relationship that requires its broadcast to the world at large?"

Lady Abercrombie narrowed her eyes but otherwise affected amusement at the question. "Aren't you a charming young lady, determined to find a cabal in a thoughtlessly tossed-off word."

Bea sat up straighter in her chair, for when she'd asked the question her reach had truly not extended so far as a secret plot. She'd merely thought the inclusion of the word *yet* was odd. Now, however, she wondered what her ladyship was hiding. "Obviously, there's nothing to be gained in revealing to all and sundry your liaison with Lord Duncan, as it will alienate your son and make the *ton* more keenly aware of your age creeping ever upward. If you planned to marry him, it would be different, for then it would be a triumph for you. But Lord Duncan hasn't reached his majority and his parents would never allow their heir to marry a woman beyond childbearing years. So I ask again: Why did you say *yet*?"

Her ladyship sent the duke a resentful look, as if he were responsible for this act of effrontery disrupting the tranquility of her Chinese-style sanctuary, with its beautiful lotus chandeliers and playful carved serpents. "Honestly, my dear, I don't know what you're trying to accomplish with this juvenile display. Tantrums might work in the schoolroom but they have no effect here. Now, you might wish to linger longer to make preposterous insinuations, but Kesgrave, at least, has the mature judgment to recognize when it is time to leave."

She rose to her feet, and the duke, impelled by courtesy, stood as well, but Bea stayed firmly planted in her seat. She was determined to get a reply to her question, yes, but she was also cradling a sleeping lion in her lap. She assumed all maxims advising one not to disturb the slumber of dogs applied double for the slumber of lions.

Thoughtfully, Bea said, "As you have no cause for the story to get out, your word choice must imply that someone else will be spreading the news. Could it be Lord Duncan?" She paused a moment to consider the prospect. "He would have some motive, for a tryst with an older, more experienced woman would burnish his reputation among his fellows, I'm sure. But is that worth the alienation of his friend? I don't know the gentleman well enough to speculate, but let's say for now that Lord Duncan has chosen to honor your request to remain silent about the affair. That means that some other party knows about it and plans to publish the information." As soon as she said the word *publish,* the missing piece of the puzzle slipped into place and she understood why she had said *yet.* "The Earl of Fazeley discovered your relationship and planned to include details of it in his memoir."

Lady Abercrombie laughed gaily and complimented Beatrice on her remarkable imagination. "You are indeed a delightful child. We must do all we can to make you fashionable. It will be my project for the season. First, we shall introduce you to Lady Jersey and secure your vouchers for Almack's. Then we'll go shopping, for surely we can improve on that serviceable but dull gown you're wearing. Who is in charge of your care? Your aunt and uncle, did you say? Vera Hyde-Clare never did have an eye for color or style. No bother. We shall take care of it, I promise."

Having spent her whole life pretending to be one thing or another, her ladyship affected sublime indifference beautifully, but Bea wasn't fooled. She understood the deal on offer: If she would leave off talking about Lord Duncan and the affair, then Lady Abercrombie would provide her with the social success all young ladies dreamed of. It made sense, of course, that that would be her quid pro quo, as popularity was clearly the thing the other woman valued most.

Before Bea could assure her she was content with her obscurity and adequate wardrobe, Kesgrave said, "Fazeley was Duncan's godfather."

Lady Abercrombie sighed and sat down. "Well, if you're determined to deprive me of the dignity of my lie, then, yes, Duncan told Fazeley about our dalliance and Fazeley came to me threatening to publish it in his memoir if I didn't give him a substantial sum to forget about it. Naturally, I'm too stubborn to succumb to coercion and told him to do whatever he thought was best. It's a scandal, of course. George will rail at me for the betrayal, as he's very much like his father in many ways, and his sisters will lament the embarrassment, but at the end of the day it will be a tempest in a teacup. Indeed, I fully expect George to thank me when he calms down, for if one's friends are so debauched as to dally with one's mother, it's better to know before they have the opportunity to dally with one's wife."

Her tone was convincingly light and resigned to the prospect of exposure, and Bea wondered if it was an effect she was only able to achieve now that the threat had passed. Fazeley's death had solved an awkward problem for her, which provided her with an inducement to seek it. But would any woman be so rash as to end a man's life simply to avoid an uncomfortable scene with her son? Bea thought rather not, but, she reminded herself, she had only Lady Abercrombie's word as to the nature of the secret the earl held. Perhaps in truth it was something considerably more scandalous.

There was no way to know without having access to the book.

Thinking of the book, she looked at the duke to gauge his reaction to the news that Lord Fazeley's memoir was not only genuine but also the chronicle of salacious deeds the gossipmongers feared it would be. His expression, however, gave nothing away, and when he did speak, it was only to observe that Lord Duncan should have known better than to confide in his godfather.

"He's just a boy," her ladyship said, excusing his naïveté. Then she turned to Bea, her expression a mix of exasperation and impatience. "Really, my dear, it's a rather ordinary dagger. A little flashier than usual but still fairly mundane. I'm not sure it's worth all this bother. Indeed, no dagger is. I've half a mind to donate my entire collection of knives to the British Museum, for they either gather dust in a glass case or cause me to be subjected to an unjust interrogation in my own drawing room."

"If you're going to donate anything to the museum, perhaps it should be your drawing room," Bea said in an attempt to be a little cutting but it somehow came out fully admiring.

"La, it's perfection, is it not?" Lady Abercrombie asked with almost childlike delight as she tilted her head back to gaze in wonder at her own coved ceiling. "Getting all the details right was simply the most challenging experience of my entire life. The bamboo canopy over the side table is the third one. I had to send the first two back because the stalks didn't match. Imagine sending irregularly sized bamboo stalks to Mayfair!"

Bea professed horror and assured her she could not.

"It took the workmen five tries to get the chandelier in the center of the room. You'd think they'd appreciate achieving perfection, but they resented the obligation every step of the way," she explained with a shake of her head. "And do not let me start talking about the wallpaper, for how an artisan can advertise himself as an expert on the Oriental design and not know what a pagoda looks like is one of the great scandals of the modern era."

But of course it was already too late, for having begged her visitor not to get her started on the wallpaper she had already gotten herself started on the wallpaper and could not finish until the whole terrible truth was out.

Despite herself, Bea found herself fascinated by the widow's devotion to a vision and her determination to see it carried out to the last minor detail. She felt the triviality of the undertaking, the emphasis on appearance and spectacle that accompanied everything the other woman did, but she also perceived the consequentiality of it. It required an astute mind to stay abreast of the hundreds of particulars that went into such an elaborate presentation.

She had little doubt this woman could conceive and execute a plan to carry out a murder with military-like precision. Maybe she did it herself. Maybe she recruited an underling. Maybe she hired an associate.

Finding the discussion of the room's interior design to be not as restful as tales of salaciousness and extortion, the lion cub raised his head, roared softly and climbed down from Bea's lap. Kesgrave was likewise disquieted by the new subject and interrupted their conversation on the proper composition of a dragon's scale to announce their departure. The hour grew late, and he had to return Miss Hyde-Clare to her home before her uncle began to wonder where she was. "We don't want to ruin the surprise."

Lady Abercrombie promptly agreed, for she was particularly fond of surprises, and wished Bea luck in her dealings with Lord Duncan. "I cannot believe he will deny you the pleasure, especially if you offer him a generous price. His parents hold the purse strings unduly tight."

Bea thanked her for the word of advice and bid her good day as she stepped into the hallway, where her maid waited with her pelisse. She expected to depart immediately, but Lady Abercrombie could not be made to take a brusque leave of Kesgrave. As effortlessly as she'd assumed the role of decorator when discussing the drawing room, she adopted the part of accomplished flirt in making

her goodbyes, teasing and cajoling her guest on his inde-
cent haste. Now, as he had before, the duke quickly fell in
line, uttering foolish phrases and extravagant praise, and
Bea kept her head tilted down so he would not read the
disdain in her eyes.

By the time they stepped outside again, she was feeling churlish and impatient with Kesgrave for a variety of
reasons, not the least of which was she knew how he
would respond if she raised her suspicions about Lady
Abercrombie.

"Tilly?" he would say in that tone of baffled fondness. "Tilly the delightful scatterbrain?"

Kesgrave thought far too little of the widow to take
her seriously, something her ladyship had been relying on
for years.

Once again Bea thought about the monumental undertaking of the drawing room and knew the woman was
far more substantial than he gave her credit for.

Wishing for the opportunity to tweak his ego in private, she suggested they walk the half dozen blocks to
Portman Square. As Annie trailed several steps behind
them, she said, "I'm surprised you didn't explain that it
was char or perhaps trout."

The duke tilted his head, looked at her with baffled
blue eyes and said, "Excuse me?"

"When Lady Abercrombie and I were discussing
which fish the scales on a dragon most closely resemble,
I'm surprised you didn't volunteer an informed opinion,
such as suggesting that it was probably char or trout," she
said, referencing a conversation they'd had months ago at
Lakeview Hall. Naturally, she had no expectation of his
remembering it. "That sort of attention to detail is one of
your chief delights."

"Char and trout are fish indigenous to the Lake District and cannot be found in China, which is where most
depictions of the dragon derive. Presumably, artists rendering them employ local species such as silver carp," he ex-

plained, his voice steeped in pomposity and his bearing regal as he corrected the profound ignorance of her comment.

And then he relaxed his shoulders and grinned, revealing the truth of his intentions, and she felt a confounding twist in her belly. While surrounded by the ostentation of Lady Abercrombie's drawing room—a condition that applied as much to the duke's manners as to the gilded serpents—she had been unable to imagine ever feeling comfortable in his presence again. Once she had seen that aspect of his character, that intimidating society creature plying flattery like wine, she'd believed she would always see it. But that assumption was wrong, for here was her Kesgrave again.

Oh, that was dangerous—to think of him as hers.

She closed her eyes, inhaled deeply and revised her thought: Here was the familiar Kesgrave.

When she opened them again, she said, "Lord Duncan is a likely prospect. He must have been quite angry when he discovered his own godfather had betrayed his trust. It was exceptionally contemptible that Fazeley used someone else's secret to extort money."

"On the contrary," the duke said, "it's quite unexceptional. I'm fairly certain that's how blackmail works. One discovers another person's immoral or embarrassing deeds and threatens to expose them to the world, as there's no money to be made in threatening to expose one's own sins."

"I stand corrected, your grace," she said with a nod of her head. "I wonder how many other victims there are. The fact that he threatened Lady Abercrombie with exposure in his book indicates to me that he made a regular habit of coercing money out of fellow members of the *ton*. There could be dozens of people who wanted to harm him. A truly successful blackmail scheme would entail multiple payments from a variety of targets. Perhaps someone became tired of paying the fee or simply didn't have pockets deep enough to cover it any longer. If only we had the book, then we would know the scale of the problem."

"But we don't have the book," he said calmly, "nor will we try to get it."

It was an astonishing implication, to insinuate that she would gain illegal entry into a dead man's town house, and Bea halted in her steps to stare at him, determined to understand how this remarkable thing had happened. Of all the people in all the world to credit Beatrice Hyde-Clare with unmitigated courage and daring, *how* had it turned out to be the high-handed Duke of Kesgrave?

Almost at once, she began to wonder if she could actually be the woman he perceived her to be. How did one go about breaking into a gentleman's residence? The first step would be to acquire the skill of opening a lock with an instrument created for just such a purpose. Where did one go to learn something like that? Were there schools or tutors available for hire?

Displeased with her silence, he repeated the injunction. "I said, nor will we try to get it."

"Yes, yes, I know," she insisted, her eyes darting to the street, where a high phaeton helmed by a stern-faced driver rumbled past. "I don't know why you would think otherwise."

That statement, at least, was true enough.

"That's because you cannot see the shifty look in your eye and I can," he explained with only a hint of amusement.

"Shifty," she repeated softly, flattered by this unexpected description as well.

Surely, a shifty woman could figure out how to sneak into Lord Fazeley's home without anyone being the wiser.

"And there it is again," he said, sounding a note of satisfaction, as if he'd just caught her in the act of stealing a biscuit from the tea tray. "I must insist, Miss Hyde-Clare, that you tell me exactly what you are thinking."

"That we must arrange an interview with Lord Duncan," she said honestly, as she started walking again. The detour to Lady Abercrombie's home was more time-consuming than she'd expected, and the hour grew late.

"There is much we do not know, such as how he felt upon discovering his godfather's betrayal and what he did with the knife. If he doesn't have a satisfying answer to the latter, then we may be sure he is the murderer."

"Yes, we do need to find out what he knows," Kesgrave agreed pensively, as an abstracted expression swept across his face.

"Ah, now I see," Bea said.

His eyes came into focus as he considered her. "See what?"

"How shifty looks," she replied. "You intend to interview Lord Duncan on your own. *And* you will use your advantage as a male in society to do it. Please do not insult me by denying it."

His smiled faintly. "That I'm a male in society? Rest assured, my dear Miss Hyde-Clare, I will never try to deny to you that I am a man."

She growled at his playful tone, which served not only as a distraction but also as an uncomfortable reminder of his flirtation with Lady Abercrombie.

Although her reaction only amused him further, he addressed her concern seriously. "I thought only of moving the investigative process along more quickly by raising the matter with him this evening if I could find him at his club or a particular gaming hell that he is known to frequent. If that is what you meant by taking advantage of my position in society, then I must concede you are correct."

It infuriated her to think of all the options that were available to him but not to her, and rendered impotent by the implacable forces that constrained her choices, she lashed out at the duke in the harshest terms she could think of. "I must admit, your grace, you do indeed know how to take advantage of your position in society, which, after today's display, I can only assume is as a charming lapdog. I would never have thought you could manage feats of excessive subservience because at the Skeffingtons' you wore such a supercilious sneer, but I see now you just needed the right hand to pet you. And what a lovely hand it was. How did you describe her skin? Like the finest Limoges. How sweetly you fell in line with her expectations, how eagerly you debased yourself to please her. You are clearly a skilled sycophant. If only I had realized it sooner, then I wouldn't have been so in awe of you."

'Twas a thoroughly punishing speech, and she delighted to see the Duke of Kesgrave cringe multiple times. But he did not blush and he did not offer the self-justifying defense she'd expected.

Rather, he said softly, "You were in awe of me?"

Startled, she blinked at him several times, wondering how the conversation had gotten so far off course. Only moments ago, she had been tossing humiliating insults at his head. "What? No. Of course not."

"But you just said it," he replied.

Bea could not believe that was true and repeated the speech quickly in her head: lapdog...Limoges...eagerly... sycophant...awe.

Well, yes, there it was.

She'd gotten so carried away with her slights, she had foolishly and inadvertently revealed a truth about herself. Of all the horrible mistakes she could have made! Mortified, she tried to think of something cutting to say and only came up with *lapdog* again.

Kesgrave laughed, then asked if she was sure she would be attending the Leland ball the next day. "You are positive your aunt will not figure out some way to make you miss it?"

Although she couldn't imagine what one thing had to do with another, she was grateful for the change in subject and said she was certain as they turned left onto her block.

"Very good," he said. "We will interview Lord Duncan then."

Amazed, she realized her speech had worked—not the effusive barrage of insults to deflate his ego but the one accidental compliment that puffed it up.

Rather than marvel in silence, she said, "Thank you, your grace."

"You're welcome."

As they approached her house, Kesgrave wondered if he should bid her goodbye there, rather than in full view of the front windows, but Beatrice felt confident the precaution was not necessary.

"Remember, if you will, Aunt Vera's response when Mr. Skeffington suggested we were working together in the Lake District to identify Mr. Otley's killer," she said. "I believe she fell to her knees laughing at the implausibility. Even if she observed you in my company right now, she would dismiss it as some sort of trick of the light, for her mind would not be able to process the information in any other way. Trust me, your grace, I know my aunt's prejudices intimately."

He gave her a dubious look. "Your aunt may be a little injudicious at times, but I think in this you are greatly underestimating her. She will hear your maid's report that you spent the day with me and won't be able to dismiss it as easily as you think."

Bea knew this observation to be true and once again felt annoyed by the demands of decorum. And yet, as she looked over her shoulder at Annie, she wondered if there might be a way to gain her silence. Perhaps if she paid her the respect of treating her as an equal in the subterfuge.

"Annie, do you see the Duke of Kesgrave here?" Bea asked, her tone lilting in such a way as to make the expected answer perfectly clear.

"No, miss, I do not," Annie answered primly, but her eyes twinkled with amusement. "I see a hack returning us to the house after a long and exhaustive day at the British Museum."

"You see there?" Bea said with a pert smile. "We are covered. And tomorrow, when Aunt Vera accosts you at Lady Leland's ball, she will introduce me to you as if we've barely met."

"Impossible," Kesgrave said.

"I wager a shilling she will," Bea added confidently. "Furthermore, she will remind you of our visit to the Lake District and studiously avoid any mention of Mr. Otley's death or even the Skeffingtons. And she will say we all had a lovely time, which will include Mr. Otley, who somehow managed to enjoy himself despite his untimely demise."

"You are making it impossible for you to win," the duke pointed out. "If you had stopped at an introduction, you probably would have had a fair chance of prevailing, but now you've set the parameters too narrowly."

She smiled and said, "We will see."

"Indeed we will," he agreed. Then he tipped his hat, bid her good-day and continued down the street.

CHAPTER SIX

Bea's aunt realized that the evening was not going according to plan when Matilda, Countess of Abercrombie, called Lady Cowper over to meet Miss Hyde-Clare.

"I assure you, my dear, this young lady has the most delightful sense of humor," she said, "so you must be sure to invite her to everything this season."

Although the introduction was all Vera Hyde-Clare had ever wanted—validation from a high-ranking member of the *ton,* attention of an Almack's patroness—she opened her mouth to offer several clarifications such as her niece's humor was more dull than delightful and the lady wasn't *precisely* young. She immediately closed it again because she wasn't lost to reason, but it was difficult to maintain her composure during the exchange, and Bea, witnessing her struggle, reached over and squeezed her hand.

Aunt Vera, fearing some strange, private message in the gesture, looked more frightened than ever.

Bea's attempt at sympathy, however, had been entirely genuine, for she herself felt an uncomfortable mix of agitation, trepidation and enjoyment. With her rough treatment of Lady Abercrombie the day before, she'd hardly thought she'd made an ally, and yet this evening, at the Leland ball, the countess had greeted her with the fervor of a cherished friend.

The push for popularity was particularly disconcerting on this night of all nights because the Hyde-Clares had decided, in a council of war that included all relevant parties, even extended family members such as Aunt Vera's sister, Susan, and her husband, Lawrence, that Bea would fade quietly into a corner and remain there until dinner. During the meal, she would disappear quietly into her chair and then return quietly to her previously claimed spot along the wall.

Like any good plan, it wasn't entirely without its opportunity for error, but with patience and vigilance, it could be relied upon to minimize trouble.

By *trouble*, of course, Aunt Vera meant any situation in which her niece could be irreverent or impertinent or disrespectful or satirical or indeed open her mouth to say anything other than yes or no.

The implementation of such extreme measures would not have been necessary if Bea had simply agreed to stay home. Her family had attempted a thoroughly persuasive argument by pointing out the patently obvious truth: The horror of finding Mr. Otley's violently slain corpse combined with the terror of being trapped in an abandoned shed married to the devastation of Mr. Davies's death had succeeded in corrupting her judgment.

Pointing this out was futile, of course, for the young lady's judgment was too corrupted to grasp patently obvious truths.

It was Bea's visit to the British Museum immediately following the announcement of Mr. Davies's death that had convinced her relatives something was truly wrong with her ability to reason, for what young lady of clear intent chose to pass an entire afternoon amid its creaky halls filled with old rubble from dead civilizations? Furthermore, the destination was too much of a non sequitur for any of them to breath easily, for it bore no relation to anything Bea had ever done before. Aunt Vera could recall her niece going to the museum only once, and on that occasion she practically had to be tugged there by her sleeve. Without question, this was a woman whose behavior could not be relied upon to be either rational or beneficial to her family.

Given Bea's sweeping lack of success and her general discontentment at society functions, her relatives were taken aback by her refusal to sit out the ball. Her insistence that she must attend only reinforced their belief that she must not, but short of tethering her to the bed and locking her bedchamber door, they could not figure out how such an objective might be achieved. A brief discussion about which bed sheets might best be used as a restraint was halted by Uncle Horace, who lamented the high cost of linens.

With no other option available to them, the Hyde-Clares settled on their plan to confine an unhinged Bea to a quiet corner and approached the first glittering event of the season with restrained enthusiasm. The amazing circumstances of the Earl of Fazeley's mysterious death, for how could such a high stickler for fashion find himself undone in such an unfashionable section of town, added fizz to the evening, and Uncle Horace and Russell were eager to compare theories with cronies. Aware that her relations could have information to which she was not privy, Bea tried to discover these opinions, but her interest was deemed unnatural and seized upon as further proof she was not well.

All seemed fine at first, for they arrived without incident and proceeded through the receiving line without calling undue attention to themselves. As they walked through the crowded ballroom, Uncle Horace excused himself to talk to an associate about an upcoming prizefight in Wanash, Russell went off to join a group of friends by the refreshment table, and Mr. Thorpe came to claim Flora for his dance. Aunt Vera, her arm loosely threaded through her niece's, inspected the available corners for the greatest seclusion and settled on the one to the right, with its generous fig tree.

Their progress across the floor was almost immediately impeded by Lady Abercrombie, who greeted Bea with familiarity. Aunt Vera was, to be sure, disconcerted to discover the two had met and wondered aloud when that felicitous event had taken place.

"Why yesterday, of course," her ladyship said smoothly.

The idea of a woman so beautiful and popular spending any portion of her life in a dreary museum filled with broken pots and chipped statues was beyond anything Aunt Vera could comprehend, and she stared in amazement. Before her aunt could express her astonishment and perhaps discover the truth by accident, Bea explained to Lady Abercrombie that they were on their way to the refreshment table.

"May we get you a glass of ratafia?" she asked.

But her ladyship was not listening, for she had spied her dear friend Lady Cowper only a few feet away and insisted she come meet her new protégé.

This shocking development woke Aunt Vera from her stupor, and she looked around the room as the other woman approached, a trapped expression on her face. Bea, who also hadn't anticipated such a reception, stiffened her shoulders and worried she would lapse into muteness as soon as the exalted figure greeted her.

No, she thought forcefully. She would not regress to sullen silence without a fight.

Bea smiled at the elegant patroness of Almack's, who was well-known for her kindness and charm, and felt instantly soothed by her graciousness. She managed to conduct a reasonable conversation without stuttering or mumbling or apologizing.

After Lady Cowper was called away by her husband, the lively widow introduced Bea to Mrs. Clavering and Lady Holland and the Dowager Duchess of Padstow, who squinted her eyes and leaned in.

"Making your first season, are you?" she asked.

As startled as she was amused by the question, Bea considered the best way to answer it, for she wanted neither to embarrass the older woman with the truth nor mislead her with a lie. Finally, after a moment of silence, she said, "My seventh."

Her grace frowned sharply and stepped forward to examine Bea more closely. After a moment, she said, "No wonder. You've got a very plain face."

Far too familiar with her attributes to take offense at this observation, Bea smiled and said, "I'm quite wan as well and have absolutely no conversation."

The dowager nodded. "That spray of freckles across your nose does not do you any favors either."

"And do note the dullness of my hair, which is far too limp to be of any interest," she said with a smile, then added, because the older woman's honesty had charmed her, "Unlike your beautiful curls."

The dowager's austere expression lightened as she said, "I wouldn't say *no* conversation."

"You make it easy, your grace," Bea replied, the sincerity in her tone indicating the comment was no mere frippery.

The Dowager Duchess of Padstow simpered.

Lady Abercrombie clapped in admiration a few minutes later while Aunt Vera chastised Bea for speaking so flagrantly about her advancing years.

"You did not have to reveal an actual number," she pointed out. "A simple no would have sufficed in answer to the question, or, if you want to be more effusive, then you could have said, 'No, I'm not.'"

"Nonsense," Lady Abercrombie said, "pretense will get you nowhere."

Bea knew her ladyship's denunciation of pretense was only a pretense, for the woman was artifice piled on top of deceit wrapped in the pretty paper of artfulness, and she couldn't help but wonder what game she was playing with this display of support. Surely, her ladyship wasn't genuinely interested in bringing drab Beatrice Hyde-Clare into fashion. No, she had another reason for her actions, and Bea could not decide if it was nefarious or benign. Either she was aware of Bea's suspicions and thought to distract her from her pursuit with attention or she was amused by the challenge of making a plain-faced spinster the hit of the season.

Both possibilities struck her as equally likely.

Aunt Vera, who had never met a peer whose opinion she didn't instantly adopt, rushed to agree with the beautiful countess and promptly garbled Sir Walter Scott's maxim about tangled webs and deception.

"Exactly," Lady Abercrombie said with gleeful satisfaction, although the quoted lines had been so mangled it was difficult to say precisely what she was agreeing with. "Stay the course, my dear Miss Hyde-Clare, and you will be the height of fashion by Easter."

At this announcement, poor Aunt Vera made a strangled sound.

Fearful that the other woman was choking, Lady Abercrombie whacked her on the back to clear the blockage and announced it was time to find her protégé a dancing partner. Bea opened her mouth to protest while her ladyship examined the candidates in the immediate vicinity, her absorption in the activity so complete she thoughtlessly continued striking Aunt Vera. Wanting to free herself but not wishing to appear rude, the latter took small, inching steps away from the countess's hand, accidentally bumping into an impeccably dressed gentleman with a Bedford crop.

He turned to offer his apologies just as Lady Abercrombie exclaimed in approval and urged him with undeniable persistence that he lead Miss Hyde-Clare onto the dance floor for the next set. Perceiving no way to escape, he submitted to the treatment and held out his hand, which Bea, whose demurrals had gone unheeded, accepted with mortification.

As they crossed to the dance floor, she turned to the unfortunate gentleman, who had been cornered by the widow, and plainly owned her embarrassment, which was made especially acute by the fact that Michael Barrington, Viscount Nuneaton, was already known to her. He had made up one of their number at Lakeview Hall, as he was a cousin of their host. Buried in the country, he had seemed like a reluctant attendee, indifferent and bored by the company, an attitude she had originally found off-putting but ultimately discovered to be more affectation than conviction. By the end of their stay, Bea found that she liked him quite well.

"I'm sorry this happened," she said now, "but I hope you know I was as powerless as you to stop it."

His lordship insisted he had not been powerless at all. "Trust me, Miss Hyde-Clare, my skill at avoiding tasks in which I have no interest is well-honed. You need only apply to my father if you require confirmation."

As the dandy she recalled lounging in the Skeffingtons' drawing room appeared to have no interests at all, she found this difficult to believe but thanked him anyway for his graciousness.

"I assure you, I'm being quite sincere," he said as they took their place in the quadrille. "I had every intention of calling on you next week."

Bea laughed at the idea of the languid peer calmly subjecting himself to her aunt's energetic chatter. "Now I know you're only being polite, my lord."

"One is loath is argue with a lady, but in fact I'm not," he insisted. "As Skeffington's cousin, I'm determined to discover all that transpired during that ghastly week, but Kesgrave will give me damnable few details about the investigation into Mr. Otley's death. I'm hoping you will be more forthcoming."

"Of course," she said smiling as the music started and the dancers began to move. "That makes more sense."

"I'm curious to know more, yes," he conceded, "but that is not my sole motivation. I find you a woman of daring and intelligence and think I would enjoy your acquaintance."

Once again, she pictured the indolent gentleman in the Lake District determined to be bored by everything and knew herself to be the recipient of a very great compliment. "I think I would enjoy that as well," she said honestly, for she'd had few friends in her life and certainly none who were male.

Following the head couple, they danced into the center of the square and paused their discussion while performing the intricate move. When conversation was possible again, Nuneaton asked how she had passed the holidays and she entertained him with tales of her family's attempts to discover what she would like for a Christmas gift. "And Flora was convinced I wanted a new reticule so she left magazines out opened to images of various reticules and would watch to try to gauge which one I lingered over the most. Sadly, I didn't linger over any at all, as I am pleased with my reticule and unaware that I required a new one. In the end, she picked out the design she liked best and when I didn't use it for two weeks, asked if she could borrow it."

Nuneaton chuckled in appreciation and said he would have to try that ploy with his sister, who was most urgently in need of a new pair of Hessians.

The music ended soon after, and rather than consider himself free from the obligation Lady Abercrombie had imposed, he escorted her to the refreshment table. After he secured her a glass of lemonade, he asked what she thought of the earl's murder.

Bea was taken aback by the question and feared that she had somehow revealed her interest, but before she could issue a denial, he added, "Your deftness in handling Mr. Otley's demise leads me to assume you at least have a theory as to how Lord Fazeley contrived to meet such an unfortunate end."

Of course it had been a general inquiry and not specific to her actions, she thought. The earl's death was the topic on everyone's lips. "I believe it had to be connected in some way to the book he was contracted to write," she offered.

"Ah, so you believe the memoir is real and not another creation devised to draw attention to himself, such as the Fazeley Flow," he said, revealing his opinion on the matter. "I have attempted the knot for which he is famous, Miss Hyde-Clare, and I must tell you it's a great hoax. It's merely the Maharatta tie combined with the Trone d'Amour and employing the stiffness of the Oriental. If it does require half the kitchen staff to achieve, it's only because Fazeley insisted on eating a joint of mutton whilst getting dressed for the evening."

"Naturally, I will defer to you on all matters of men's dress," she said somberly, although the picture he painted was highly amusing, "but, yes, I do believe the memoir is real and does contain the sort of salacious secrets one might be moved to violence to protect. If I have learned anything from my experience at Lakeview Hall it is that everyone has secrets."

Nuneaton tilted his head curiously. "Even you?"

Recalling Mr. Davies's brief life and unfortunate death, she laughed self-consciously and said, "Even me. But bearing in mind I'm a twenty-six-year-old ape leader, you will perceive that my secrets are far from salacious."

"Really, my dear, you are being rather hard on yourself," he said kindly. "You're not quite in ape leader territory yet."

Perhaps if his tone had not been so sympathetic, she might have been able to let the remark pass without comment, but she detected just the slightest hint of pity and that she could not bear. "I'm afraid you don't know me well enough, my lord, to comprehend my aversion to flattery, but I truly have no use for Spanish coin," she explained, glancing at him out of the corner of her eye, for she worried he would take umbrage at her frankness. "If we are to be friends, then you must not descend to flummery."

He accepted this edict with a firm nod but added, "If we are to be friends, then *you* must learn how to accept a sincere compliment, as my comment stemmed from a genuine belief that you are not as high up on the shelf as you believe. To please you, however, I will concede you are several rungs up the ladder."

Appreciating his contorted efforts to oblige her request, she said, "You just want me to tell you about my investigation into Mr. Otley's death."

"Desperately," he said with exaggerated vehemence.

The fierceness in his voice made her laugh and she tried to assure him it was not that interesting a tale, but her mirth was too intense.

"Good evening," said a voice sharply from behind her.

Bea, who hadn't realized the Duke of Kesgrave was already in attendance, ceased laughing at once and turned to greet him. Her delighted smile frayed at the edges as she met his stormy expression. She was taken aback for a moment, for she had done nothing to provoke his anger, and then remembered the interview with Lord Duncan. Kesgrave had wanted to conduct it by himself the day before. He had been forced to cool his heels for a full four and twenty hours just to gratify her wishes. No wonder he was scowling.

His annoyance was such that he even took it out on poor Nuneaton, responding to his friend's eager greeting with a clipped nod.

Unsure how to proceed, for she had little experience cajoling dukes out of their sullens, she said in a playful tone, "Lord Nuneaton was just expressing his interest in knowing more about the events at Lakeview Hall. He claims you have been stingy with the information, which surprises me, as it is at the intersection of your two chief pleasures: details and long narratives."

Although Bea had known his delighted grin was too much to hope for, she thought her teasing would convince him to unbend at least a little bit. But he remained stiff, his shoulders rigid as he looked down at her from his superior height. All at once, she felt as she did the first time she'd met him, in the Lake District, like a pesky ant daring to intrude on his picnic.

It was not altogether shocking, of course, that he would look at her with condescension, for they were in a dazzling ballroom in London, not a hallway in a remote backwater. Here, he demanded the respect and dignity she was too irreverent to pay him.

Embarrassed to have misunderstood the situation so egregiously, she straightened her shoulders and offered an apology for teasing him. "I beg your pardon, your grace, I don't know…"

But she trailed off when she noticed her aunt charging across the ballroom floor toward her. She turned her head to the left and saw Flora striding with equal determination. Looking to the right, she spotted Russell taking large, leaping steps forward. Aunt Vera, slightly out of breath, reached her first and, like a general issuing orders to his lieutenants, told her children with a look to stand down. At once, Flora and Russell stopped moving, spun on their heels and walked in the opposite direction.

"My lord duke," Aunt Vera said, pressing a hand against her chest as she slowly regained her breath, "what a pleasure to see you. And Lord Nuneaton too. 'Tis a double honor, to be sure." She tittered nervously as she looked from the two peers to her niece and then back again. Kesgrave's glower did little to put her mind at ease, and she grimaced at Bea before recalling their company. "Of course you remember my niece, Miss Hyde-Clare. She was part of the delightful company at Lakeview Hall. You will excuse her, I trust, if she is in any way—" She broke off awkwardly rather than put ideas into their heads, for maybe Bea hadn't been inappropriate or clever. "We are lucky she decided to join us this evening, as she has had some unpleasant news of late. Unpleasant *not* in the way of Mr.... That is to say, we thoroughly enjoyed out visit to Lakeview Hall, despite certain elements that..." She coughed awkwardly, then tried again. "Despite unexpected developments, I'm sure everyone had a delightful time, as we did."

Throughout her aunt's remarkable speech, Bea, still deeply mortified by her assumption of familiarity with the duke, kept her eyes trained on the refreshment table to the left of Nuneaton's shoulder. It was difficult, of course, for Aunt Vera was saying almost the exact words she had predicted she would say the day before. When she stopped just short of mentioning Mr. Otley, Bea almost tilted her head in Kesgrave's direction, but she managed to resist. A moment later, however, when her aunt insisted everyone at the house party had had a delightful time, she could not stop herself and sought Kesgrave's gaze.

He was already looking at her—and grinning.

She smiled in return and felt her whole being lighten.

Now they could go find Lord Duncan and discover if he'd plunged the knife into his godfather's back.

But of course they couldn't go right then, for her aunt was there and remained determined to stay as long as necessary to ensure her niece did nothing to embarrass or shame the family. To help the situation along, she pointed out the lovely corner in the northeast section of the room and observed that the fig tree would provide gentle respite. "I think you will benefit with a rest before they announce dinner, my dear," Aunt Vera said with anxious concern. "It has been an eventful evening so far, what with Lady Abercrombie's attentions and your quadrille with Lord Nuneaton. Yes, I feel very strongly that a respite amid the fig leaves is exactly what you need to restore your health."

Although Bea knew her health required no restoration, she decided it was better to appease her aunt now in order to defy her later. She was just about to observe that the fig tree did indeed look welcoming when Kesgrave spoke first and invited her to dance.

Horrified, Aunt Vera said, "Oh, no."

Bea understood her alarm, for she felt it too. The music playing now was a waltz, and the thought of being held by the Duke of Kesgrave had a very unnerving effect on her composure. She had danced only a few waltzes in her life and had yet to develop a nonchalance about them.

Despite her apprehension, it did not occur to her to turn him down, for she knew the duke had a purpose in proposing the scheme. If he wanted to waltz, then he desired the opportunity to discuss their plan. She agreed smoothly while her aunt refused on her behalf, and Nuneaton, amused by the display and seeking to be helpful, drew the older woman's attention by marveling at the beauty of her necklace.

Bea sent him a grateful look.

Kesgrave was quiet as he led her to the dance floor, which only increased her anxiety, and by the time he put his hand on her shoulder, her heart was racing at a dizzying pace. It was perfectly absurd, and yet she could not help sparing a glance at the fig tree in the corner. It did indeed look restful.

Realizing the silence only made it worse, she looked at the duke as they began to move across the floor and said, "You owe me a shilling."

He readily conceded the truth, then chastised her for placing such a cautious bet. "You knew your subject far better than I. If you had offered one hundred times the amount, I still would have taken the wager and you would have earned a small fortune."

"I'm content with my winnings," she said. "Vindication is its own reward. Perhaps next time you won't be so confident you are right."

He smiled but said nothing, and Bea, succumbing to the pleasure of his firm, steady grip, relaxed into the sensation of sweeping around the room. She closed her eyes to soak up the feeling.

And immediately opened them again as a wave of irritation washed over her. She was waltzing with the Duke of Kesgrave, yes, but they weren't truly waltzing. They were conducting important business by way of the only means available to them.

"What do you think is our best strategy for confronting Lord Duncan?" she said. "Is he here? Have you seen him? I own that I did not look for him myself, for as soon as I arrived, Lady Abercrombie swooped down and demanded my attention."

"He is here, yes. He entered the card room about twenty minutes ago. I propose we wait until after dinner, as we will have more success if we don't disturb his play," the duke said.

Bea agreed with the soundness of this plan on all its points, for she knew men did not deal with interruptions in their gambling with equanimity, at least not her uncle or Russell. "If we are looking for a quiet corner in which to hold the discussion, I can recommend one with a calming fig tree."

Kesgrave's laughter was deep and rich, and Bea, struck by the beauty of the sound, lost her place and stumbled. 'Twas only a misstep, and the duke's firm grip immediately steadied her. She tilted her head to thank him for his quick response and found the words dying on her lips when she saw the way he was watching her—with an unnerving intensity that bore no resemblance to reality. Nothing could explain it. Nothing at all.

And then the last strains of the music faded and Kesgrave's hands released her, causing an odd, sudden chill, and she realized it was the waltz. The waltz explained it.

Bea had no time to feel foolish, for Flora was immediately at her side, not, as Bea supposed, to ensure her safe passage to a quiet corner, but to giggle and gush over her dance with the duke, who left her with her cousin with only the most cursory of nods.

"How elegant you looked!" she said as soon as she could be sure Kesgrave was out of earshot. "How graceful! How regal! You made such a beautiful pair, I could have melted with envy."

Her effusive praise made Bea laugh, for never before had her cousin used the word *beautiful* in reference to her. "It was all the duke's doing. He's a masterful dancer. I merely went where I was led."

Flora dismissed this statement as false modesty, which was another novel experience for the two cousins. Bea, enjoying the other girl's admiration, decided not to press the issue.

After a while, Flora was claimed for the next dance by Mr. Grevail, a birdlike young man with sharp shoulders and a narrow chin. Her cousin had no sooner vanished into the crowd of dancers than Russell appeared at her side to assure her he was there and ready to provide her with whatever support she needed.

"We have divided the rest of the evening into half-hour shifts," he explained, "and this is my stint, so please don't have any one of your weird freaks or starts during the next twenty-eight minutes."

Her aunt's solution to being unable to confine her to the corner was, in effect, to bring the corner to her. Bea appreciated her ingenuity. "Who has the next session?"

"My father."

The image of Uncle Horace standing guard over her in the Lelands' ballroom made her smile. "Very well. I promise to have no weird freaks and starts while you keep watch."

Although Bea would have kept her word regardless, she did not have a chance to break it, for her attention was claimed and held by an endless stream of guests who wanted to meet the woman whom Lady Cowper had called charming and with whom the Duke of Kesgrave had waltzed. The conversation was mostly repetitive, the same general questions about her family and her interests, so she found it easy to supply answers and her mind did not go blank as it had so often in the past.

True to his word, Russell remained at her side, interjecting only occasionally and squeezing her hand in goodbye when his father appeared to serve his shift. She introduced Uncle Horace to Mrs. Everston and her sister, who both congratulated him on having a delightful niece.

He was so surprised by the comment, he said, "Really?" Then, quickly recovering, he repeated the word but changed the inflection: "Really!"

The two ladies chortled and Bea laughed and her uncle looked at her with an expression that could almost be described as fond.

No, not fond, Bea realized. Proud.

How startling to finally earn his approval after twenty years.

More startling yet was the feeling of relief and happiness that accompanied it. 'Twas almost as if she valued her uncle's approval.

Bea was immediately distressed by the thought, for she knew this moment of popularity was fleeting and she would soon return to the corner with the fig tree.

Dinner could not come fast enough for her, and she

was thrilled to hear it announced not too long after her uncle's stint had ended and Aunt Vera's second one began. The meal was sumptuous and delicious, but Bea hardly tasted her food because she was too distracted by the family rota. If one of her relatives was assigned to stay with her at all times, then she would not be able to sneak off to conduct a private conversation with the duke and Lord Duncan.

It consumed her thoroughly, and yet in the end it presented no problem at all, for her aunt had failed to schedule shifts for after the meal. With her niece's fragility and the recent hardship the poor girl suffered, Aunt Vera had naturally assumed the family would be well gone by the time the dinner bell sounded.

Grateful for her aunt's lack of faith, which seemed to be the one constant in her life, Bea slipped away from the table when she saw the duke and Lord Duncan stand up. She kept a safe distance behind them, pausing to admire a painting of Lord Leland's grandfather when they were stopped by Nuneaton, who, noting the unlikeliness of the pairing, expressed interest in joining them for a smoke after he finished dinner. Kesgrave was agreeable and told him to find them on the south balcony. Then he turned, reversed directions and led Duncan to the north terrace.

When Bea stepped outside in the chilly early-February air, the two men were leaning against the balustrade at the far end. Nearer to the door, a group of gentlemen were discussing Lord Liverpool's latest speech to Parliament, and a pair of ladies sitting on chaise longues argued in quiet, harsh tones. Both parties seemed wholly engrossed in their activity, which emboldened her to stride across the balcony to Lord Duncan, look the surprised young man in the eye and demand he tell her everything about his brutal slaying of his godfather.

In the golden glow of a dozen torches, Lord Duncan turned white.

CHAPTER SEVEN

Although Bea's experience with eliciting confessions was limited to a single case in which the murderer had owned the deed openly rather than allow someone else to point the finger, she was certain the sudden paleness of Lord Duncan's visage was tantamount to an admission of guilt.

It was obvious beyond a shred of doubt that this young man had done something wrong and was terrified that it had been discovered. His eyes, a deep shade of brown and already a little too large for his narrow face, widened like saucers and moved shiftily around the balcony, darting from Bea to Kesgrave to the gentlemen discussing Liverpool to the French doors that led inside back to Bea again.

He was considering his options, Bea knew, trying to decide if he should flee into the ballroom or brazen it out.

No, not brazen, she thought. There was nothing bold or brash or unabashed about the boy standing before her all but shivering in fear.

With none of Lady Abercrombie's steel or insouciance, he was merely a grown man of twenty years cowering in terror. Bea derived no pleasure in the spectacle, for it was impossible to look at him and not feel sympathy for his plight.

And yet that plight was naught but a situation he'd created with his own actions. Nobody compelled him to raise his hand in violence and end his godfather's life. It seemed very simple to her: If one did not want to be confronted with one's evil deeds on a balcony during the first ball of the season, then one should abstain from committing evil deeds.

The logic was immutable, its application requiring only the barest minimum behavior in terms of human decency: Do not kill.

Although she had determined to say nothing else until Duncan addressed the charge, she began to wonder if it was a futile resolution. The longer the silence stretched, the deeper the young lord's apprehension grew. His collapsing suddenly in a faint at her feet did not strike her as entirely impossible.

That would not do, for if he was unconscious, she would never get any useful information from him.

Very well. She would speak.

"I must insist, Lord Duncan, that you take several slow, deep breaths to calm yourself down," she said, her tone brisk. "Your excessive panic is not helping your situation, for it only serves to convince me of your guilt. Now do get control of yourself and explain to us what happened with Lord Fazeley."

Nodding frantically, Lord Duncan inhaled for several seconds and exhaled for just as long. With every breath, a little more of the color returned to his face.

"There you go," Bea said soothingly. "Don't you feel better?"

Although he was less in danger of falling to the ground from immoderate respiration, the wild motion of his bobbing head presented a new risk and she had to advise him to stop. "You're making this harder than it needs to be, Lord Duncan," she said impatiently.

The young man ceased his nodding at once and managed to utter an apology without stumbling or stuttering his words.

Finally, she thought, progress.

After another moment, he added quietly and with enviable calm, "I did not kill my godfather."

Bea thought it was a paltry denial in light of his previous conduct, but Kesgrave nodded pensively and said, "Tell us about the dagger."

"I knew it," he said with a deep sigh as he rested his weight against the balustrade for support. "When I read the description in the newspaper, I knew at once the murder weapon was the jade knife Lady Abercrombie had given me. Your accusation merely confirms it." He closed his eyes as he took another deep breath. "The knife was mine for a while, but I sold it almost immediately to my godfather. Its garishness appealed to him, and he had determined to wear it as an accessory as a direct rebuke to Brummell, who, as you know, decries anything that isn't simple, plain and elegant."

Although Bea knew little of the history of ornamental weaponry, she was fully aware of the rivalry between the two dandies. They espoused diametrically opposed philosophies of manner and presentation, and neither could stand to leave the other to his preference. "When did you sell it to him?"

"Last month. Lady Abercrombie"—he blushed here as he said her name—"made a gift of the piece to me for Christmas, and when I returned to town I showed it Fazeley. My intent was to sell it to an agent at an auction house, but he made an offer and I was delighted to be spared the effort."

"Did you tell him why Lady Abercrombie gave you the dagger?" Kesgrave asked.

"Well…I, uh, yes," he stammered as the flush in his cheeks turned a vibrant pink. "I mentioned that our relationship had…ah, deepened and grown and that she gave me the dagger as a keepsake of our deepened bond."

As his blush intensified, Bea marveled at how young he looked. He was only a little younger than Russell—twenty, perhaps twenty-one—and yet appeared many years his junior. "You seem reluctant to talk about the love affair," she said boldly and wondered how a man who had indulged in lascivious activities could flinch at the phrase *love affair*.

And yet he felt compelled to deny it. "No, of course

not. I'm a man of the world and appreciate the…ah, the attentions of an older woman. It serves to…hmm… deepen my worldview."

Bea shook her head, for his bashfulness was too pronounced to allow for pretense. "You are, Lord Duncan, quite spectacularly reluctant. I can only imagine how you must have felt when your godfather took the very private information you had shared and used it to blackmail your paramour."

His huge eyes grew impossibly larger at her observation, and he rose to his full height to protest quite strongly. "Now, I say, Miss…ah, Miss…"

Realizing he didn't know her name, he trailed off.

"Hyde-Clare," she supplied promptly. "Miss Hyde-Clare."

He nodded and aired his objection again. "I say, Miss Hyde-Clare, you are flagrantly misrepresenting the events. What I and Tilly…that is, Lady Abercrombie and I…had was fleeting at best. To describe her as my paramour is woefully off the mark."

Confused by the vehemence of his rebuttal of such an insignificant point, she glanced at Kesgrave to see his reaction, for she did not know enough about male affairs to judge if his lordship's outrage was justified. He wore an expression of faint amusement.

Reassured, she returned to the point that she considered to be the more salient one. "So you were not angered when you discovered his betrayal?"

His indignation was as fleeting as his relationship with the beautiful widow, for at this question his shoulders collapsed and he pressed against the balustrade again for support. "He did not betray me. He approached Lady Abercrombie with that bargain upon my request."

Amazed by this revelation, Bea stared at the young man, whose stuttering and blushing had led her to believe he was an innocent who had merely stumbled into a situation that was far more complicated than he could handle. His timidity in discussing his love affair with Lady Abercrombie had all but convinced her he was too fainthearted to commit murder and she had gone back to considering the countess to be the more likely culprit. But the revelation of his venality altered her perspective, for a man who would send another man to blackmail his lover with information he himself had supplied had no conscience at all.

The question then became, of course, why would Lord Duncan strike down his godfather? If he felt no compunction in sharing private information with him, the motive could not center around the exposure of a secret.

Perhaps it had something to do with money, as both Lord Duncan and the Earl of Fazeley appeared to be in need of it. Had Lady Abercrombie lied about refusing to comply with the blackmail threat? Had she handed over a large wad of cash that the earl refused to share with his godson? Could that serve as the source of their discord?

While Bea tried to organize her thoughts, Kesgrave asked Lord Duncan to explain why he'd sunk to blackmail.

Once again, the young man cringed at the accurate description of the event and Bea felt a renewed sense of irritation at his childishness. "I needed the blunt. My parents are miserly and refused to cover my gambling debts and Fazeley cheated me on the value of the knife, which turned out to be worth four times what he paid," Lord Duncan said defensively. "He refused to give me a shilling more, for a deal was a deal, he said, and a gentleman must abide by the original terms. It was infuriating, the way he talked about it, as if the rigid code he himself had established was somehow out of his hands. But he said he would help in any other way he could. So I suggested a way that would be beneficial."

Bea found it infuriating that the earl's so-called rigid code applied only to gentlemen and that exhorting money from a woman was perfectly in line with his principles.

Before she could voice her anger, Kesgrave made the same observation, only with far less passion.

Lord Duncan perceived no contradiction in his godfather's unwillingness to renegotiate terms with a gentleman and his willingness to defraud a lady. "'Twas a lark, and turning it down would have been very fainthearted indeed," he said, his brows drawn in confusion, as if he could scarcely believe he had to explain something so basic about human existence to a man of Kesgrave's ilk.

"She could well afford it," he added sullenly, as if the problem was the amount, not the act. "Judging by the knife she gave me as a *token,* she could manage a king's ransom without noticing. And we asked for a mere fraction, a sum so modest she could have covered it with the funds set aside for lion food alone. Refusing the pay was pure churlishness on her part."

Heaving a sigh, Bea looked at the duke to see what he thought of his cowardly defense and was pleased to note his ducal sneer. Now Lord Duncan was the ant. She would have to be content with that, for she could not vent her spleen on Lady Leland's balcony in view of other guests.

Calmly, she said, "Were the rumors true? Was Lord Fazeley writing a book about the *ton* and its foibles?"

"Oh, yes," Lord Duncan said. "He had an arrangement with a book publishing firm, the name of which I cannot recall. He was of a literary bent, you see, and was very proud of his writing style. It was to take the form of a memoir, a comprehensive chronicle of the daily comings and goings of a popular society figure and detailing the very business of life, with all its elements, both large and small, trivial and consequential, commonplace and extraordinary. It was to be a Very Great Event in the life of the beau monde."

Bea thought it would be a Very Great Disappointment if the earl's book contained the same lurid pomposity his godson used to describe it. "Was he mentioning members of the *ton* by name in his book?"

Lord Duncan's modesty applied only to love affairs with women old enough to be his mother and charges of murder, for, on much firmer footing now, he scoffed at her question. "A mere moment ago I said it was about the daily life of a popular society figure. Pray tell me, my dear Miss…"

He trailed off, uncertain, and Bea smothered the urge to remind the contemptuous young man that she'd told him her name only mere moments ago, "Hyde-Clare," she said.

"Do tell me, Miss Hyde-Clare," he said, the disdain that much stronger now that he had a name to which to apply it, "how my godfather would be able to write a book about his daily life *without* mentioning members of the *ton*? So many passages and details would have to be elided as to render the work unreadable."

She ignored the provoking condescension and focused on the part of his answer that was relevant to her interests. "Had his lordship contacted any of the subjects included in the book and offered to elide particular passages or details in exchange for payment?"

The young man inhaled sharply at the suggestion, threw his shoulders back and took one large step closer to Beatrice so that he could stand directly in front of her as he delivered his reply. "You *dare* suggest my godfather would act with such dishonor and disgrace! If you were a man, Miss Hyde-Clare, I would tell you to name your second."

His anger at the injustice of the charge was so sincerely and finely honed, Bea could only stare at him in astonishment. She could not believe the hypocrisy, and yet she knew breathtaking hypocrisy of this magnitude was the base on which the whole entire world was built. Men of a certain class and breeding were free to do whatever they wanted, and everyone else had to step cautiously and apologize. It was maddening and inevitable, and she felt desperately helpless that there was nothing she could do to convince this sniveling boy who could not hear the phrase *love affair* without recoiling in embarrassment that he was a speck of mud on the heel of the world.

Because he wasn't a speck. He was a young lord with a kingdom at his feet.

While Bea struggled to calm her anger, Duncan turned to Kesgrave and said, "I'm confused, your grace, why you would choose to associate with a female such as this inadequate example, with an inelegant mind and limited intelligence. A man of your talents and accomplishments can seek the company of any woman, for none are above your touch. I do not say this to be critical, for I would never presume to censure the behavior of an out-and-outer such as yourself, but I would like to comprehend your thinking."

Bea, as well, would like to have a better understanding of the duke's behavior, for it still seemed antithetical to his ends to allow her to investigate Lord Fazeley's death alongside him. She was too furious, however, at the young man's remarks to allow Kesgrave to respond. She'd been willing to end the conversation on a polite note rather than addressing the glib double-dealing of his self-serving opinions. She'd resolved to exit the balcony by way of the high road. But resisting this final provocation was simply beyond her capability.

She raised her head to look at him, a study of defiance and confusion as he tried to understand the low company of such a high stepper, and recalled the trapped little boy cowering in the corner, his head bobbing, his eyes darting. He had regained his composure, yes, but the other creature wasn't so very far behind.

Smiling faintly, she leaned forward and said in a snappish burst, "Love affair."

Lord Duncan jumped back.

Bea said it again, this time drawing it out mockingly. "Love affair."

Prepared for the attack, the young man managed to hold his ground. But a pinch of color appeared on his cheeks as he figured out what she was doing and the self-conscious realization that she knew how easy it was to discomfit him discomfited him further.

She grinned at him now. "Love affair. Love affair."

His eyes grew wide and huge as he tried to contain his reaction. The harder he fought it, the darker he became: Pink turned to fuchsia turned to red.

It was, she thought, the most satisfying feeling she had ever experienced in her life. No, she would never convince him he was a speck of mud, but for a few moments she could make him feel as if he were. "Love affair. Love affair. Love affair. Love affair. Love affair. Love aff—"

"*Beatrice!*"

Aunt Vera's horrified screech tore through the night, and Bea swung around to find her entire family standing only inches behind her. Uncle Horace's face was as red as Lord Duncan's, and Flora's chin might as well have scraped to the ground, her mouth was open so wide in shock. Only Russell seemed unaffected by the display, as he was too busy staring at his hero, Kesgrave, to notice what his cousin was doing.

"Aunt Vera," Bea said, her own face now bereft of color as she imagined what the scene must have looked like to one outside of it, "you must let me—"

Her aunt bit out the word *no* with a viciousness Bea had never heard her use before. She rushed to explain. "But it's not—"

"*No!*"

At this unexpectedly vehement denial, Lord Duncan started and, sensing an opportunity to slip away unnoticed, took several steps backward. Watching him make his escape, a scurrying little creature afraid of his own shadow, Bea sneered at the cowardly display. Any man with an iota of self-respect would have stayed firmly rooted to the spot and enjoyed his tormentor's disgrace.

The duke, also noting Lord Duncan's exit, turned to Aunt Vera and addressed her with his customary urbanity, which, under ordinary circumstances, rankled Beatrice. Now she was grateful for it. "My dear Mrs. Hyde-Clare, if you would allow me the opportunity to—"

But no, she could not.

Aunt Vera's shame and horror at finding her niece spouting the words *love affair* over and over again like a deranged child to a peer of the realm in front of a leader of the *ton* was so pronounced it compelled her to do the one thing Bea had thought impossible: interrupt a duke.

A *duke*.

"You are very kind, your grace, to try to offer excuses for Beatrice," Aunt Vera said evenly and with hard-won dignity. "But I must not let you debase yourself by allowing you to become embroiled further in our family drama. You cannot know the strain my niece has been under in recent days, and I fear you in your generosity have allowed her to influence your behavior in a way I'm sure you will find repugnant upon later reflection. I trust you will believe me when I say we are very grateful for your kindnesses. Good evening, my lord duke."

Kesgrave's shock at hearing such a speech from her aunt was exceeded only by her aunt's at delivering it. He seemed inclined, at first, to register an objection, for his back had stiffened at the mention of his debasement. But now he merely bowed over her hand and bid her good night.

Bea watched, appalled by how quickly he had capitulated to her aunt's wishes.

But you're a *duke*, she wanted to shout. Stand up to her!

Unaware of her silent exhortation, Kesgrave walked away from the shocked little group without a glance, not even a fleeting one out of the corner of his eye at Bea. Just like Lord Duncan, she thought, as she realized what her aunt said was true. Upon later reflection—in this case mere seconds—he'd examined his own behavior and found it wanting.

She had driven him to a disgust of himself.

Bea could not say how that made her feel, for she was at once desperately sad their strange and wonderful association had come to such an ugly end and bitterly angry that his disgust could be so easily earned. He was the Duke of Kesgrave, a man who set the fashion, not followed it. If his impervious condescension conveyed anything, it was a sincere indifference to the opinions of others. And yet here he was, presented with an opportunity to use his arrogant disdain for good and he scampered away because her straitlaced aunt disapproved.

Had she really influenced his behavior?

She recalled the scene in the British Museum: Heatherton Hall, the dagger, Mr. Goddard's contempt for females, Kesgrave descending seemingly from on high to secure her access to the archive like a deus ex machina in an ancient Greek drama. Nobody had asked him to interfere. Nobody had tapped him on the shoulder and suggested he sort the matter out. Nobody had nudged him on the back until he was suddenly in the middle of the drama.

No, he'd inserted himself willingly and with seeming eagerness.

Indeed, he had been the one who had continued the association after she had resolved to proceed with the investigation on her own. The only reason she had known about Lord Duncan's involvement was the duke had brought her to his interview with Lady Abercrombie. If not for his interference, she would, at that very moment, be comfortably ensconced in the northwest corner of the ballroom next to a fig tree.

If anyone was to blame for that evening's debacle, it was Kesgrave himself.

How dare *he* feel debased by *her*!

As outraged as she was by the sweeping unfairness, Bea knew it was futile to argue—with Kesgrave, with her family, with herself. Assigning blame to the proper party did nothing to alter the truth: She had fulfilled her family's worst expectations of her. If their understanding of the cause was less than astute, their grasp on the outcome was accurate.

For Bea there was nothing to be done but to accept the disgrace because she had earned it and earned it well. As they crossed the ballroom, her eyes tilted down, she caught sight of Lord Duncan. His lips were curved in a repugnant grin as he correctly interpreted her situation.

Now he's brave, she thought in contempt.

The carriage ride home felt interminable to Bea, as her aunt alternately whimpered in despair and promised her niece everything would be all right. Squeezing the girl's hand with unexpectedly strong force, she'd assure her all she needed was a nice, long rest, then turn to the window and moan quietly, her hand still clutching and crushing.

Bea felt no small fissure of trepidation at the mention of a nice, long rest, for she couldn't hear those words without picturing the ward for madwomen at Bethlem Royal Hospital. She didn't truly believe her aunt would consign her to an asylum, and yet hours later, as she lay in bed trying to sleep, she couldn't quite shake the image of women struggling to move freely in well-stained white jackets designed to confine their movement.

She knew it was merely exhaustion making the matter feel worse than it actually was, and in the morning, after only four hours of sleep, her prospects did not look quite so grim. Damage had been done to her family's perception of her, yes, but given their already low opinion of her, the harm could not be hugely significant. It would not require much to repair the injury, she thought. A few days of agreeing with everything her aunt said, a few sessions where she talked about her sadness at Mr. Davies's death, a promise to keep an open mind in the future. Yes, she would say, let's visit Chancery Lane and inspect law clerks.

It would be galling to feign emotions she did not have, but it was an improvement on Bedlam and it was certainly better than letting her aunt break all the bones in her left hand.

Wasting no time in the implementation of her scheme, Bea called for her relatives' attention at breakfast and apologized for her behavior. "I see now that you were all right to be worried about my frame of mind, for I seem to have been far more affected by recent events than I allowed myself to realize. Perhaps if I hadn't been so determined to pretend everything was all right, I would have noticed my own weakness taking hold. I cannot explain my behavior last night on the balcony with Lord Duncan"—or, rather, she would not—"but I can promise you it will never happen again. The circumstances that made that moment possible no longer exist, so there can be no risk of a recurrence. I thank you all for your patience and understanding during this difficult time and promise in the future to heed your guidance. Whatever you prescribe, dear aunt, I will gladly comply without complaint. I am yours to instruct."

It was a fine speech, certainly a little excessive at times, with its dear aunts and guarantees of compliance, and Uncle Horace, looking up from the *London Daily Gazette*, said he was relieved to hear it. Then he immediately returned to his newspaper, which caused Aunt Vera to tsk-tsk in disgust as she examined her niece thoughtfully. She was not as easily swayed as her husband, but she seemed willing to consider the possibility that her niece was finally on the mend.

Bea bit her lip to keep from smiling and announced she would spend the day in her room quietly reflecting.

Aunt Vera applauded the plan and promised she would have Mrs. Emerson send up a light repast later in the day so she would not have to interrupt her introspection by coming down for food.

Bea wondered if by "light repast," she meant bread and water.

The rest of the day was uneventful, as Bea spent a quiet afternoon finishing the biography of George Stepney and starting one about Isaac Newton. In the evening, Aunt Vera and Flora went to Mrs. Yardley's rout and Uncle Horace visited his club. Russell, claiming disinterest in his friends' plan to attend the theater, invited Bea to play cards in the drawing room with him and, while teaching her the particulars of vingt-et-un, proceeded to interrogate her about the Duke of Kesgrave's interests. His idolatry, having progressed through the silent worship phase, required details so that a firmer connection could be established. Amused, Bea did her best to oblige, but she couldn't be sure that what she had to offer was of any value.

At breakfast the next morning, she kept her head down and did not say much, which earned her aunt's approbation. She pronounced herself pleased with Bea's progress, then related the important events of the night before, which consisted, among other things, of the Duke of Kesgrave's bestowing his attention on her for a full twelve minutes.

"We conducted a spirited conversation on the many uses of beetroot," she said.

At this dazzlingly intriguing tidbit, Bea's lively mind perked up, for she at once began to speculate at the substance of the conversation on the humble vegetable. Kesgrave, with his catalogue of facts on all mundane topics, could no doubt fill a full hour with the many ways of preparing beetroot pies and beetroot jellies and beetroot juices and beetroot poultices. He would be a veritable storehouse of beetroot information: the year it was discovered, the best method for its cultivation, how medieval monks used it to change the color of their hair.

Poor Aunt Vera, compelled into admiration for a vegetable she could hardly bring herself to swallow.

Bea could not wait to mock the duke for his beetroot sermon, which must have been as tedious as his lecture on the Battle of the Nile. She would even look up information about the root vegetable herself so she could drop a few fusty facts into the—

And then she remembered Kesgrave's fainthearted retreat two nights before.

She would have no opportunity to mock his ostentatious pedantry.

Disconcerted by the realization, she excused herself from the table and disappeared into her room for another quiet day of penance and contemplation. She picked up the Newton biography where she left off: in the middle of his years at the King's School in Grantham facing off against a bully. She was deeply engrossed in his building of a sundial when Flora knocked on her door to report that Lady Abercrombie was downstairs.

Bea looked up in surprise. "Lady Abercrombie?"

"Apparently, she is sincere in her efforts to make you fashionable, for she keeps calling you her protégé," Flora explained as she swept into the room. "Mama doesn't know what to do with herself. She's beside herself with excitement at hearing a peeress describe any member of her family in such intimate terms while also terrified that your mind is too weak to handle her patronage. She is, at this very moment, trying desperately to steer her attention toward me, pointing out my dewy complexion and biddable nature, but her ladyship is deeply resistant. I'm too insipid to be worthy of her sponsorship."

Sunk in disgrace, Bea had not thought of Lady Abercrombie since the scene on the balcony and she now pondered the other woman's motives for bestowing attention on her drab, uninteresting self. It was possible, yes, that the countess had slain Lord Fazeley in a desperate attempt to keep her brief love affair with her son's friend secret, but Bea decided it was highly unlikely. Having seen true cowardice in the form of Lord Duncan, she believed her ladyship was too bold and honest for such a despicable act. She would have scorned the earl's offer and brazened out the scandal.

Similarly, she no longer considered Lord Duncan to be a viable candidate for her list of suspects, for she could not believe he would ever have the nerve to cold-bloodedly murder his uncle. In the heat of the moment—heart racing, anger seething—yes, she imagined he would be capable of overcoming his own cravenness, but the earl was stabbed from behind on a busy street. That circumstance did not indicate a furious reprisal in the midst of a passionate disagreement.

It was just as well she was confined to quarters, for it appeared as though her list of suspects had dwindled to nothing. Not only had her dignity and respect for the duke ended on the balcony, but her investigation had too.

Although Bea was inclined to feel sorry for herself over the pitiable state of affairs, she was determined not to wallow in her failures and resolved to find humor in Lady Abercrombie's interest. Clearly, the countess needed a new project, for the limitations of making a lion cub fashionable were readily apparent, as one could not bring a wild animal into a ballroom or pressure a viscount to dance with it.

The image of Nuneaton dancing with Henry made Bea smile, and she rushed to assure her cousin that *insipid* wasn't the correct word. "The right one is *quiz*. You aren't enough of a quiz to excite her interest. She's looking for a challenge, which I present in spades. You should have heard her delight in telling people I was in my seventh season. Perhaps if you are still unmarried in six years, she will consent to take you on."

"You are being far too ungenerous to yourself," Flora said as she made herself comfortable on her cousin's bed. "You have age, yes, but also a fearlessness that must come with it, for you never used to be like this. You were always so quiet and timid, and now you are browbeating young lords with excessive repetition: love affair, love affair, *love affair*. I cannot imagine the circumstance that supports such an attack, but I'm convinced your behavior was entirely in line with it."

Bea did not expect her young cousin to be so astute and expressed sincere gratitude for the demonstration of faith.

"Of course," she said, then added with a sly look. "Mama, however, is thoroughly buying it."

Although the implication was clear, Bea chose to appear confused. "Excuse me?"

Flora laughed. "Your humble apologies, your promises to do better, your endless mea culpas spread throughout the day. I'm finding it a bit too much, but Mama is persuaded you are sincere. Now that you've acknowledged the fact that discovering Mr. Otley's body at Lakeview Hall has had a corrosive effect on your emotional well-being, she's confident you will return to normal and stop embarrassing the family. It has been a very impressive performance. I can only hope if I step out of line one day to achieve a display half as accomplished."

As flattering as the speech was, Bea could not rule out

the possibility that her cousin was a spy sent to gather information behind enemy lines. "I hope I've given Aunt Bea some comfort, for her peace of mind increases my own. I understand your cynicism, but I assure you it's unfounded. It wasn't merely the horridness of Mr. Otley's corpse that has undermined my ability to think clearly but also the shock of Mr. Davies's unexpected demise. The two events affected me far more strongly than I'd realized, with my emotional well-being, as you put it, getting progressively worse until I accosted poor Lord Duncan on the balcony."

Flora's lips twitched. "Ah, yes, poor Lord Duncan. I cannot wait to discover what he did to deserve it. You must promise me to reveal all one day."

Unable to make such a compact, she looked away from her cousin and examined her room for a distraction, settling, after a moment, on a pack of playing cards on her escritoire. "Russell taught me vingt-et-un last night. It's a game of chance, but there's also some skill involved. I feel I showed some talent for it, which, I suppose is what every gambler who cannot break himself of the habit believes. Shall we play? Just for ha'pennies, of course. I have no intention of wresting your pin money from you."

Realizing she would get no useful information from her cousin, Flora stood up and announced she should return to the drawing room before her mother noticed she was gone. "Lady Abercrombie is so captivating with her jewels and ebullient manners, Mama cannot turn away. Even as she was explaining my many fine points as a protégé, she had her eyes firmly fixed to the widow. I must admit, I find her a little overwhelming and am grateful she takes no interest in me."

Her cousin's description of the visit made Bea desperately tempted to look in on it, and she wondered what harm could come from peering discreetly into the drawing room to observe the proceedings sight unseen.

No harm obviously, if she didn't get caught.

If Aunt Vera did discover her, however, it would set

Bea's efforts to demonstrate good sense and decorum back two days. Her aunt must believe she was sincere in her displays of penance.

Putting thoughts of Lady Abercrombie out of her mind, Bea returned to her book and read quietly for the rest of the afternoon. She had dinner with her family, who then went en masse to the opera in Covent Garden to keep their engagement with Lady Marsham, with Russell grumbling the entire way out the door that he didn't want to see *Artaxerxes* again and Aunt Vera telling him over and over that he had yet to see it once.

Amused by their antics, Bea bid them good night, then made herself comfortable before the fire in the drawing room with Newton and a cup of tea. Sir Isaac had just presented his reflecting telescope to the Royal Society when Dawson entered the room to announce a visitor. It was a surprising communication, to be sure, for the hour was a little after ten, which was, by all accounts, an unusual time for social calls. She could only imagine it was either one of her uncle's cronies or a friend of Russell's.

"And have you explained to him that nobody is at home?" Bea asked reasonably.

Dawson nodded. "But he's here to see you."

Now that was a strange development, for Beatrice Hyde-Clare had had few callers in her six previous seasons—there may have been one or two when she first made her appearance in society—and certainly none at unconventional hours. Unable to imagine who it could be, she was grateful her aunt wasn't there to either censure her for the other person's behavior or insist she turn the guest away. "All right, Dawson, show him in, and ask Annie to come sit in the drawing room to lend the proceedings decorum. Thank you."

Bea marked the page of her book and laid it on the side table next to the settee. Then she stood up to greet her visitor and was amazed when the Duke of Kesgrave entered the room.

CHAPTER EIGHT

He was dressed in evening clothes: black silk breeches, pristine white shirt, elaborate cravat, shoes polished to a high shine. His blond curls, a little longer than fashionable, swept across his forehead, and his brows were drawn in anger.

Or was it irritation?

Perhaps it was impatience.

Bea, who could not understand what the Duke of Kesgrave was doing in her aunt's drawing room at ten o'clock at night, was further confounded by the fact that he was in her aunt's drawing room at ten o'clock at night seemingly annoyed with her.

What had she done to cause his ire? For two days, she had been confined to her house, demonstrating solemnity and respect and repenting for the very scene on the balcony that he had deserted at the earliest opportunity. Furthermore, she had not been abroad and could not have created new resentments. What ancient grievance had he dug up to pester her about now?

While she was still trying to reconcile the oddness of his appearance, Kesgrave stepped forward and said, "You must forgive me for interrupting."

Although his words were imperious, his tone was not,

and Bea, more confused than ever, assured him that she did. Then she gestured to the settee and asked him to sit down. Annie, entering the drawing room, confounded her further by bestowing on her a nod and a faint smile of approval, as if endorsing the enterprise. She settled into a chair across the room by the window, close enough to provide respectability while far enough to allow for discretion.

Bea regained her seat by the fire and wondered what activity had been disrupted by this visit, for he certainly was not dressed like a man who had been spending a quiet evening at home.

"Would you like some tea, your grace?" she asked, determined to be as gracious as possible. Revealing her anger at his desertion would give the matter too much importance. Months ago, at Lakeview Hall, when they were discussing possible culprits in the murder of Mr. Otley, Kesgrave had suggested they were colleagues working toward a common goal. The idea appealed to her then and it had appealed to her on the night of the Lelands' ball. But the concept was untenable, for in order to be colleagues they would have to be equals and recent history had demonstrated all too clearly that they were not.

The duke appeared ready to turn down the offer of tea and it was hard to say who of the two was more surprised when he agreed to a cup.

Bea put the request to Dawson, who immediately disappeared to fetch a second teacup. Then she felt the side of the pot to confirm the brew was still hot and waited for the duke to speak. He held his peace until the cup was delivered and when assured of their privacy, said, "Your cousin tells me you are being held prisoner."

His forthright tone was tinged with amusement, making it clear that he didn't believe Bea had been trapped in her home against her will. But the fact that he was there seemed to indicate some concern that her situation was a little more fraught than normal.

"If it was Flora, she was teasing you," Bea explained.

"If it was Russell, he was trying to get your attention. Both would appear to have succeeded beautifully, although perhaps Russell would deem the exercise a failure, as the attention he would seek is for himself."

He smiled and admitted it was Flora. "I attended the opera as well this evening and saw your family there. When I inquired after your health, as your absence was notable, your cousin said you were in fine spirits for a prisoner. Your aunt was not amused."

As impressed as Bea was with her cousin's daring, she feared it would mean only harsher treatment for her, as Aunt Vera would no doubt hold her responsible for Flora's impertinence. Having displayed it first, Bea would always be considered the model.

"Reports of my imprisonment have been greatly exaggerated, your grace, no doubt for comic effect," she said calmly. "I am indeed in fine spirits and am welcome to leave the house whenever I wish. That I choose to confine myself to quarters for the present is no concern of yours. You must not worry that I'm suffering cruel consequences for my outburst the other evening. Although you were not there to see it, for you had already beat a judicious retreat"—devil it, she hadn't meant to mention his desertion—"my family treated the matter with all the calm equanimity one would expect from a Hyde-Clare." Realizing she lacked the self-control to stay clear of the issue, she allowed herself to wade in deeper. "I do hope your presence here isn't an attempt to expatiate guilt, for you have nothing for which to atone. You were merely exercising your right as a man to remove himself from an awkward situation you were powerless to improve. 'Twas not as if you could have explained to my family that, although my methods certainly appeared unconventional, Lord Duncan's behavior had warranted such a response. My aunt would never have believed you, as you are only a duke and she's in no way in awe of dukes."

Although Bea wasn't sure if the intent of her speech

was to make Kesgrave feel ashamed or to simply vent her spleen, she was disappointed and insulted that he responded with laughter. "Miss Hyde-Clare, you must be in even more awe of me than I'd understood if you do not realize that my defense of you would have only made matters worse. Any explanation would have been either incomplete or so complete as to have you confined to this house for the rest of your life," he said, his blue eyes alight with humor. "No, I did not come here to make amends or apologize. I came to give you an update on our investigation."

There were so many surprising things about his statement, Bea didn't know where to rest her thoughts, for it all seemed strange and improbable. Only a few hours before, she had resigned herself to the fact that there no longer was an investigation, and yet here was the Duke of Kesgrave in her drawing room late at night assuring her that there was. Even more remarkable was his determination to probe the death of the earl with her help. His ego seemed to make many odd twists and starts. Additionally, he had left the opera during intermission to come to her house to provide her with the update. Surely, when he had had his valet tie the Mail Coach earlier in the evening, he hadn't thought to himself that he would leave the performance in the middle to pay a call on Miss Hyde-Clare. It simply did not make sense.

And yet he was there.

Extraordinary.

Rather than reveal these thoughts, Bea said, "And what updates do you have for me?"

"I had my steward visit every book publisher in the city, and he reported back that not a single one has a publishing contract with Lord Fazeley," he explained.

Bea nodded as she considered the information for several seconds. Then she said matter-of-factly, "So your update is that you have no update."

Kesgrave stiffened at her incomplete understanding of the situation and explained with exquisite condescension,

"With your limited experience with worldly affairs, you're clearly incapable of appreciating the complexities involved in the gathering of information. The acquisition of knowledge is not merely the discovery of a positive, my dear Miss Hyde-Clare. It's also the confirmation of a negative."

Watching him stand on his consequence, Bea conceded to herself that she was a perverse creature, for the thing that had annoyed her to distraction when they first met delighted her now. Hoping to increase his stiffness with additional offense, she said, "You missed the second half of *Artaxerxes* to tell me you have nothing to tell me?"

He inhaled sharply, feeling the prick to his ego keenly. "It appears I did," he said, his tone cold. "And now I will bid you good night."

"No, please," Bea said quickly, reaching out a hand to still his movements, for she had not intended to drive him away. "I'm sorry. I was only teasing. Truly, you have no idea how pleased I am to see you."

This declaration, made without a hint of self-consciousness, seemed to surprise the duke, and Bea felt almost certain she discerned a spark of pleasure light up his eyes. "You are?"

The truth was, she could not recall ever being so happy to see anyone step into her drawing room, but obviously she could not admit *that* to the duke. Indeed, she could barely admit it to herself. "Yes, for I most particularly wanted to ask if beetroot may be used as a clothing dye," she said irreverently, "and if so what ratio of beetroot juice to water would you suggest?"

As she had only her aunt's report to go on, Bea wasn't sure the duke would understand the reference she was making or perceive himself the subject of further mockery. If he did comprehend either, there was a very good chance he would storm out the door in a huff, as this provocation, coming so closely on the heels of the other, might be more than his dignity could withstand.

She was pleasantly surprised, then, to see him settle

into the settee and explain how his dissertation on the usages of beetroot was meant to torment her aunt with its dull specificity. "As a reprisal of sorts for treating you so harshly the night before at the ball. You have made me aware that my comprehensive knowledge, although an enviable thing in almost all circumstances, might not be entirely welcome in the social setting. Your aunt, however, appeared to enjoy it immensely. Indeed, her interest in the topic, chosen, of course, for its extreme banality, which even I can realize, was so strong, she asked a series of follow-up questions that I did not know the answer to. I resorted to pure fiction to maintain the appearance of expertise. I believe I did a reasonable job of coming up with an explanation for why taking beetroot with garlic will sweeten sour breath."

Bea laughed at his bewildered tone and his willingness to invent facts to suit his needs. It was not something she'd imagined him doing comfortably, unbending enough to play fast and loose with the truth, and discovering he could raised him in her estimation. "She was toadying, your grace. You are an esteemed personage, and she was not only grateful for the attention but leveraging it for maximum effect. While you were running through a recipe for beetroot powder, she was picturing how she must appear to her friends, deep in conversation with a duke for ten minutes. No doubt, it was the height of her social career. We may call it enlightened self-interest, and I can only assume it happens to you all the time, which is why you did not realize your displays of comprehensive knowledge are off-putting."

Kesgrave considered her thoughtfully for a moment, then said, "You are merciless, Miss Hyde-Clare."

It was impossible not to giggle at such a charge, for she did not have enough power to give or withhold mercy. As an orphan, she had been buffeted by other people's whims for twenty years. "I?" she asked with interest. "In what way?"

"You would leave me nothing—no social interaction unexamined, no kindness unscrutinized, no compliment unrifled for hidden motive," he said. "Must I go back to my babyhood to find one person who did not have a secret agenda in our dealings?"

"I sincerely hope not, as the nursemaid who swaddled you probably wanted a great many things," she replied with a gentle smile. "That said, Nuneaton seems genuine in his regard for you, and you are almost equals. Certainly, there are one or two others."

Kesgrave leaned forward as if to add to the list, and Bea, delighting in the absurdity of a duke cataloging his popularity, felt a stab of disappointment when he merely picked up his tea and took a sip.

"I did not come here solely to give you an update," Kesgrave announced, firmly changing the subject.

Bea swallowed her disappointment and said with irrepressible amusement, "You mean, you did not leave Covent Garden in the middle of a performance solely to give me an update."

He responded with one of his withering looks, but the effect was ruined by the smile that immediately replaced it. "Yes, I did, you brat, but only because it was so deadly dull, not because I found the prospect of your company impossible to resist. You hold yourself in high esteem."

In fact, she did not. Although there were several explanations for his presence that did not include a tedious theatrical production, there was no version of events in which Beatrice Hyde-Clare's company was impossible to resist. Rather, she assumed his visit could be attributed to a combination of factors such as guilt over deserting her on the balcony, concern for her welfare after Flora's comment, eagerness to share his knowledge and a desire for conversation with someone who was familiar with the particulars of the project.

He couldn't very well discuss Lord Duncan's childish decision to blackmail a former paramour rather than curtail his gambling or ask his parents for more blunt with Viscount Nuneaton.

"I'm surprised to hear that, as I was given to understand from several reviews that the production is excellent, with many fine performances. Mrs. Beatty's portrayal of Mandane, in particular, is meant to be entrancing."

"If you are entranced by the sound of a horse gargling salty water, then, yes, that is an entirely accurate description," he said with little sympathy for the poor soprano who sang the role. "But I did not come to give my assessment of the opera. We must discuss our investigation into Fazeley's murder and establish what our next steps will be."

Although she was hardly inclined to be sentimental, Bea thought *our next steps* might very well be the three loveliest words in the English language. How startling and inexplicable that the Duke of Kesgrave was the one to say them.

"What do you make of your steward's inability to discover the name of the earl's publisher?" she asked. "Does that mean he lied to his godson about signing a contract or is the firm simply unwilling to come forward?"

She made no mention of Lord Duncan's staggering hypocrisy, though the fact of it still burned hot in her throat, because she could not be certain that Kesgrave did not share his point of view to some extent. The young lord's low opinion of women—his apparent belief that blackmailing one of Lady Abercrombie's sex did not rise to the insult of blackmail—was not novel among the men of the *ton*. Indeed, she imagined it was a universal that cut across the social order regardless of wealth, class or education.

If Kesgrave agreed with him, she truly didn't want to know.

"I suspect it's the latter," he said. "If the manuscript is the revealing document Fazeley promised it would be, then more than a few members of society with secrets to keep might be moved to halt its publication by way of a legal action. That being the case, the publishing firm would be wise to deny all knowledge of it, especially to the steward of a duke, until the book was available for purchase, at which point the damage would be done and any attempt to stop distribution would only increase interest and sales."

Conceding the validity of his argument, Bea suggested sending around a less impressive personage to make the inquiries. "Perhaps an orphan whose family is not illustrious enough to merit mention in Lord Fazeley's book."

Kesgrave shook his head. "No, I believe the damage has been done and anyone else asking questions would be met with the same suspicion. We need to devise another approach."

At this statement, Bea nodded pensively, as if giving the matter serious thought, but it was only a pose. She knew what they had to do, for it was as plain as the nose on her face. Every contract had at least two signatories, and if the first party would not divulge its participation, then it was necessary to consult the second one. Given that the second party in this situation was departed meant they had no choice but to break into his town house and look through his things. It was the ideal solution in more ways than one, for it gave them access to not only the earl's private documents but also his manuscript. Lord Duncan's outrage at the notion of his godfather using his memoir to exhort money from his peers was all well and good, but Bea was hardly inclined to take a sniveling hypocrite's word for it. If they could find the work, they could confirm for themselves if blackmail was a possibility and, if so, who was vulnerable to it.

As obvious as the solution was, Bea knew the duke would not easily fall in line with it. He would consider it too dangerous or too undignified or too much of a violation of the unwritten code of conduct that governed the way gentlemen treated each other.

Very well. He would have to be maneuvered.

Sitting up straight with a sudden start, she said with feigned excitement, "I've got it! You can buy all the publishing companies."

Rather than reject the outlandish proposal out of

hand, he quirked an eyebrow as he examined her. "*All* the publishing companies?"

"Yes, all, that way we may gain access to all their contracts," she said.

"In the entire country or just the city?" he asked in a tone so neutral she could not tell whether he was considering the idea or mocking it.

"We can start with the ones in the city, and if they don't yield results, move on to the rest of the country," she said reasonably. "There's no need to make rash purchases."

"So I may buy them one by one," he said as he weighed the value of the plan. "Buy the publishing firm, examine its contracts and if it doesn't have Fazeley's, buy the publishing firm down the road or a few streets over. It's not the most efficient method for acquiring information but it has its merits, namely that it's safe and reliable, which, ultimately, makes it an excellent scheme. Very well, Miss Hyde-Clare, you've persuaded me. I shall buy all the publishing companies."

Although Bea didn't doubt for a moment that the Duke of Kesgrave could afford to purchase every publishing firm in the kingdom—and that, in itself, struck her as a travesty—she knew he was far too meticulous and fond of regulation and order to actually do it. The acquisition of just a single firm alone would require weeks, if not months, of inspection, examining the accounts for irregularities and confirming the soundness of the business model. Even if he wanted to act recklessly to move the investigation along, he would not be able to bring himself to sink money into an enterprise he knew little or nothing about. He simply did not have the constitution for irresponsibility.

Bea could not say why she found that so charming.

Clearly, he agreed to her implausible plan only to tease her and she wondered if she should propose another unlikely scheme or simply suggest they break into Fazeley's residence posthaste.

Noting the humor gleaming in his eyes, she decided

to let him have an opportunity to recommend a solution. "All right, then, what's your plan?"

"Am I not acquiring a monopoly on books?" he asked.

"We both know you could never bring yourself to buy anything without first establishing its soundness as a business concern," she said.

The duke's lips quivered as he looked at her with faint amusement. "I don't know how you can make the responsible stewardship of the Matlock family legacy sound like a bad thing. And yet..." He trailed off as he shook his head. "I think we should establish a more direct course to discovering the information. I will gain entry to Fazeley's residence and search through his private documents for the contract. His father is away in Scotland and has probably only just gotten word of his demise. He will not have had a chance to get the house in order yet."

His readiness to violate the law in the pursuit of the truth delighted her, for she had not expected his morals to yield to practicality so easily, but she took exception to his intention to go alone. Naturally, he would resist the idea of her accompanying him even though she had successfully snuck into the private rooms of several men during their stay at Lakeview Hall.

She decided not to argue with him about it—at least not yet. The more she knew about his plan, the more easily she could figure out the best way to infiltrate it. "By what method will you use? Will you pick the lock open using a special tool like a burglar or shatter a glass pane to open a window at the back of the house?"

Although he was sitting next to her on the settee, Kesgrave peered down at her as if towering above her, his handsome features—his light eyes, his firm mouth— arranged in a pose of arrogant amusement. "My dear Miss Hyde-Clare, I will use the front door."

She peered at him with suspicion, knowing it could not be as simple as he made it sound. "How?"

And yet, from his perspective, it was indeed. "I am a duke," he said.

Kesgrave had given this answer to her before to other questions, as it seemed to be his response to most problems. All complicated issues or unexpected obstructions could be resolved or cleared with the assertion of his importance. He once told the Skeffington heir that matters were decided by order of precedence, and it appeared he believed it wholeheartedly. No doubt history and the world had contrived over and over to affirm this belief.

She found his self-regard maddening.

"Even the Duke of Kesgrave cannot march up to the door of a dead man's residence and demand access to the property," Bea insisted with impatience.

Kesgrave raised an eyebrow. "Who said *demand*? I shall have my steward express interest in the location with the agent in charge of it. It is a rental, and the owner will be worried about next month's expenses. The Duke of Kesgrave is a desirable tenant, so I'm confident Stephens will be able to arrange for an inspection tomorrow afternoon."

As much as it pained Bea to admit it, his plan was sound. Why sneak around a house crouching in shadows when you could brazenly walk its floors? In determining its suitability for his needs, he could open any door and look through any drawer and enter any room without raising suspicions. Truly, it was the ideal way to rifle though a dead gentleman's private things in search of a contract that may or not exist.

If Bea wished she had thought of it herself, she was practical enough to acknowledge the limitations of her outlook, for she was neither a duke nor a man. She felt the unfairness deeply but knew there was nothing to be gained in railing against it. Instead, she focused her attention firmly on the future and tried to discern how she might take advantage of Kesgrave's many advantages. His methods were aboveboard and overt, which meant he could not argue that the undertaking was dangerous in any way or that her participation would put her at risk. He would try to, of course, because he was a man and a duke, but the claim would ring hollow and have no sway. Whether he liked it or not, she *would* accompany him on that inspection tomorrow.

As determined as she was, she knew there was no harm in beginning the discussion with a display of admiration. Flattery was, to be sure, a low technique, but she had not met many people who could withstand its lure. "I hope you will not think ill of me when I admit that my instinct was to impugn your scheme and outline all the ways in which it wouldn't work. But I find I cannot do that because it's a very good ruse and much better than anything I was privately devising. Well done, your grace."

He titled his head at a curious angle as he smiled. "I believe that's the first compliment you've ever intentionally paid me."

Acceding this point silently would have furthered her agenda, but she couldn't refrain from pointing out that intentional compliments were not necessary, as he frequently pulled thoughtlessly spoken words out of the air and used them to praise himself.

Kesgrave knew at once exactly which assortment of thoughtless words she was referring to. "You needn't feel embarrassed by your admission of being in awe of me. I assure you, most people are."

Bea had to clench her teeth at the satisfaction in his tone, for the alternative was to pour a cup of tepid tea over his head. Then she forced a smile so stiff it was almost ferocious and said, "How clever of you to rely on that for your plan. That shrewdness is what I'm in awe of."

"Thank you," he said, noting nothing amiss in her tone. "Your admiration means the world to me."

"And being so clever, you will have no trouble figuring out how I may fit into this scheme," she added.

The duke's right hand flew to his heart as if troubled by some sharp and unexpected pain. "Ah, now your compliments make sense. You are trying to manipulate me into allowing you to join my tour of Fazeley's residence tomorrow. It strikes me as an unlikely path to success, but you are welcome to continue making the attempt if you believe it will bear fruit. So far you've praised my intelligence and the overwhelming sense of wonder my presence inspires in your breast. Next you might consider admiring my face, which I've been led to believe is pleasing, or my skill with horses, as I'm a notable whip. I'm also a deft boxer and can tie my own cravat in a pinch."

"Don't forget your ego, which is the largest in London," she said.

"An accomplishment of which I'm particularly proud," he replied, "as the competition among Corinthians is quite fierce. Ritterdale erected a statue of himself on his front lawn, which made me fear he might take the title, but fortunately, humbler heads prevailed and he decided to have it face away from the street."

"What an anxious few minutes for you," she observed with an overabundance of sympathy, "and yet you speak of it with such equanimity. Truly, I *am* in awe of you."

"And still you try to flatter me into compliance," he asked with a hint of wonder. "You are dogged, Miss Hyde-Clare, a trait that I must admit I find particularly attractive in a woman. So many females give up at the first sign of resistance or fail to make convincing arguments. See, there, now I'm trying to flatter you into accepting my refusal without further discussion. I expect it won't work, which demonstrates with clarity how unequal flattery is to the task of persuasion. Perhaps we should both try another method, like threats or intimidation."

"What about rational discussion?" she suggested, her heart still beating just a little faster than normal at the thought of the Duke of Kesgrave finding something—anything—particularly attractive about her. Knowing it was a tactic curbed her pleasure but could not eradicate it entirely. "No tricks or diversions. Honest dealing on both sides. Like colleagues in the House of Lords coming up with solutions to policy issues."

He considered her proposal for a long moment, as if

looking for a trick or a diversion, then, perhaps recognizing it as the very thing he himself had said when they were drawing up a list of suspects at Lakeview Hall, agreed. "Very well. I will go first. Your joining me on a tour of Fazeley's residence is untenable, as there's no way I could arrive with an eligible female in tow and not ruin both of us."

Bea thought of several responses she could make to this observation, such as pointing out the fact that, at six and twenty, she was not an eligible female or marveling at his obsession with his own ruination, which he had also displayed during their visit in the Lake District. But she wanted to respect the parameters of the discussion that she herself had set up, so she calmly addressed the cause of his concern. She started by acknowledging its validity. "It would be most unusual if the Duke of Kesgrave arrived to look at a house accompanied by a young, unmarried female. It would be assumed that I was either your mistress or your fiancée, both positions of which, as you yourself indicated, would be disastrous for me. There is no reason, however, why the Duke of Kesgrave cannot look at a house in the company of a young man."

"No," he said.

He could have at least considered it before rejecting the notion entirely out of hand. "Why not?"

"You said a rational discussion," he pointed out, aggrieved by the deception. "Your proposing to dress up as a man and accompany me to look at a house is not rational. It's ludicrous."

"Why is it ludicrous?" she asked. "I think I would make a very convincing fellow. I have the shoulders for it. I know this because my aunt has lamented many times over the years that they're too masculine." She jumped to her feet and stood before him, throwing her shoulders back and demonstrating her stance. "See? Aren't they manly? Aunt Vera says I should have a rapier in my hand, for I have the build of a fencing master."

Forced to his feet, Kesgrave stared at her as if she

were mad. "Your shoulders aren't manly. They're lovely. Quite lovely."

Bea delighted at the praise—of course she did. She was human and female and twenty-six years old, and she had never had a beau and felt awkward around people and much preferred the company of books to the *ton* and nobody had ever complimented her on any aspect of her physical appearance before. That her shoulders could be quite lovely, that any part of her body might rise to the level of quite *anything,* was revelatory to her. Hearing the words repeat themselves in her head, she felt a sudden and inexplicable urge to throw herself into his arms.

What an utter disaster, she thought, wondering if this was what a tendre felt like. She could not believe it was so and yet how wholly appropriate for the middling Beatrice Hyde-Clare to aim so comically high.

Her mind raced, but her expression remained tranquil as she said calmly, deliberately, with precision and intention, "Now, come, your grace, we agreed to no more flattery."

He seemed surprised by her remark and started almost guiltily, as if caught in the act of doing something wrong. "We agreed to be rational," he said stiffly.

Bea took a deep breath and sat down again. "Rationally, then. There's no rational reason why you can't tour the residence tomorrow in the company of your steward. If you were truly intending to lease the property, you would probably bring him along to take notes and observe its condition. Additionally, there's no rational reason for anyone to suspect I'm not who you say I am. You are the Duke of Kesgrave. No one would dare question what you say."

A fleeting smile appeared on his face as he rested his arm against the mantel. "Now who's breaking the prohibition against flattery?"

She continued as if he hadn't spoken. "I will look the part. My cousin Russell is taller than me, to be sure, but his build isn't much different from mine and I'm confident his clothes will fit me well enough. And no one will even notice I'm gone because I'm being held prisoner. I've spent the past two days in my room reading, and the only person who has visited is Flora. And she did so only because Lady Abercrombie had visited to discuss my mentorship."

"Your mentorship?" he asked with such confusion the word sounded foreign.

Bea shook her head, unwilling to allow such a deep and long digression. "I have the clothes. I have the opportunity. I have the interest. I have an astute mind that might notice something you miss, not because you aren't observant but because two sets of eyes are better than one."

"I appreciate the argument, for I do think you've made it in good faith, but I cannot see my way toward encouraging such irresponsible behavior," he said.

Even before he said the words, she knew he remained firmly opposed and decided it was better to let the matter drop. Clearly, he would not be convinced and continuing to argue would serve only to antagonize him further. For what she had in mind—her alternative plan that would go into effect when he refused to be rational—relied to a certain extent on his goodwill. So pulled her face into a sharp scowl, as if angry at him and her own powerlessness, and then made an elaborate display of trying to talk about something else. She floundered for a topic, then realized Lady Abercrombie and her mission to make Bea the height of fashion was the ideal topic. She began the narrative as a distraction, but she quickly got carried away as she explained the beautiful widow's plans and her aunt's attempts to redirect her efforts to her own daughter, Flora. She had barely explained that she felt like a novel oddity to be shown off in public before Kesgrave called her Tilly's new lion club.

"Yes, precisely," she said, smiling in perfect accord.

They discussed the likelihood of her ladyship's plan succeeding. Kesgrave thought it was high if the patronesses of Almack's had already accepted her, and she rushed to explain that it was only Lady Cowper, who was known for being the kindest of the cohort, and Lady Sefton, who could not bring herself to revoke anyone's vouchers for ill-considered behavior. The duke assured her Lady Jersey could not be far behind, and Bea grimaced in mock horror at such an august personage rendering judgment on her.

"Not nearly as august as I," he said, only half-teasing, "and you have yet to wither under my attentions, though I have made every effort."

Bea laughed at the slightly disgruntled note in his tone.

Indeed, she laughed at everything he said and passed a remarkably pleasant hour in his company discussing Lady Abercrombie's absurd scheme and her dazzling drawing room and Sir Isaac Newton's telescope and how to optimize a seemingly weak pair of cards in vingt-et-un. At midnight, he announced his intent to leave and Bea nodded, for it seemed very late to her and she had no idea when her family would return. In an extremely and surprisingly charitable mood, she walked him to the door, thanked him for his visit and bid him good night. She did not, however, tell him she would see him tomorrow.

But obviously there was no question that she would.

CHAPTER NINE

Having never assumed the identity of a steward before, Bea decided to adhere closely to the familiar—namely, Mr. Wright, her uncle's steward for more than twenty-five years. He was a serious gentleman, diligent in his habits, respectful of the family, quiet and sincere. He wore his gray hair closely cropped, squinted behind a pair of spectacles and labored under a pronounced stoop made worse by years of crouching over a desk for hours at a time.

Naturally, she could not adopt all his habits, as she had no inclination to turn her hair gray, nor any idea how to do it. Powder, she supposed, was the usual method, but that would make a mess and leave a trail everywhere she went. Achieving the hunched look, however, was easily accomplished by rounding her shoulders forward, an uncomfortable pose she would be able to hold for only a few minutes at a time. Locating a pair of spectacles was a slightly harder challenge, and after considering the problem from every angle, she had no choice but to borrow a pair from Mr. Wright's office. If Dawson thought her appearance belowstairs was odd, he did not remark upon it to her.

Hopefully, he would not remark upon it to anyone.

He had, of course, mentioned the duke's visit the night before to the various members of the household, but as none of them could wrap their head around the implausibility of the Duke of Kesgrave's visiting plain and spinsterish Bea, they each assured him he had misidentified the caller. As much as Bea wanted to be insulted by their certainty, she was too grateful for their intransigence to take a pet. If they suspected Kesgrave's interest, they would discover her secret activities and she would be sent to rusticate in the country once and for all.

Having collected the spectacles and perfected her stoop, she turned her attention to depressing familial interest in her afternoon activities. Over breakfast, while Russell complained about the tedious opera the night before and Aunt Vera gushed about the wonderful time they all had, Bea made a great show of crying into her porridge. She was still incapable of producing tears on demand—and rather thought if she was going to continue down this route of deceit and investigation despite all her resolutions to deal honestly with the world, she might work harder to cultivate the skill—and had to settle for hiccoughing a great deal. But it was enough to convince her relatives she was deeply distressed about something and after a small bit of coaxing she revealed that *Artaxerxes* was Mr. Davies's favorite opera.

To their credit, the Hyde-Clares were a liberal family who readily accepted that a lowly law clerk from Cheapside had a sincere fondness for opera.

Aunt Vera was delighted by her niece's demonstration of grief, for it meant she was no longer denying her emotions and the depth to which Mr. Davies's death had upset her. "You go rest in your room, my dear. Don't exert yourself on our account."

Once in her room, Bea assembled the other aspects of her disguise and realized she had forgotten to steal footwear from Russell during her raid on his wardrobe the night before. She rather thought her uncle was closer in size to her than her cousin, but sneaking into her cousin's rooms to take something carried less risk. While she was there, she helped herself to a bicorne hat.

At one o'clock, she examined herself in the mirror to evaluate her appearance. The total effect could be better, she admitted, for her lack of side whiskers made her seem very young while her stoop and the awkward way she shuffled around in Russell's overlarge shoes indicated great age. But she wore the clothes in a convincing manner, with her manly shoulders filling out the unadorned white shirt and her breasts flattened against her chest by a stiff cotton band. The light-colored breeches, which were snug on her cousin, were loose and long, which gave them the appearance of being handed down from an older brother, a condition that was in line with her career as a steward.

Lastly, she inspected her face for signs of unwelcome femininity but saw only the same visage with little to distinguish it staring back at her. The only thing of note was the spray of freckles across her nose, but surely men were as subject to the effects of the sun as women.

Satisfied, Bea cautiously opened the door to her room, peered into the hallway, confirmed it was empty and quickly dashed down to the ground floor. Unobserved, she raced through the corridor toward the front door, breezed through the entrance without anyone noticing and walked the several blocks to Chesterfield Street, where the earl had taken a house two doors down from his rival, Brummell. The *ton* speculated he had chosen the location so that he could observe the Beau daily and prepare remarks on the inadequacies of the other man's sartorial choices. The earl, affronted by the conjecture, ardently denied such reports, insisting he had a natural talent for stinging set-downs and required no effort to issue one.

Bea found number eight among the row of redbrick houses, assured herself all she needed to do to carry off the deception was exude confidence and marched up the steps. She knocked firmly on the door, which was opened several moments later by a dour-faced man who offered a fierce scowl in greeting. It required all her courage not to run away.

"Good afternoon," she said deeply, accomplishing a light tenor that was sufficiently unfemale, if not resoundingly male. "I am Mr. Wright, the Duke of Kesgrave's steward, here to inspect the house for possible lease, per my conversation with the agent who manages the property."

Although the expression of the imposing butler's face did not change, Bea felt his disapproval. "We were told to expect the duke."

"As you should!" she said with more force than was necessary. Did it make her sound defensive? Suspicious? Like a woman dressed in her cousin's clothes pretending to be her uncle's steward? Should she smile to soften the severity? Were ingratiating smiles of compensation an essentially female thing?

The silence stretched as Bea considered her response. Lord Fazeley's butler, who appeared to be the archetype of the intimidating London servant, stared at her.

Finally, she said, "The duke will be along presently. I cannot claim to know the specifics of his schedule, nor can I hope to influence his movements. He will arrive when he arrives, and in the meantime he requested that I begin the inspection on my own, as I'm familiar enough with his likes and requirements to make an initial judgment as to the property's viability. As you can imagine, the duke has standards of a very exacting nature that are difficult for most people or situations to meet."

"Exacting standards" was precisely the sort of thing the earl's butler understood, and he smoothly stepped aside to allow Bea to enter. The hallway was narrow and elegant, with carved moldings and wide-plank floors. She pursed her lips, nodded thoughtfully and tilted her head forward as if examining a very small detail that only someone with her expertise would notice. She took out a notebook she'd brought with her and made a nonsensical note about the shape of the front door.

As she recorded her observations, the butler hovered, and fearing he might hover for the whole of her visit, she said, "I'll just show myself around. If I have any questions, I will seek you out."

He opened his mouth as if to protest the arrangement, so she quickly added, "This will leave you free to listen for the duke's arrival."

Although the grimace remained firmly affixed to his face, he agreed to this arrangement and even called it very good.

Bea smiled in gratitude and then immediately worried that men did not engage in that kind of smiling either.

"You will drive yourself mad," she muttered, entering the drawing room, which, though elaborately styled, did not have the excesses one had come to associate with his lordship. As a renter, he was not free to redecorate the room to conform with his preferences, but she would expect a few elements of extravagance to make the room feel comfortable to him.

She passed through the double doors into the dining room, which was also quite refined, with light colors and a long table that was either new or had been treated very well. Determined to appear interested even if the butler wasn't keeping a close watch, she inspected the sideboard, looked under the duggard at the floor and sat at the seat at the head of the table to confirm its comfort.

After checking the parlor, she stood at the bottom of the staircase and wondered what would be the logical next move for an actual steward in her circumstance: head upstairs to look at the bedrooms or go down to examine the kitchens and other servant offices?

Deciding her employer's creature comforts should come first, she climbed to the first floor and looked in the room at the front of the house. As she'd expected, it was the master suite, lavishly decorated and filled with compartments for storing private documents.

Perfect, she thought.

The bedchamber itself seemed the least likely place to find the contract or the manuscript, but it behooved her to be thorough, so she checked every drawer and cabinet. She discovered an unexpected number of literary works among his things and admired the care he took with his books. As well-read as they appeared, none had broken spines or bent pages.

Next she searched the dressing room and found herself in awe of the extent and depth of his wardrobe. It hardly seemed possible that one person could have so many waistcoats in so many colors and patterns or so many pairs of pumps and boots, all seemingly similar, though no doubt quite different in small but significant ways.

Other than the sheer magnitude and variety of his collection, there was nothing interesting in the dressing room and she moved on to the sitting room. As soon as she observed the writing desk, she felt a fissure of excitement, for this felt like the room where a gentleman might store his contract to publish a book.

She looked briefly through the cubbies and the smaller drawers on top, once again determined not to miss anything in her haste. No, nothing of note, she thought. Just nibs and fasteners and sealing wax and scraps of paper. She opened one of the larger drawers and shuffled through several sheets of paper, which, upon further scrutiny, turned out to be letters. She read the first one and immediately dropped it back into the drawer when she realized it was from a lover. All the letters were, although their authorship varied. Judging by the dates on the missives, Lord Fazeley had been carrying on four affairs at the same time. She did not know enough about the mating habits of the typical male to judge, but four seemed to be on the high side. Certainly, it required a lot of effort to juggle the expectations and requirements of four women. How did he keep them all straight in his mind?

Perhaps he did not and that was what led to his death.

Based on what Lord Duncan had told them, she'd assumed the pending publication of the revealing memoir served as the cause of the dandy's murder. But she knew from her investigation into Mr. Otley's death that a romantic betrayal, even one many years in the past, could fester and seethe and erupt in a violent attack.

Bea recorded the names of the women in her notebook—Autumn, Lila, Susan, Carla—then returned the letters to the drawer and slid it closed.

The next compartment contained a diary describing the earl's daily activities in quite extensive detail. The entry from the day before his death recorded not only his waking time but also the hour he had breakfast, what he consumed during the meal, how long the event lasted and what he said to the footman as he was clearing the dishes from the table ("Careful, Rogers, you missed a crumb"). It described his grooming habits, including precise measurements for tooth powder (used to clean his teeth as well as his fingernails) and something called Dr. Hamley's Improving Tonic. He chronicled the conversations he had with various members of his staff: with his valet, selecting his clothes for the day; with his housekeeper, picking the menu for dinner; with the groom, choosing a bridle for his morning ride. His movements outside the house were just as closely followed: where he went, what he did, whom he talked to. A disagreement with Lord Crestor over the proper fit of one's waistcoat warranted two lines. Mr. Manley's confidence that ceremonial daggers would soon be the rage with Lord Fazeley's support earned four. His romantic dealings received the same treatment: dinner with Lucy, who admired his cravat, which he described as a modified version of his famous invention, the Fazeley Flow; and a later supper with a dancer named Susan, during which he had three glasses of wine and a flute of champagne.

As a narrative it made tedious reading, but as a chronicle of the way a certain type of gentleman lived his life it was a fascinating study, and Bea sat down at the escritoire to read more. She turned to the previous day, which bore a close resemblance to the one after: He woke at the same hour, breakfasted on the same meal, groomed with the same care, conversed with the same men, dallied with the same women. Only his wine consumption seemed to change, dropping to two glasses with Susan and rising to one with Lucy.

Bea flipped to two days before his death and read. She flipped to three days and read. She flipped to four. Over and over again he reported the same general facts of his general existence. There were variations, of course. On the day he perfected the simplified Fazeley Flow, a project that had taken three days from conception to completion, he recorded a two-hour practice session with his valet. On the day he ended his liaison with Autumn, he included a trip to the jeweler to buy what he called his usual trinket to lessen the pain of parting: a gold necklace with a pear-shaped ruby pendant. On the day he went to Lady Abercrombie's to exhort money on behalf of his godson, he described the underwhelming quality of the teacakes she served, criticized the oolong as weak and aired his resentment at having to compete with the interior of a drawing room for sartorial dominance.

It was an astounding document, at once riveting and tedious, and Bea wondered at the voyeuristic impulse in her that kept her glued to the chair as she continued to read. It was, she supposed, the novelty of being exposed so deeply to the way a mind worked, even if it was a dull mind.

Try as she might, she could not pull herself away.

And so the duke found her an hour later, bent over the desk and wholly engrossed.

The first she heard of him was when he spoke: "I must congratulate you, Miss Hyde-Clare, on making the most rational decision available to you."

She startled at the sound of his voice but quickly smoothed her movements, for she'd known this moment was coming and had prepared for it. And yet she hadn't prepared for the reasonable sound of his tone or the calm way he regarded her. She'd anticipated cajoling an angry duke out of his fit of temper and worried now that his placidity indicated a devious scheme of his own.

Carefully, she closed the diary and stood up. "Thank you, your grace. I trust you understand why I could not leave things the way they were."

"Naturally," he said mildly.

"And I did not lie about my intentions," she pointed out. "I merely ceased discussing the matter when you made it plain such a course was futile. There is a difference, you'll own, between a lie and resisting a futility. And you never expressly sought my agreement, as you did not consider it necessary. Presumably, the Duke of Kesgrave is accustomed to his dictates being followed without their actually being issued."

At this charge, he smiled faintly and said with pronounced sobriety that he was relieved to hear that it was, of course, ultimately his fault. "When you didn't immediately lay the blame for your presence here at my self-regard and duchy, I feared our interactions might have humanized me in some alarming way. It's comforting to know I'm as imperious as ever."

She knew he was teasing, for he did not truly consider himself imperious, a fact that made him all the more commanding. "I did not immediately begin with your culpability as a sign of respect, which, I'm sure you'll agree, is your due."

"It's a comfort to me, Miss Hyde-Clare, to know you are worrying about my consequence even when I'm not," he said.

"'Tis something I cannot forget," she said, matching his light tone. It was an effort, however, because she was no longer joking. That he was a duke with every option available to him was never far from her mind, and yet even as she recalled that she pictured the future he most likely imagined for himself: Incomparable wife, cherubic children, beautiful home, serene existence. In many ways, his narrow expectations for himself were as limiting as her own prospects. The different was, he didn't know it.

Kesgrave stepped further into the sitting room, looked at the book in her grasp and held out his hand. "May I?"

She felt a juvenile impulse to hide the diary behind her back and blink innocently at him as if she had nothing to surrender. But she restrained such childishness and passed it along.

As he opened to the first page, he said, "I trust you also won't forget to apologize to Stephens."

"Stephens?" she echoed, wondering if that was the name of the butler who had answered the door.

"Stephens is my actual steward," he explained. "He is the man whose nose you put out of joint by pretending to be him. He got very stiff with Jones when Jones told him he was already there and then positively churlish with me when I, perceiving what you had done, rushed to assure Jones that I did in fact possess two stewards and that one had indeed been dispatched before us as an advance party to inspect the property. Unaware of your deception, Stephens believed that I had hired a second steward without telling him and that my trust in this new, untried fellow was so high, I sent him here to inspect the property on his own. He's now in the kitchens nursing his displeasure, which I have no doubt he will make me feel keenly after we leave here. So do, please, if you remember, take a moment to reassure him that his place in my heart has not been usurped by another—for his sake, of course, not my own, as I know my discomfort means little to you."

Bea found it impossible not to laugh over the scene he described, and although he made a great show of being offended, she could tell from his sanguine expression that he thought it was amusing too. Feeling in charity with him, for she had gotten her way and was genuinely appreciative of his not revealing the truth to the terrifying butler, she said, "That is Lord Fazeley's diary, which contains the minutiae of his daily existence. I can only assume he used it as a reference to recall the details of particular interactions for his memoir and perhaps to help him keep abreast of his own romantic liaisons. As you will see, he was quite generous with his favors. We cannot know if any of the women to whom he devoted his attention objected to the others, but I feel fairly certain we should add jealousy to the list of possible motives."

"Hell has no fury…" Kesgrave murmured.

Nodding, Bea rose and indicated to the chair, but he refused to sit while she remained standing.

Next to the escritoire was an ornate mahogany bookcase with brass accents and a cabinet below for storing items. Bea opened the compartment on the bottom, which was filled with ledgers, more diaries, and bills of sale for clothing, including—

No, she thought, bending her head closer to get a better look at the number. That couldn't be right.

How could the earl spend three hundred pounds on a greatcoat? That was more than the price of her court gown. It was little wonder he'd decided to sell his memoirs to a publisher. Even if his estates were equal to the challenge now, his extravagant tastes would eventually require subsidizing by one method or another.

Despite Lord Duncan's vehement claims to an inviolate ethical code, blackmail struck her as more and more likely. If the earl's morals were as hypocritical as his godson's, perhaps he'd limited himself to exhorting money only from the women of his acquaintance. Perhaps one of the women whose letters were in the drawer had a husband she hoped to shield from the truth of her lapsed fidelity.

As she closed the cabinet door and turned her attention to the drawer in the bookcase, Kesgrave said, "If I had not met Fazeley and talked to him on many different occasions, I would think him quite mad from reading this account. He is like Narcissus falling in love with his own reflection in water and slowly dying because he's unable to look away. It's vaguely monstrous."

Well familiar with the myth, Bea agreed with his assessment while she sifted through the many papers in the drawer. There was the lease for the Chesterfield Street residence and a copy of a speech for the House of Lords, which struck her as odd until she saw the subject was a tax on silk.

Obviously, he could not let that atrocity proceed unabated.

"Ah, this is interesting," Kesgrave said a few minutes later. "On January third he mentions delivering the manuscript to his publisher."

She halted in her search as she turned to look at him. "That was four weeks ago. Does he mention the name of the firm or the name of its owner?"

"No, the description is terse. No names, no directions, no indication of how he got there. He simply mentions that he brought it to the offices. Do note, however, that the pains he took in dressing for the errands are described in detail as is the repast he had afterward to celebrate the accomplishment. Glasses of sherry are also recorded."

"How many?" she asked, curious despite herself.

"Three."

"Well, at least we know he submitted the manuscript, which supports our theory that he was killed because of something he revealed in it," she said. "Whoever was worried about its publication must have felt compelled to act because he knew the day his secret became public was drawing ever closer. If only we had the manuscript, we'd be able to figure out who that person is."

"I will keep reading," Kesgrave says. "Perhaps he mentions the publisher in an earlier entry."

She nodded and returned her attention to the drawer. A moment later, under a clipping from a newspaper dated six months before—reporting, of course, on the rhetorical brilliance of his silk-tax speech—she found the contract.

"I have it," she said, her eyes focused on the document as she tried to quickly identify the name of the publishing firm. "His contract is with…hmm…Sylvan Press. Do you know it?"

Kesgrave left the diary on the desk and peered over her shoulder to look at the contract. "I have heard of it. I believe they specialize in Gothics in the style of Mrs. Radcliffe and Mr. Lewis. A memoir would be a departure for them, but Stephens nevertheless paid a call to their offices to inquire if they held the deal with Fazeley. They claimed to have no knowledge of it, of course, but that was only to be expected."

"We need to see that manuscript," Bea murmured, her mind already working on the problem as she pondered what would be the best approach: honest dealing or subterfuge. As a publisher seeking the largest numbers of readers, Mr.—she looked at the bottom of the contract for a name—Cornyn would no doubt welcome the notoriety that would come from the truth being revealed. Here, he could announce in all his advertisements, is a book to die for. But your copy will cost you only ten shillings.

No story she could make up would be as persuasive as the truth.

But how to put her argument to Mr. Cornyn? She could show up at his office as Miss Hyde-Clare or Mr. Wright. To which persona would he respond more positively?

She scoffed at herself for even posing the question, for Mr. Cornyn was a man and men always responded more positively to other men. If he was inclined to allow either interloper to peruse the earl's manuscript, it would be Mr. Wright.

Kesgrave, who'd never in his life worried about his favorable reception, assured her that they would see the manuscript presently. "I'm sure Mr. Cornyn will be delighted to supply me with the copy so that I may examine it myself."

Although Bea felt the usual compulsion to pillory his arrogance, she let the moment pass because this time it would help her achieve a goal she strongly desired. "But they resisted your efforts before," she said.

In noting his previous failure, she was merely pointing to a simple truth, but somehow she'd still managed to prick his ego. "That was because I sent Stephens in my stead," he explained crisply, "and although he is imbued with all the powers of my personage, he's lacking the force of my person. It will be a different matter when I present myself personally to Mr. Cornyn or his associates. I assure you, no one will resist my efforts."

If he spoke to the publisher with the same crushing confidence, she was inclined to agree with his assumption. Bea folded the contract in half and slipped it into her leather satchel. "Let us go, then."

The duke looked at her, seeming to notice for the first time the details of her outfit: the ill-fitting breeches, the awkward perch of her hat, the drooping collar. "My dear Mr. Wright, you must fire your tailor at once, for he clearly has no respect for you or any regard for human decency. Simply looking at you, I feel pummeled by his scorn."

Bea dismissed his criticism as being stingy. "Certainly, I could never rise to your level in either taste or execution, but you must admit I make a very fine man. Can't you just see me with a blade in my hand, thrusting and parrying on a turret staircase? I've found Aunt Vera to be right about very few things, but on this I think she's on the mark."

Kesgrave smiled faintly as he said, "Remarkably, that ridiculous image evades me entirely."

"You'll see," she said, "after I take lessons at Angelo's and perfect my technique."

The duke shook his head as he picked up Lord Fazeley's diary. "Truly, I don't know if the prospect amuses or frightens me more."

Before Bea had a chance to assure him he should be terrified, a red-haired man in black trousers and coat walked forcefully into the room, and spotting Kesgrave by the writing desk, approached him with stiffened shoulders. "Your grace, based on my inspection of the kitchens alone, I cannot give my imprimatur to this house. They are filthy, poorly ventilated, sparsely equipped and too small to accommodate the sort of large dinner someone of your august status is accustomed to hosting."

"All right, Stephens," Kesgrave said amiably. "We shall take our leave."

"Furthermore," he continued, in too high dudgeon to hear the duke's swift acquiescence, "there's no wine cellar at all, just a space next to the larder for storing bottles, and the buttery is half the size of the one in Berkeley Square. I don't know what freak start brought us—"

He halted his speech abruptly.

Ah, Bea thought, now he heard it.

The color rose in Stephens's cheeks as he realized he had been about to criticize his employer. Horrified, he apologized at once. "I cannot explain what has come over me except that seeing a kitchen so disrespectful of your position or requirements offended me with such intensity I forgot myself. It will not happen again."

"Stephens, it is knowing that you will be affronted on my behalf that allows me to keep a cool head when abused by a kitchen," Kesgrave said gravely. "You are right to be appalled, and I trust it goes without saying that your opinion is all I need to make a decision."

The red-haired steward, who was only a little taller than Bea, seemed to rise a whole foot at this praise. "It does indeed, your grace. And I trust it goes without saying that I will work my hardest to continue to be worthy of your faith."

As sincerely affecting as Bea considered the scene between the duke and his employee, she found this announcement to be a little too heartfelt for her cynical bent and a giggle rose in her throat. She quickly turned it into a cough, which drew the attention of Stephens, who had been too upset to notice her before. Now he glared at her with a mixture of abhorrence and triumph.

Kesgrave also turned to her. "Mr. Wright, I believe I may dispense with your services in the future."

He spoke so seriously, as if Mr. Wright actually existed. Beatrice felt the laughter well up again, and it was all she could do to squelch it. After a few calming breaths, she said in her practiced tenor. "Of course, your grace. I understand."

Stephens grinned widely at his rival's misfortune and said, in an attempt to be gracious in victory, that he hoped his grace would provide the other man with a letter of recommendation. "Leave off mention, of course, of his ability to inspect a house, for if he had any skills in identifying what suited a duke's dignity, you would never have set foot in this residence."

"I shall do exactly that, Stephens," Kesgrave said. "Thank you for the advice."

The older man made no attempt to hide his delight and stared at his employer worshipfully as he said, "Of course, your grace. Of course."

Bea had witnessed the way society bowed and scraped at the duke, including, most intimately, her aunt, but that deference paled in comparison to the way his own employee treated him. No wonder the man was insufferable.

"In fact, Stephens, why don't you return to Berkeley Square right now and write the reference for me?" he asked. "Be as generous with the complimentary adjectives as you feel appropriate. I will deposit Mr. Wright at the employment agency where I found him."

Although Stephens was clearly reluctant to leave Kesgrave alone with the other steward in case he tried to worm his way back into the duke's good graces, he could not argue with his employer. "Very good, your grace," he said.

His tone was mild, but the warning glance he sent Bea on his way out of the room seethed with menace. If she were truly a steward looking for a position, she would have been quaking silently. Since she was not, she turned to Kesgrave and said with disapproval tempered with wonder, "You lied to your own staff rather than risk riling his temper again."

"Of course," he said briskly. "You may think we rule the servants, but it's very much the other way around. If belowstairs is unhappy nothing in the household runs smoothly. I'm terrified of Stephens and my butler, and surely I don't have to tell you the havoc an angry cook can wreak on one's domestic tranquility. You may call it cowardice—and given your consistent lack of regard for my dignity, I can only assume you will—but I'll lie to them every time if it will spare me days of discomfort."

Bea, shaking her head, did not disappoint. "You are a true profile in courage, your grace."

"Quite," he said, gesturing to the doorway that led back to the staircase. "Now, do you want to continue to mock me or should we pay a call on Mr. Cornyn?"

She laughed at the naïveté of the question, and as she crossed the floor, assured him she could quite easily do both.

CHAPTER TEN

The proprietor of the Sylvan Press was so determined to avoid an interview with the Duke of Kesgrave, he insisted that Mr. Cornyn was away from the office and would not return for the rest of the day. Unperturbed by this development, Kesgrave calmly announced he would try again on the morrow. Flinching, the clerk in the brown waistcoat brushed a stray lock of hair off his forehead and amended his statement to include the rest of the week. The duke remained placid in the wake of the updated information and insisted he could come back the following Monday with little trouble. Now the gentleman laughed nervously as little beads of sweat began to form at his temples.

"Forgive me, your grace, but I am a complete ninny," he said, pressing his hand against his forehead to discreetly dab at the perspiration. Then he tugged at the left sleeve of his shirt, alternatively raising it and lowering it as his jittery fingers seemed to move of their own volition. A tattoo of a sea turtle on his forearm peeked out and then quickly disappeared. "Mr. Cornyn will be away for the rest of the month. I don't know how I got the timing confused."

Before Kesgrave could open his mouth to frustrate him further, the clerk tilted his head toward the back of the office and said, as if unable to maintain the ruse a moment longer, "To be completely candid, your grace, Mr. Cornyn is away for the rest of the year but wishes to keep the matter secret, as publishing is a very competitive business and he doesn't want his colleagues in the other companies to know he's pursuing exciting new options. You are, of course, encouraged to return in January. Shall we arrange a date and time now or would you rather drop by at the moment most convenient to you as it presents itself?"

The clerk blinked his eyes nervously as he looked at Kesgrave to see how this development had been received, then glanced away just as quickly. He seemed incapable of staring directly at the duke, as if, like the sun, his magnificence would burn his eyes. The condition of the office did little to mitigate this impression, for the small, shabby room, with its excess of ragged furniture—desks, bookshelves, storage cabinets, an armchair that was clearly never used for sitting, as it was stacked high with documents—gave Kesgrave a sort of pristine glow.

Bea wasn't surprised in the least that Mr. Cornyn would lie to evade the duke's attention, and although she found this act cowardly, she sympathized with the impulse. He could not be the first man to try to evade his notice with an increasingly elaborate fiction. Her compassion, however, was undermined by his inability to accomplish the thing with any skill or conviction. People were free to invent all the stories they wanted, but they owed their audience the courtesy of imbuing the tales with certainty. Either act as if the invention were wholly true or tell the whole truth. Bea firmly believed those were the only two options available, and watching Mr. Cornyn fail so egregiously at the former made her annoyed that he hadn't simply employed the latter.

Kesgrave, who seemed unbothered by the man's inability to lie convincingly, insisted that the clerk reveal the proprietor's direction so that he may address him directly in his current location. "Do not trouble yourself with the inconvenience to me. I have concerns in many parts of the country and can assuredly combine my visit with Mr. Cornyn with an estate matter that needs attending to regardless. Now do, my good man, tell me where I may find your employer so that we can conclude our business here swiftly."

The clerk's eyes fluttered up at Kesgrave as the beads of sweat began to trickle down the side of his face and his fingers fiddled with his sleeve. Then he glanced down at the counter he was standing before, then over at the front door with a trapped looked on his face. Seemingly unimpressed by his prospects, he rested his elbows on the counter, laughed awkwardly and said, "Goodness gracious, I perceive the problem now. It seems that I've made a rather shocking mistake, your grace, and must now correct it. When you said Mr. Cornyn, I naturally assumed you meant my father, as he had been the proprietor of this company for more than forty years. He only recently ceded control to me so that he may devote himself fully to discovering talented new authors. The mix-up was entirely my fault, and I truly do regret it."

Hearing the note of sincere remorse in his tone, Bea smiled with approval, for that was how you told a whisker. Of course she didn't believe for a second that his father was out and about, for, based on Mr. Cornyn's age of fifty or so years, the elder Mr. Cornyn was far too old to be gamboling around the countryside interviewing writers. But she appreciated his progress as a fabulist.

Kesgrave appeared satisfied as well and graciously congratulated the man on his recent promotion. "I'm sure your father's faith in you is well-deserved. Now, as my steward had explained to you previously, I'm interested in seeing the manuscript submitted by Robert Hanson Crestwell, Earl of Fazeley. On that occasion you denied knowledge of the work, but presumably that was another misunderstanding. Perhaps you thought he was referring to a work by another gentleman called Fazeley."

"No, that wasn't a mistake," Mr. Cornyn said, surprising Bea with his sudden sharp swerve into honest dealing. "I denied all knowledge of the manuscript to your man in hopes that your interest in the manuscript would subside and the matter would quietly go away."

"Quietly go away until you print it, so that you may create a very large stir?" Bea asked, remembering to use Mr. Wright's tenor. Next to the duke's fine tailoring, she felt as shabby as the office and it was little wonder the owner of the firm had paid her scant attention until she asked the question.

"Good God, no," he said, visibly shuddering at the idea. "That book must never come to light!"

His vehemence delighted Bea, for it validated her theory that something in the manuscript was so shocking it had led to his lordship's vicious slaying. "Why?" she asked as she leaned forward on the counter. "Is it too salacious?"

He stiffened his posture, as if offended by the notion. "Sylvan Press is a respectable establishment that prides itself on its enthusiastic treatment of all things salacious," he explained tightly. "We have a reputation for finely wrought sensationalist stories to uphold. Consider, I beg you, what we've published to great success: *The Monk's Vendetta*, *The Widow's Revenge* and *Moll Sawney's Terrible True Tales of Newgate*, which was written by an actual prisoner of Newgate. These titles are magnificent examples of our aesthetic, of which the Earl of Fazeley's submission fell well short. It was, in a word, dull."

This pronouncement was the last thing Bea had expected to hear. "Dull?" she repeated, as if unable to comprehend the word.

"Dull," he confirmed, shaking his head sadly. "As dull as ditchwater. A work with so much potential to stun and amaze was merely a tedious catalog of Lord Fazeley's personal habits and concerns. On and on it went, listing the drams of port he'd consumed, the number of minutes he spent straightening his hair, the number of strokes he used to shine his Hessians. I couldn't possibly foist such a stultifying chronicle on the public. My readership would be appalled!"

"And your father," Kesgrave said.

"My father…" Mr. Cornyn said, faltering in confusion. But it lasted only a moment, for he immediately insisted with alarming vehemence, "Indeed, *yes,* my father! He entrusted me with the business he'd built, and I could not let him down by publishing a book that fell so far below his standards for interest and relevance. There were a few bright spots among the dross, anecdotes that I felt could be expanded into engrossing stories, but Lord Fazeley resented any implication that his writing required improving. I am, as you probably realize, an experienced editor and have helped many fine authors produce final works that are substantially better than the initial manuscript they submitted. Publishing is a process of collaboration, which Lord Fazeley considered beneath him. He insisted his book was already perfect and demanded its prompt return so that he might seek another publisher."

Bea had little trouble believing the publisher's description of events, for she could not imagine the earl calmly submitting to the notion of imperfection in any matter. As a self-proclaimed arbiter of fashion, he'd taken far too much joy in ridiculing the failings of others to readily admit to any of his own. "Did you give it back?"

Mr. Cornyn glanced briefly at the door along the back wall before answering. "Naturally, I said he could have it just as soon as he returned the fee I had advanced him in expectation of its publication, per the agreement in the contract he'd signed, by which I expected him to abide."

"And he did not?" Kesgrave asked.

The publisher pressed his lips together in a display of anger and disgust. "He did not think it was incumbent upon him to follow the terms of the contract when I was the one who had found fault with the book. The money I paid him might not have seemed like a very great sum to him, but it was, I assure you, a significant amount to me," he explained, his tone defensive as if he expected his august visitor to trivialize the expenditure. "I could not on principle simply hand over the manuscript without getting something in return."

"Of course not," the duke said, calming his concerns. "You're a businessman, after all. And how did Fazeley receive this news?"

A gentle flushed crept up his neck. "A small tussle might have ensued," he said. "His lordship felt that he had the right to search the premises for his property and I disagreed. I merely tried to constrain him to the other side of the counter, and it lasted only a moment because he feared snagging his waistcoat on the wood. After straightening his clothes, which had gotten quite mussed in the struggle, he promised to send his solicitor to deal with me, as I did not deserve the honor of his disagreement, and marched out of the building."

The memory of the event agitated him so much that he began to fiddle again with his sleeve. Bea, observing his anxiety, sought to establish the date of the exchange. "That was Tuesday, correct?" she said, her tone firm, although she was in fact making an educated guess.

Responding as she'd hoped to the confidence in her tone, Mr. Cornyn immediately agreed to the date and then, realizing the timing aligned inauspiciously with the earl's death, tried to amend his statement by stammering that he couldn't be quite sure what day of the week it had been. "Perhaps Monday? Could it have been Saturday? I would need to consult my calendar to be sure."

But he'd reverted to the uncertainty with which he'd proclaimed his own absence upon their arrival and, as if discerning the difference in his tone himself, gamely conceded that it had indeed been Tuesday.

"You are on Catherine Street," Bea pointed out.

Mr. Cornyn lowered his head, as if the observation were also an indictment. "I know."

"The Strand, where the *London Daily Gazette* is located

and Fazeley died, is only a block away," she added, although it was entirely unnecessary. Mr. Cornyn knew exactly how unfortunate the situation appeared: the dispute over the contract, the ensuing tussle, the publishing office's close proximity to the place where the victim fell.

"I understand your concern and in no way resent the implication that I was somehow involved," he said with such calm that Bea felt inclined to believe him. "We exchanged words, to be sure, but I did not wish him ill or grievous harm over a publishing contract. Indeed, I cannot believe anyone would be so depraved. We left the matter civilly, with the earl determined to refer the matter to his solicitors. I cannot imagine what happened so soon after he departed this office that caused him to end up with his own knife in his back, but it had nothing to do with the Sylvan Press. As I said, he was peeved when he departed but resolved on a course of action that he felt confident would ultimately deliver satisfaction. I returned to my usual business of running a publishing company, which is a consuming occupation. In fact, we had a book due to the printer that day and it required all my attention. If you don't believe me, my daughter and my associate were here and can attest to my description of events. Would you like to talk to them?"

Bea thought this suggestion was a fine idea, for she was not inclined to take at his word a man who had already told them several lies. At the same time, she was at a loss to ascribe to him a motive for ending Fazeley's life. If Mr. Cornyn truly wanted to recoup his investment, he stood a far greater chance of getting his money back while the earl was still alive. Killing him accomplished nothing, and as the publisher had observed, he would have to be quite depraved to murder someone over a contract disagreement.

"Yes," she said, glancing at the pair of empty desks pressed between the wall and two squat storage cabinets. "Where is your associate now?"

"At the printing house delivering a manuscript. We

are a small concern and cannot afford to own a press our-
selves, so we contract with one nearby," he explained, his
manner calmer now that he had been granted permission
to provide corroborating evidence of his innocence. "It's
also on the Strand, so he should be back in a few minutes.
And my daughter is just upstairs. She and I live together
above the office with my sister. As you can imagine, the
space is somewhat tight with so many people and Esther
enjoys spending time down here, observing the business. If
you'll excuse me, I will fetch her now."

But Bea did not want to excuse him, for she feared
any time spent alone with his daughter would provide him
with an opportunity to ensure her version of events
aligned perfectly with his. Instead, she offered up herself as
messenger and found herself the object of the publisher's
horrified gaze. It was only then that she remembered she
was dressed as a young man. She'd grown so accustomed
to speaking as Mr. Wright, she had completely forgotten
she wasn't herself.

Was an apology in order?

Did young men apologize?

She thought of her cousin Russell, who rarely, if ever,
admitted to any wrongdoing. Should she emulate his stub-
bornness or show contrition at her inappropriately bold
suggestion?

Kesgrave, mildly amused by her predicament, pointed
to a bell pull on the wall near the counter and asked if perhaps Mr. Cornyn could ring for her.

"Yes, of course," he said, shuffling over to tug the
cord at once. "I'm sure she will be down momentarily."

"While we are waiting," Kesgrave said, "tell us about
the knife."

Bea and Mr. Cornyn looked at the duke in surprise,
although only the latter repeated the word *knife* with a
vaguely trapped expression on his face.

"You mentioned that Fazeley had been stabbed with
his own knife, which means you recognized it from the

description in the newspaper," Kesgrave explained logically. "Tell us about the knife."

As Bea had missed that piece of information herself, she regarded the duke with respect and murmured, "Well done, your grace."

Kesgrave kept his eyes trained on the publisher, but his lips twitched at the compliment.

"'Twas only a guess," Mr. Cornyn said quickly, his eyes darting from the front door to the one in the back of the room as he waited impatiently for someone—anyone—to enter the office and bolster his story. His anxiety was so acute, Bea thought she could detect a new thin layer of sweat starting to form, this time above his lip. "I don't know for certain if the jade knife found in Lord Fazeley's back was the same jade knife he wore about his person when he visited my office. It seems unlikely there would be two blades matching that description in circulation that day, but I could not rule it out as a possibility. As I said, my conclusion was only a guess."

The proprietor's anxiety about appearing guilty had the unfortunate effect of making him appear guilty, Bea thought.

"The knife Fazeley wore was jade?" Kesgrave asked.

Mr. Cornyn nodded firmly. "Jade and shaped like a horse's head. Quite intricately carved, as well. It was very eye-catching and not just because the handiwork was so fine. It's unusual to see a gentleman sporting a dagger as decoration and I congratulated his lordship on how well the knife looked on him, as I knew he would appreciate the compliment. Although it was not mere puffery," he hastened to add, suddenly fearful of appearing too calculating. "I sincerely admired the way he wore it. As a chronicler of his time, Lord Fazeley lacked the flair necessary to excite his reader's interest, but as a dandy, he wanted for nothing. I tried to tell him that the second was a more impressive accomplishment, but he was not in the mood to listen. The brief tussle followed soon after and then his lordship left."

As persuasive as Bea found his mild description of the events, she still found his propensity to lie troubling. "If everything is as you say, then why did you lie about having the manuscript to the duke's man when he inquired? That does not strike me as the act of a person who has nothing to hide."

"I feared for my life as well," he said stiffly.

Bea furrowed her brow, as if uncomprehending, and turned to the duke to see if his understanding was more developed than hers.

Perceiving her suspicion, Mr. Cornyn explained with a moue of impatience. "We do not know what motive inspired the murderer to act, and it could very well have been the threat of the manuscript. His lordship had let slip the possibility of a memoir chronicling the follies of the *ton* to excite interest, and there's every reason to believe someone feared the book would reveal a dire secret. That was, after all, the only reason I'd commissioned the work in the first place, as Lord Fazeley promised many remarkable revelations. What I did not realize at the time is that he meant remarkable revelations about himself. But nobody knows that, of course, so as long as the murderer remains at large, I fear my life may be at risk too."

"Papa!" a soft voice gasped in surprise. "How could you not tell me you were in danger!"

Bea looked toward the back of the room, where a lovely woman with auburn curls, almond-shaped eyes and a dainty nose stood staring at her father in shock. She was young, perhaps a year or two older than Flora's twenty, and tall, with a generous figure that was shown to advantage in the unadorned silk dress. Although her beauty wasn't as ostentatious as Miss Otley's, a diamond of the first water with whom they'd spent time in the Lake District, she was just as much of an Incomparable. Indeed, in her simple gold necklace with a red pendant, she shone twice as brightly as the other woman in her diamonds.

"I did not want to worry you," Mr. Cornyn said soothingly as he spared an angry look at Bea, as if it were her fault he had been forced to do so now. "I'm sure I'm just being fanciful, and yet I see no harm in taking a few precautions if I can. But let's not dwell on the things we cannot change. Do come here so I may introduce you to the Duke of Kesgrave."

Her eyes widened in surprise as she noticed her father's company, which was far more illustrious than that to which she had grown accustomed. Earls, Bea thought with amusement, weren't nearly as impressive as dukes.

Miss Cornyn complied with the request, gracefully navigating the small, crowded room until she reached the counter. Realizing the wooden obstruction made proper introductions awkward, the publisher raised the worktop so they could both pass through. After Miss Cornyn made a neat curtsy to Kesgrave, she turned her attention to Bea, who noted her eyes were a deep bottle green.

"It's a pleasure to meet you, Mr. Wright," Miss Cornyn said softly.

Bea sketched the sort of bow she had observed her cousin Russell do a hundred times and assured the young lady it was a pleasure for her too.

As Mr. Cornyn explained why her presence had been requested, Bea found her eyes drawn again and again to the vibrant red necklace she wore at her throat. There was something about the piece—the pear-shaped drop pendant surrounded by seed pearls—that struck her as familiar. Did Flora have something of a similar design? Or perhaps Aunt Vera? For the most part, the Hyde-Clares were too sensible to spend their money on lavish accessories, but there was that stunning emerald necklace her aunt took out of the safe for special occasions like the Leland ball. Did it bear a resemblance to the one Miss Cornyn wore now?

No, Aunt Vera's beloved piece was a choker.

Bea was so consumed by the sensation of familiarity, she didn't realize she was being introduced to Mr. Cornyn's associate until she was called upon to greet him. It was only then, as she turned her head to meet the outraged glare of Mr. Hill, that the impropriety of her interest occurred to her. Yes, she had been examining the necklace, but to everyone else it looked as if she was admiring Miss Cornyn's bosom.

And it was, she thought, her embarrassment rising, a generous bosom to admire.

Impersonating a man was rife with unexpected pitfalls.

Mr. Cornyn, wisely perceiving no threat to his daughter's virtue from the duke's steward, explained the many valuable services his associate performed as Bea struggled to recover her composure. She kept her gaze firmly away from Kesgrave's, for she could easily imagine the humor that must be lurking there.

"Truly, he's indispensable to the firm, as he has a remarkable eye for detail," Mr. Cornyn said. "As the publisher, it's my responsibility to make sure the books we publish are coherent and sensible and thoroughly entertaining to the reader. My concerns have to do with the story itself, with the themes and issues it's addressing and its ability to surprise. As an undertaking, it's quite huge and sometimes the details get lost in the process. That's where Mr. Hill's contribution becomes invaluable because he reads every single word and makes sure they all adhere to their correct spellings and that none are missing. And, of course, he does all the coordinating with the printing house on my behalf, which provides me with further opportunities to craft interesting and well-told tales."

Mr. Hill, several inches taller than Bea and as spindly as a foal, thanked his employer for the praise and blushed when Miss Cornyn reaffirmed it with her own words of appreciation.

"I'm grateful to you both, of course," Mr. Hill said firmly, "but I'm sure the duke did not call to discuss me. Let us return to the matter that concerns him."

"Right you are," Mr. Cornyn said fervently. "Right you are. He and his steward are here to discover what happened to the Earl of Fazeley's manuscript."

At the mention of the deceased peer, Miss Cornyn shuddered in horror, and Mr. Hill, observing her distress, responded with a sympathetic look. The young lady, however, was too distracted to notice.

"Do forgive my daughter," the publisher said with a sad shake of his head. "We were all so upset to discover what had happened to his lordship. It is so unusual to see the death of someone you know described in the newspaper."

"And the last time you saw him, Miss Cornyn, was on Tuesday?" Bea asked matter-of-factly.

Finding the question indelicate, Mr. Hill sent her another disapproving look and answered on the young lady's behalf. "Yes, that was the last time she saw him. I, as well. He and Mr. Cornyn had a brief conversation about a project we were working on, and then his lordship bid us good day and left."

As much as Bea appreciated his discretion, she did not have the patience for it. "That's not exactly what happened, is it?"

The young man flinched at her tone and conceded that perhaps his lordship had not offered a thoughtful goodbye on his way out. "His leave-taking might be described as rude by another, for he made a vulgar gesture that is not fit for mixed company, but it's not for me to remark upon the manners of my betters," he said, putting enough emphasis on the last word to make his true opinion of the earl known.

"He was quite cross when he left," Miss Cornyn said. "He and Papa had had a business disagreement, and he felt he had not been treated with the respect he deserved. His leave-taking was therefore abrupt. It made for an awkward few moments after his departure, for we were all uncertain if we should try to appease his lordship. But my father announced that he had much work to do, and we all returned to our various occupations. I believe that was the day the Harrison manuscript was due to the printer, was it not? There was much to get done."

Mr. Hill accepted the rebuke silently, then confirmed the timing of the earl's visit and looked at the duke to ascertain if he was satisfied with these accounts. By any measure, they substantiated Mr. Cornyn's claim that Fazeley had left the office in a peevish mood and the publisher had remained behind to address important tasks.

Kesgrave nodded his assent and announced they would leave them to their business as soon as Mr. Cornyn provided them with Fazeley's manuscript.

"Naturally, I will compensate you for the work," he added before the publisher could object. "I'll meet the terms of your original contract. Does that sound fair?"

Mr. Cornyn, who had never expected to get value out of the manuscript, smiled brightly and said that was more than fair. "But as you read it, I pray you remember that it's not our typical style. As I explained previously, we have a reputation for sensationalism to maintain and I fear Lord Fazeley's tedious tome might do it irreparable harm."

To the publisher's delight, Kesgrave promised to always consider Sylvan Press to be twice as lurid and shocking as Minerva Press.

"Wonderful," he said, beaming. "Wonderful. I tucked it up in my apartments upstairs as an act of precaution. It will take me a moment to get it."

Mr. Cornyn dashed off to get the manuscript, and his daughter apologized for not offering refreshments. "If I had realized you were here when Papa requested my presence, I would have brought a pot of tea with me and some biscuits as well. We are a small concern, but I try to observe the proprieties."

"You succeed," Mr. Hill assured her with admiration so ardent it revealed more about his feelings than perhaps he'd intended.

Seemingly oblivious to his affection, Miss Cornyn, striving to be the ideal hostess to a duke in circumstances that were less than hospitable to her goal, explained that she would offer her guests a seat except the only available options were a pair of rickety chairs. "As Mr. Hill can attest, you are much safer waiting here."

Indeed, the young man rushed to do just that, telling a tale of bruised dignity and scraped knees, which Kesgrave, despite his penchant for superciliousness, listened to with an affect of interest. It was the sort of act of kindness and consideration Bea didn't expect from him, and she found herself staring at him with surprise and perhaps a little bit of confusion. As if aware of her attention, he turned to look at her, his eyes pulled together, as if perplexed himself.

Embarrassed by the sudden scrutiny, she turned toward Miss Cornyn and her gaze settled again on the shiny jewel at her throat. "That's a lovely necklace," she said, drawing closer to admire the piece and to inspect it more fully. Although the stone, about twice the size of Bea's thumbnail, caught the light with the intensity of a ruby, she knew a publisher's daughter could not afford such a dazzling gem. "Is it a garnet?"

Miss Cornyn, who had also been listening to Mr. Hill's unfortunate treatment at the hands of a recalcitrant chair, turned to Bea with a faint smile on her lips. "Yes, of course. A garnet with charming seed pearls."

The pearls were indeed lovely, Bea thought, but the garnet was something more—shiny and sparkly and brightly faceted. Without thinking, she reached for the pear-shaped pendant and lowered her head to examine it.

At once, the room became silent.

Bea looked up to find Mr. Hill, who had broken off his sentence abruptly, staring daggers at her.

Devil it!

It had slipped her mind again that she was a man and could not freely study the bosoms of unmarried young women.

Or any woman.

As if burned by the stone, she dropped the pendant, stepped back and hastily apologized for letting herself get carried away by its beauty. She was clearly talking about the necklace, but Mr. Hill thought she was flirting with Miss Cornyn and glared even more severely.

Offended by the conclusion—for if she were the type of man who flirted with the daughters of publishers she would do it with far more grace—Bea opened her mouth to protest, but Mr. Cornyn returned at that moment with Fazeley's manuscript. He was also carrying half a dozen novels that he insisted the duke had to read to counterbalance the monotony of the earl's memoir.

"Well, obviously, you don't have to read them if you do not desire to," he amended immediately, "but if you are curious to try one, I strongly recommend you start with *The Devil's Covenant,* which has many of our most popular elements, including a mysterious stranger, a foreboding castle and a beautiful young lady trapped in a loveless marriage with her cruel stepfather."

Kesgrave promised to send his man around with the appropriate funds posthaste, then solemnly thanked the publisher for his generosity.

The proprietor of Sylvan Press smiled happily as he offered the cumbersome stack of books to Bea, who, surprised at the shabby treatment, stared at him in confusion before recalling that she was not only a man but the duke's man. Of course the burden fell to her to carry the pile.

She submitted without complaint, the heavy stack resting awkwardly in her arms, and waited impatiently as the duke thanked Mr. Cornyn for his help and promised to read *The Devil's Covenant* with all due haste.

Mr. Cornyn gushed appropriately at Kesgrave's gracious condescension and asked him to please keep him in mind if he should ever desire to publish a chronicle of his ducal experiences. "Without question, Sylvan Press would be delighted to bend its rule about sensationalism to accommodate the gravity of your situation," he explained.

Kesgrave pronounced himself to be touched by the consideration and pledged to keep the offer in mind should he ever feel moved to pen such a work. "And please give my regards to your father on his travels," he added with a touch of humor. "You may assure him I think you're doing a fine job taking care of the legacy he bestowed on you."

"Grandfather is traveling?" Miss Cornyn said in confusion.

Her father darted an anxious glance in her direction and immediately began to speak quickly in hopes of distracting from the moment. "Yes, traveling the countryside in search of new authors. It's something I should do in his stead, as he's too old to be knocking about. But I've always preferred to stay close to home. I've never even been outside the confines of London," he said with a nervous laugh as he played with his shirt cuff. "Regardless, I appreciate your kind words and will eagerly pass them along. Thank you, your grace."

As soon as they stepped outside into the bright sunshine of Catherine Street, Bea said, "You were cruel to tease poor Mr. Cornyn. He's quite the worst liar I have ever seen. I feared he might fray his shirtsleeve, he was fiddling with it so much."

"Here," Kesgrave said, reaching for the stack of books she carried. "Do let me take them."

Bea danced lightly away and said chidingly, "Think of what it would look like to observers: you weighed down by a pile of Gothics while your man walks empty-handed at your side. Surely, it would be alarming proof that your faculties are on the wane. No, your grace, I have too much respect for your importance to expose you to such vile speculation. And do recall how close we are to the Strand. Any one of these fellows we see around us might work for the newspaper. Your humiliation could be the *on-dit* as soon as tomorrow."

"Once again, Miss Hyde-Clare, you do not comprehend what it means to be a duke. The very moment I decide to carry a pile of Gothics while my man walks beside me unburdened *that* becomes the fashion. By the end of the week, we will see marquesses holding packages for their footmen and viscounts opening doors for their butlers."

He was teasing her, of course, but at the same time he was not.

Indeed, it was true: She did not comprehend what it meant to be a duke. It was a mistake she made more and more because he seemed to act like one less and less. She could not picture the toplofty lord she first met at Lakeview Hall listening with such respect as a lackey at a publishing company detailed his misadventures with a rickety office chair and marveled at the change. Was the difference in him or in her perception of him?

The question distracted her so much, she did not realize they were tracing the earl's last steps until they reached the Strand. As they turned the corner, she examined the scene thoughtfully, noting that the landscape was made up primarily of establishments that published newspapers— *London Daily Gazette, Daily Advertiser, The World News*—and the neoclassical wonder that was Somerset House.

The idea that the earl, fresh from his argument with Mr. Cornyn, would march into a newspaper office to report his ill treatment was inconceivable. His destination had never been the *Gazette*. That had simply been the door he had stumbled against after the knife was plunged into his back. The *London Daily Gazette* was off to the left, across from Somerset House, the large public building that housed several administrative offices, the Royal Academy of Arts and the Society of Antiquaries of London.

Obviously, Fazeley had no cause to visit the Salt Office or the Navy Office or the Stamp Office or the Hawkers and Pedlars Office, and it was far too early in the year for summer exhibition at the Royal Academy. That left only the antiquarian society, which wasn't the most unlikely direction for a man who had decided to make ceremonial knife-wearing fashionable. Perhaps he wanted one of its members to evaluate his jade dagger or suggest another weapon, maybe a sword, that would look just as dashing about his waist.

Such an errand was in keeping, she thought, with the meticulous man who made a record of every grain of rice he consumed.

Very well. He had been en route to the Society of Antiquaries of London at Somerset House when he was accosted from behind right about—Bea stopped several feet from the door of the *Daily Gazette*—here.

Immediately, she was knocked from behind as a man in a brown hat scowled at her for halting suddenly in the middle of the busy sidewalk. She was bumped again, this time from somebody walking toward her, and she realized how easy it must have been for the killer to plunge the knife into the earl's back and escape undetected. With so many people jostling and being jostled, Lord Fazeley wouldn't have noticed anything was amiss until after the blade had been fully inserted and by then the perpetrator would have disappeared into the crowd.

It was a clever way to commit a murder, she thought. In sight of dozens of people and yet hidden from the view of any one person in particular.

As clever as it was, it didn't account for the troubling fact that the earl had been attacked with his own weapon. Her theory of the stranger approaching from behind did not account for how he removed the dagger from the front of his victim. That part simply did not make—

"We must move," Kesgrave said, wrapping his fingers around her elbow and pulling toward the buildings that lined the sidewalk.

As she emerged from the crush of people, her shoulder was jolted again, this time by an elderly man who growled, "Watch where yer going."

Angered by the unfair abuse, she opened her mouth to tell him to watch where *he* was going, but her grip on the books slipped and the pile fell to the ground. She immediately dropped to her knees to pick them up, grabbing the two tomes nearest to her as several pages of his lord-ship's manuscript escaped their ribbon and blew away. Horrified, she threw her body on top of the stack to contain the rest of the pages, landing on her elbows with a thud as Kesgrave ran off to chase the unruly sheets down the block. Scrambling to her knees as pedestrians on the busy sidewalk growled and tripped around her, she scooped up the earl's memoir and winced in the pain from the scrape on her arm. Ignoring the sting, she pivoted on her knees to gather the other four books and found herself suddenly shoved backward onto the sidewalk as pain exploded in her right eye, then her left.

She was under attack.

CHAPTER ELEVEN

The world around Bea darkened and dimmed as a hulking figure climbed on top of her, wrapped his hands around her neck, squeezed threateningly and leaned forward. "Stay away," he said before bashing her with his fist one more time and running off.

Stunned as much by the violence as the pain, Bea lay there, on the Strand, her head on the stone, her arms clutching the manuscript, only a few feet from where the earl had died.

She could not get her mind to work—to cry for help, to call for the duke, to pick herself up, to gather the rest of the books, to chase after her attacker.

It was the pain. The punishing jabs to her face hurt with an intensity she could not have imagined, and already her bruises had swollen so magnificently, her vision was impaired. Her throat ached from the pressure he had exerted. He had impeded her breath for only a second, but it was enough for her to know what choking felt like.

Stay away.

The threat, echoing in her ear, spurred her first coherent thought: Stay away from what?

Mr. Cornyn's publishing house?

That made no sense, she thought, for the only point of danger associated with the firm remained clasped in her arms. She retained possession of Lord Fazeley's manuscript, so the work itself could not have been the motive for the assault.

As she considered the question, other parts of her brain began to function as well, and even before someone kicked her thigh—*and* yelled at her for lazing about—she knew she had to get off the ground.

Sit up, she ordered herself.

And yet, as a wave of pain slashed from ear to ear, she realized it was too ambitious a plan.

Fine. Just move.

Quickly, before another impatient pedestrian abused her, she pushed herself up and over...up and over. Now she was only a foot away from the building. One more roll and she could lean against it for support. She would do that just as soon as she had the wherewithal to raise her head.

In a moment, she thought, remaining still for several seconds.

And perhaps a few moments more.

"Good God!" Kesgrave yelled, suddenly there, suddenly cradling her head in abject horror as he examined her face.

No, she thought with a perverse sort of humor, she could not presume to know with what kind of horror he examined her face, for her sight was too impaired. The swelling in her eyes had reduced the view of the world to a mere play of shadows, and the duke's appearance was no more distinct than her attacker's.

For all she knew, Kesgrave had been her attacker.

Ah, but no, she thought, as the duke shifted positions so that he was sitting on the ground next to her and gently helping her raise her shoulders from the dirt. She could not mistake his presence for anyone else's.

"Careful," he said softly, helping her lean against the wall, where there was considerably less foot traffic. "Careful."

She appreciated his concern, but she did not think it would make a difference to her wounds if she were careful or not. The throbbing in her face would continue regardless of how delicately she laid her head against the bricks.

Sighing deeply, she said mildly, "The killer objects to our investigation."

Kesgrave's laugh was a hollow sound as he said with equal mildness, "I object to the killer."

Bea closed her eyes, for there was little purpose in keeping them open, and asked if the duke had managed to find all the missing pages. "I was distracted by my own endeavor and lost track of yours."

"I did, yes, though a horse was standing on top of one of the sheets, which is why it took me so long to gather them all," he explained. "We must go. It's not good to linger here long."

Although she was in too much pain to consider or care about the ridiculous and appalling site they must present to the world, she knew the Duke of Kesgrave could not dismiss it so easily. "Ah, but think how this will burnish your reputation as a bold leader of fashion, your grace," she said. "By the end of the week, we will see marquesses cradling the bruised heads of their footmen and viscounts dabbing at the open sores of their butlers."

"Yet again you underestimate my position if you believe my reputation requires further burnishing, Miss Hyde-Clare," he said kindly. "My concern is not for myself but for you. Your bruises are going to continue to swell until we apply a cold compress. As the veteran of many bouts at Gentleman Jackson's, I can personally attest to the value of ice. To that end, I will have to ask a boy to deliver our location to my driver, Jenkins. Do wait a moment."

Bea wondered where he thought she might wander off to as she watched him approach a young boy, deliver his instructions and hand over a few coins. After a few enthusiastic nods, the boy ran off to do his bidding. She rather expected Kesgrave to stand by the curb and wait for his carriage to arrive, but instead he returned to the building and sat down beside her on the rough surface.

She resisted the urge to show concern for his clothing, which was much finer than hers, and returned to the treatment of facial bruises. "Is there perchance a compress cold enough to reduce the swelling entirely, perhaps by four o'clock?" she asked.

Kesgrave flatly said no and then pointed out that even with a magical compress being so accommodating, other telltale signs of her brawl would remain. "Your face is turning ever more purple and blue as we speak, and your lip is severely cut."

Bea knew it. Of course she did. From the very moment the villain's fist had connected with her face, she'd known there would be no way to hide the events of the afternoon from her family. Naturally, they would be horrified by the abuse she had suffered and anxious for her safety and truly sympathetic about the pain she endured, but her aunt and uncle would also be appalled by the steps she had taken to provoke the attack. Although she hadn't administered any of the blows to herself, they would hold her wholly responsible.

Choosing not to dwell on the things she couldn't change, she repeated the word *brawl* aloud and pronounced herself very fond of its hard-edged reality. "May I now call myself a brawler?"

"Between this episode and your encounter with the locked shed on the Skeffingtons' property, you've quite definitely earned the designation," the duke said gravely. "But rather than think of charming epithets for you, my dear, we should come up with a way to curb your interest in pursuing violent criminals. It does not seem to work out to your advantage."

"Ah, now you sound like Aunt Vera," she said lightly, although she was somewhat disconcerted by the sincerity in his tone. "Soon you will be calling me wan and advising me to pinch my cheeks before climbing out of the carriage."

"I did not expect such cruelty, even from you, Miss

Hyde-Clare," he said with elaborate offense, "who has no respect for my dignity. But I'm going to overlook it on account of your being driven to lash out at others due to the great pain you are no doubt in. After the relief of a cold compress, you will regret your malice and wish to apologize. Please know that I already forgive you."

"Your consideration humbles me," she said, smiling and then wincing as she felt the full severity of her lip injury.

"I should hope so," he said. "You should also be humbled by my interest. It's not every young woman I question about her compulsion to seek out murderers. I trust you will be sensible enough of the honor to respond and not insult me again as a diversionary tactic."

His tone was soft and serious, and although she had a diversionary tactic at the ready—asking archly if he knew many young women who were compelled to seek out murderers—she felt a desire to answer honestly. There was something about sitting together outside a newspaper office along a bustling London street that felt oddly private, as if the wildly public space offered the same intimacy as the drawing room.

"I would like to say I'm driven by a high-minded need to see justice done, but the truth is a lot more self-serving. I appreciate the challenge." She shifted her position slightly to look at his profile, handsome and hazy in the soft light of her diminished vision. "As a middling young woman with few prospects, no fortune and crushing shyness, I've had little opportunity to stretch my mind in new directions. I read a lot, mostly biographies and travelogues and stories about inventions and novel ideas. I love discovering new things because every bit of arcane knowledge I acquire feels as if it's part of a larger puzzle. But I'm not a fool. I know there is no larger puzzle. There is just this, the everyday existence of appeasing Aunt Vera and humoring Flora. And yet, when I came across the battered body of Mr. Otley in the Skeffingtons' library, I felt as though I'd finally stumbled upon the puzzle. Everything made sense as an odd-shaped piece waiting to fall into place, and I liked it," she said, pausing to take a deep breath before admitting to an even more self-serving truth. "Indeed, it made me feel clever, and I loved that."

Although the admission was more candid than she'd intended, she didn't succumb to the expected embarrassment or awkwardness. Instead, she felt only relief and peace, as if something that had been stirring inside her for a long time had been soothed. 'Twas a strange sensation and one noticeably at odds with the throbbing in her face.

Sitting next to Kesgrave, her sight impaired by the swelling and her view limited to only his profile, she could not read his reaction to her confession. She would find out, of course, if she gave him a moment or two to respond, but the occasion was too rife with honesty for her not to try to elicit a few truths in return. "And what is your explanation, your grace? Why do you find yourself compelled to seek out murderers? I must confess that I assumed your actions were spurred by a desire to outwit me. I figured your ego could not stand the fact that it was I, not yourself, who identified Mr. Otley's murderer and so you sought to vindicate yourself in your own eyes by identifying the earl's. You will note, I hope, that here I *do* display proper understanding of your position, as I don't believe you would bother to vindicate yourself to anyone else. But your actions since the beginning of the Fazeley affair seem to refute that charge, and I find I'm all out of theories to explain your interest."

Kesgrave laughed lightly and turned his head a few degrees, providing her with an imperfect view of his bright blue eyes. "Although your cogent, sincere and reasonable response deserves an equally intelligent reply, I'm afraid I cannot issue it. I am as confounded by my behavior as you are, Miss Hyde-Clare. I will own that I find your lack of respect irritating and have been moved by a desire to tweak your ego in return. But I do not wish to best you. Indeed, I felt an inordinate amount of pride at your astuteness at Lakeview Hall."

It was a terrible answer, terrifying and exhilarating all at the same time, and Bea ordered herself not to read into it. Just because he made it seem as if the compulsion to investigate Lord Fazeley's death could somehow be connected to a desire to be with her did not mean that it actually was. Indeed, he hadn't implied anything of the kind, merely observing that his rationale was unknown even to himself.

And yet she knew it wasn't that simple, for there was the waltz to consider and the way he had interrupted his opera outing to visit her. Although under no obligation, he had repeatedly sought out opportunities to spend time with her, and only the most hardened cynic could convince herself there was no connection between them at all. Bea's cynicism wasn't quite that entrenched, and as she thought about it now, she conceded that they did indeed have a bond and quite a strong one at that. The investigation first into Mr. Otley's murder and then Lord Fazeley's provided them with a mutual occupation that was as rare as it was engrossing. Of course Kesgrave felt a desire to be with her, for there was no one else with whom he could discuss these matters. When he had dashed out of *Artaxerxes* during intermission to provide her with an update on publishing firms in London, his intentions had been sincere. He'd felt a genuine desire to share what he knew with her, however slight the information was.

Did she believe that was all it was between them?

Bea recalled the intensity with which he'd regarded her during their waltz and knew their connection was something more than just the camaraderie of colleagues. Even so, she believed that was all it *could* be, for the Duke of Kesgrave was too firmly rooted in the augustness of his lineage to allow it to become anything else. As the responsible steward of the Matlock family legacy, he required perfection, grace and beauty in his future wife. Raised with those exacting standards, he would never be able to look at her plain face, with its pale skin and impudent freckles, and see a duchess.

As she herself could not make that imaginative leap either, she didn't blame him for it. Nor did she blame herself for finding him irresistible, for he was among the most coveted men in the kingdom. Every school miss having her first season sighed over his handsome, lithe form, and it only made sense that repeated exposure to his person would have a disruptive effect on her feelings. If her sense of judgment was so degraded that she'd actually formed a tendre for him, she knew it was only a short-lived problem. As soon as the matter of Lord Fazeley's death was resolved, their connection would be severed and her good sense would be restored.

She looked forward to that moment as much as she dreaded it.

The silence between them stretched while these thoughts raced through Bea's head, and saddened by the prospect of a future without the duke's maddening, teasing presence, she tried to come up with something to say that would reveal no trace of her true feelings. Recalling their early association in the Lake District, she began to list many of the foods that were on the dinner table during one of their meals at the country estate. "Quenelles of chicken with peas and fruit jelly, fish patties with olive paste, eels à la tartare, stuffed tomatoes, veal cutlets, poached eggs, fillets of salmon, meringues with preserves."

Kesgrave met with this extraordinary response with composure, which further endeared him to the susceptible young lady, who admired his insouciance in the face of absurdity. "If this is your way of telling me your brawl has made you hungry, a not uncommon reaction to physical exertion, I regret to inform you, Miss Hyde-Clare, that I left the quenelles of chicken in my other coat."

"I'm making a catalog of all the dishes I yearned to throw at you during our second or third supper at Lakeview Hall," she explained. "You were discussing the Battle of the Nile with our host and being particularly pedantic."

"Ah, yes," he said, as if grasping something that had evaded him for a long time. "HMS *Goliath,* HMS *Audacious,* HMS *Majestic.*"

He listed the ships now as he did then—in order of appearance in the battle, per the dictates of maritime tradition—and Bea immediately corrected him, scrambling his neat arrangement in lieu of hurling chicken. "HMS *Majestic*, HMS *Goliath*, HMS *Audacious*."

Although the comment was sparked by a contrarian impulse, Kesgrave smiled in comprehension and Bea felt a sense of perfect accord settle over her.

This feeling alone explained the compulsion to investigate, she realized with sudden clarity. She'd experienced it once before, in her bedchamber in the Lake District when they discussed who might be responsible for Mr. Otley's death, and she would gratefully do many foolhardy things to feel it again. She would certainly do nothing to end it now, and neither, it appeared, would the duke, for the happy moment endured for several minutes, interrupted only by the appearance of his groom.

"Cor blimey, miss," Jenkins said when he saw her condition, revealing that he had never believed the fiction of Mr. Wright. "Uh...I mean, sir. Or...um, mister. Whose fist did ye run into?"

As the groom helped her to her feet, she said, "I believe the fist ran into me."

Jenkins shook his head. "You gonna have a pair of shiners as bad as Fits McKinney's in '08."

"Fits McKinney?" Bea said to Kesgrave, flinching when her attempt to raise an eyebrow resulted in an angry throb.

"Prizefighter," he explained as he opened the door to the carriage. "Won a few matches but got knocked out in a brutal bout against Belcher. It was a devastating blow for Jenkins, who had laid a large bet on him."

The groom sighed heavily, shook his head and proclaimed that he'd lost a small fortune.

Bea promptly expressed her sympathy, which caused the duke to tut disapprovingly because, as he explained, the lesson had been a salutary one, for every man must learn to wager only what he could afford to lose.

"Right ye are, Duke," Jenkins said. "Right ye are."

Once they were settled in the coach, Kesgrave asked her to describe her attacker, a task that proved impossible for her. The only positive piece of information she could provide was that he was a man, and even that certainty fell apart when he asked her how she knew.

"It happened so quickly," she said. "He came at me from the side, tossing me to the ground before I even realized he'd punched me in the face. And then he was on top of me, hands around my throat, warning me to stay away, before running off. I can't imagine the whole thing took more than half a minute."

"He had his hands around your throat?" Kesgrave asked quietly.

"Only briefly," she said, "and only to underscore his point that I should stay away. But stay away from what? He did not say. It's a reference to the Fazeley matter, of course, but then why didn't he take the manuscript? Surely, that's the source of any animus anyone felt toward the earl."

Bea looked at Kesgrave—still a blurry figure across from her on the other seat but more in focus now that she was accustomed to the limits of her vision—to see if he had any suggestions. Instead of offering any useful ideas, he said, "He threatened to kill you."

Somehow he said the words in a way that was more dire than the incident itself. "Well, yes, technically he did. But I don't think it was so much a threat of death as a warning to preempt the need for more extreme action. As an attempt to do that, however, it misses its mark, for I don't know what I'm supposed to stay away from. It would have served the villain's purpose better to be less enigmatic."

The duke shook his head at her staunchly nonchalant reply and said peevishly, "I do wish you would show a little more concern about the welfare of your person."

Although she knew what he was referring to, she refused to let herself be drawn into a conversation about her safety. The only solution he could advise was her removing herself from the situation, and she was not willing to do that. "Rest assured, concern for my welfare occupies a very large part of my mind. Even now, as I try to figure out what my attacker meant by 'stay away,' I'm consumed with worry about how I will explain my appearance to Aunt Vera—the bruises as well as my cousin's clothes—and what kind of punishment I will endure. If my family does not consign me to the maniac ward at Bedlam, they will send me to Welldale House, where you will never hear from me again. There, your grace, that neatly solves your other problem, for I will be safe from assault in the country. I almost suspect my attacker is working in concert with my family to permanently remove me from London."

Something of her distress must have communicated itself to him, for he surprised her by taking the matter of her banishment seriously. "We can at least arrange for a change of clothing to mitigate your offenses."

The proposal was so charmingly naïve in its understanding of society and the world, Bea grinned widely and didn't even mind the pain. "Can you imagine my aunt's horror if I were to suddenly appear in a dress she has never seen before? Truly, I can't imagine what she would think, but it would not bode well for my future. Bedlam might be too optimistic."

"I cannot believe your thinking is anything but histrionic," he announced.

She looked at him sorrowfully. "If I do not comprehend what it means to be a duke, then you do not comprehend what it means to be an unmarried young lady. If I tell you appearing before my aunt in a brand-new dress is worse than appearing before her in men's clothing, then pray do me the courtesy of believing it."

"Very well," he said, brusquely. "Another approach. Perhaps a bribe? Jewelry has long been known to make unpleasant news more palatable. We could stop at the jeweler and pick up a trinket."

At the word *trinket*, Bea straightened in her seat and stared at the duke as Miss Cornyn's necklace flashed in her mind. "Of course. Of course," she said excitedly, leaning forward to see his face better as she revealed the truth. "It *was* a ruby. The necklace Miss Cornyn was wearing, did you not notice it? It was simple but stunning. Something about it seemed oddly familiar, and I just realized it's because it matches the description given by the earl in his diary. Recall that according to his own account he conducted several affairs at once and always ended the relationship by bestowing on the discarded young lady a ruby necklace with a pear-shaped pendant."

"He seduced Miss Cornyn," Kesgrave said, understanding perfectly.

"Yes, and when he ended the affair he gave her the usual gift as consolation, which Mr. Hill recognized from the manuscript," she said.

"Mr. Hill?" he asked in surprise.

"It had to be he. According to Mr. Cornyn, he's a circumspect reader who notices details. I wager he read the memoir, recognized the necklace from the description and stabbed Lord Fazeley in the back as an act of revenge," she said. "He's clearly in love with Miss Cornyn. You saw how he reacted to me when he thought I was flirting with her."

"Stay away," he murmured. "Hill was warning off the lecherous Mr. Wright."

She nodded. "Yes, yes. He's a young man with a deep well of rage and little ability to control it. How galling it must have been for him to see the earl there in the office, refusing to return the small amount Mr. Cornyn had advanced him on expectation of a publishable manuscript. Fazeley had taken so much from them already. This additional insult was more than he could stand, and unable to contain his fury one moment longer, he followed the earl to the Strand and viciously stabbed him in public."

If Kesgrave was taken aback by her gruesome description, he did not reveal it. Rather, he found her reasoning convincing and agreed it was likely that events had unfolded exactly as she'd described.

"Tell Jenkins to go back," she said, suddenly agitated. "We must turn around at once."

"Turn around?" he said in wonder. "Now? But you need a cold compress for your bruises before they get worse, and you are in a tremendous amount of pain and in need of rest. We can come back tomorrow. Mr. Hill will still be there."

"In need of rest?" she scoffed, insulted by the suggestion that she would be so missish as to take to her bed when there was a murderer to be confronted. "I was punched in the face, your grace, not woken from a deep sleep in the middle of the night. Do not waste any more time. Inform Jenkins of our change in plans and let us return right away. Unless you think we should collect a Runner first. I will leave that for you to decide as you handled the matter during our last investigation."

Kesgrave wanted to argue. She didn't have to see his face clearly to know he objected strongly to her plan, for it was apparent in the taut silence in the carriage and the stiff way he held himself. Ultimately, it was his choice to make, as her resources were constrained and she could certainly not hail a hack with her face swollen and purple.

After a long moment—needlessly drawn out, as far as she was concerned—he finally nodded in assent and said, "All right, I will inform Jenkins. But I want something from you in return."

Relieved, Bea nodded eagerly and slid forward in her seat. "Yes, of course. Anything."

"You must promise to cease investigating these horrible deaths that keep crossing your path," he said seriously.

She stared at him, unable to believe he would use such an underhanded method to achieve his goal. "I expected better of you, your grace, than to seek to curtail my freedom with unfair conditions."

"In the pursuit of two villains, you have found yourself twice brutalized," he said curtly. "First, you were struck over the head with a wooden plank and locked in an abandoned shed, from which you had to escape by thrashing a hole in its wall, and second, you were assaulted on a city street in the middle of the day by a man who threatened to strangle you. If you persist in this folly, you will get yourself killed and that I cannot abide."

Kesgrave spoke coolly, dispassionately, like a tutor explaining an algebra equation to a student, and yet her heart fairly leaped from her chest when he announced he could not abide the thought of her death.

You are a fool, she thought, annoyed that she could interpret for even a moment the most general display of concern for a fellow human being as a personal admission of tragedy and loss.

Annoyed now with both of them, she considered his proposal carefully and wondered what cost it would actually exact from her. Stumbling across two dead bodies over the course of little more than four months was extraordinary enough. Did she really think it would happen a third time?

No, of course not.

Truly, if it did happen again, she would start to believe the problem had something to do with her and consign herself to the ward for lunatics at Bedlam.

Ultimately, the promise he sought from her was empty.

But as worthless as the promise was, it wasn't entirely meaningless, for making it implied he had a right to restrict her movements when he in fact had no rights over her at all. Furthermore, it meant that if the highly implausible, almost impossible event did somehow happen for a third time, she would not be free to pursue it. She would be honor bound by a promise she had given under duress.

Was one obliged to honor a promise one gave under duress?

Yes, devil it, one was.

But not, she realized, to those things that aren't specifically mentioned in the promise itself. If she vowed to cease investigating deaths that crossed her path, it still left her free to investigate all those deaths she had to seek out herself.

Did she plan on seeking out deaths to investigate? Of course not. But the option remained open to her, and that was what was important.

"Very well," she said, sighing with excessive heft to make sure he understood the weight of the concession. "I promise to cease investigating the horrible deaths that keep crossing my path. There, your grace, are you satisfied? May we now proceed to Sylvan Press so that we may hold Mr. Hill responsible for the brutal slaying of Lord Fazeley? Or do you have other promises you would like to extract through devious means?"

"No others," he said mildly. "Just the one to ensure you don't meet a grisly end at the hands of a vicious killer."

"For the record, I find your high-minded condescension to be just as irritating as your usual sort," she said.

He professed surprise that she didn't find it *more* irritating.

She scowled at the taunt, a meager effort with her swelling, and resisted the urge to respond. Instead, she stared calmly out the window as he instructed the driver on their new destination. As they were returning to Catherine Street posthaste, she concluded he had decided against the necessity of a Runner. She imagined it was a reasonable decision, as it would be far easier to bring charges against a clerk at a publishing concern than a member of the peerage, and if the killer should decide to flee, the Duke of Kesgrave had the resources to find him and deliver him to justice.

They arrived back at the offices of the Sylvan Press only forty-five minutes after they had departed, and much was the way they'd left it. Mr. Cornyn was standing at the counter by the front door, his head close in conference with Mr. Hill as they examined the pages of an illustrated manuscript. Miss Cornyn, her neck still swathed in the beautiful necklace, sat at one of the desks, her eyes focused on a ledger as she recorded information in neat columns.

All three gasped when they saw Beatrice.

Miss Cornyn rushed over to offer succor, Mr. Cornyn swore in surprise, and Mr. Hill shrunk back in horror.

"I apologize if Mr. Wright's appearance startled you," the duke said solicitously. "I did everything I could to dissuade him from returning, but he was adamant that we finish our business here immediately and I was forced to agree. It is always better to conclude unpleasantness as quickly as possible."

"But what happened to put him in such a condition?" Mr. Cornyn asked confounded. "Did your carriage overturn? Were you assaulted by a pickpocket? Never say you caused this yourself with clumsiness."

"There must be something we can do to help with the swelling," his daughter said, looking at Bea, then Kesgrave. "Perhaps some ice? It helps with my father's joints, which ache from time to time."

Mr. Hill remained silent, and Bea wished her vision was better so she could see the fear in his eyes. He knew exactly why they had returned.

"Please don't make a fuss," Bea said, assuring them her injuries were the result of a minor accident and hardly bothered her now. "We are here for one purpose and one purpose only: to apprehend Mr. Hill for the murder of Robert Hanson Crestwell, Earl of Fazeley. I hope you will come without a struggle, but the duke's coachman is on hand to assure your compliance."

Although Jenkins stepped forward to make his presence felt, none of the occupants in the small office paid him any attention. Mr. Hill's face whitened to such an alarming degree even Bea could see the difference with her diminished perspective, and he looked around in every direction, as if compulsively examining the scene. Mr. Cornyn launched into an interrogation of the duke, demanding why he would let a lackey make such an astounding and erroneous accusation. Miss Cornyn began to sob at once and chant, "No, no, no, no."

"You are clearly a man of pronounced intelligence, so I do not understand why you would allow your steward to spew such nonsensical drivel," Mr. Cornyn said.

"No, no, no," Miss Cornyn wailed, her hands in fists as tears wet her beautiful face.

"Indeed, it's your duty to restrain your servants from behaving in disgraceful ways in public," he continued, "which is something even the most lettuce-headed turnip knows."

"No, no, no."

"And to permit him to make this astounding accusation *here*," Mr. Cornyn added, his tone a mix of surprise and disgust, "in the presence of my daughter, a delicate young woman who has done nothing to deserve such distress, is above all things—"

"No!" Miss Cornyn said, her voice trembling as the scream tore from her. "It was me. I did it. I murdered Lord Fazeley."

CHAPTER TWELVE

In the silence that followed Miss Cornyn's stunning admission, Beatrice tried to reorder her thoughts to make them align with the new information. It took very little imagination to come up with a reason why the beautiful young woman would want the rakish lord dead, for he had taken her innocence and then callously tossed her aside when the affair grew tedious. Perhaps she had learned from reading his memoir that she was one of an assortment and not the special bloom he had sworn her to be.

Just another plucked rose in a bouquet of plucked roses.

How she must have seethed with anger at that discovery, her fury growing and growing until she could no longer contain it, and after a meeting with her father in which the high and mighty Lord Fazeley was informed his prose was not adequate, she decided to drive the knife deeper by driving in the knife.

It made perfect sense, she realized.

"No," Mr. Hill said, his face suddenly swamped with color. "I did it."

Mr. Cornyn looked at both of them as if they had each lost their mind, and Jenkins muttered, "Cor blimey."

"He's lying," Miss Cornyn said with deathly calm, entirely in control of herself. Even the tears ceased to fall. "I killed him because he was a heartless cad. He seduced and abandoned me, and for that he had to pay."

"Good God, what?" shrieked her father.

Both confessors ignored the deeply shocked proprietor of the Sylvan Press and stared at each other imploringly.

"No, Miss Cornyn," Mr. Hill said firmly, "I killed Lord Fazeley because he was a heartless cad. He seduced and abandoned you, and for that he had to pay."

But Miss Cornyn could not let it stand and turned to Kesgrave to plea for her own guilt. "Please, your grace, do not listen to him. He's only trying to save me, but I don't deserve to be saved. I have been willful and wicked, and I deserve any punishment that comes my way."

Mr. Hill took several steps toward the duke and said, "Consider it, your grace. Miss Cornyn is too sweet and delicate to have done this evil act. But you know I'm not. You know I attacked Mr. Wright in the street not half an hour ago. You know it. I could see it in your eyes the moment you stepped into the office."

Miss Cornyn let out a strangled cry as she looked first at Bea's bruised face and then at her father's associate. She began to cry again. "But why, Mr. Hill? Why would you do such an awful thing to that poor man?"

He shook his head, as if unable to explain, then said, "It was a mistake. A horrible mistake. I saw the way he looked at you and responded with fury. White-hot fury. I feared he would hurt you the way the earl hurt you. See, Miss Cornyn, I am no good. Let me go to the gallows for you to atone for my sin. It would be an honor."

This sentiment, so sincerely expressed, only confounded the young lady. *"For* me? But I didn't do it."

Mr. Hill pulled his head back in surprise. "You didn't?"

"No, I was trying to go to the gallows for *you,*" she explained. "You killed him because of me, because of my credulity and stupidity. I could not let you hang for that. The sin is on my soul. I cannot add to it by letting you die for an act of misplaced gallantry that I drove you to. Do not ask me to bear it, for it is beyond bearing."

"I didn't do it," Mr. Hill said.

The adamant young pair stared at each other as if nothing in the world made sense.

What a ridiculous turn of events, Bea thought.

"If I may hazard to explain what is going on right now," she said, struggling in her disappointment to hold on to her patience, "it is this: Mr. Hill, Miss Cornyn believed you were the perpetrator of this heinous crime and confessed to spare you punishment. Miss Cornyn, Mr. Hill believed you were the perpetrator of this heinous crime and confessed to spare *you* punishment. Neither one of you murdered Lord Fazeley, and unless I miss my mark, you both care for each other deeply. You might want to take up the matter privately between the two of you later, assuming, of course, that you have your father's permission." Bea spared a glance at the publisher, who still seemed incapable of digesting the fact that his daughter had been seduced and abandoned by the earl. Clearly, he had no idea the event had occurred.

Despite Bea's very practical suggestion that they wait until they were alone to discuss their feelings in a more favorable setting, Mr. Hill would not be denied. He rushed to Miss Cornyn and said, "Is it true, my love? Do you care for me? Is it possible?"

Miss Cornyn blushed prettily, nodded shyly, her eyes tilted down, and insisted that she did care for him. Quite dreadfully. "But surely you can't care for me after...after...after I ruined myself."

"All you did was fall prey to a scoundrel who knew exactly how to woo an innocent like you," he said in her defense. "I could no more hold that against you than the sun for shining. But if you do not pine for him, why do you wear his necklace? Naturally, I assumed you wore it as a token to remind you of him and your great love."

Although Bea thought this was a logical supposition, as she herself had drawn the same conclusion, Miss Cornyn found it quite surprising. "I wear it because it's beautiful and I like the way it sparkles. But if you'd prefer not to see it, we can sell it to a jeweler. It's probably quite valuable, and we can use the money to buy a little house."

With this sundry detail nicely arranged, the duke reached his limit and announced it was time to go. "I have indulged you, Miss"—he broke off at Jenkins's cough, suddenly aware of what he had been about to do, and changed course—"Mr. Wright, but enough is enough. This afternoon has not turned out as any of us expected, especially Mr. Cornyn, who must now assimilate many uncomfortable truths. Let us have the decency to allow him to do so in private."

Bea, who tried and failed to find consolation in the fact that she had inadvertently united a pair of hapless lovers, agreed there was little reason to linger. Remaining in the office served no purpose other than to remind her of how wildly off the mark she had been in her conclusions. If thinking she was clever enough to identify a murderer made her giddy, then realizing she was not made her forlorn.

It was only a temporary setback, of course, for they still had the manuscript and she was as convinced as ever that its pages held the secret to the mystery. Given the earl's clutch-fisted miserliness—his refusal to deal fairly with either Lord Duncan or Mr. Cornyn—she thought blackmail was still a likely possibility. Despite the publisher's insistence that there was nothing interesting in Fazeley's tedious accounting of shirt collars and fish servings, she felt confident she would find something. Perhaps the monotonous details formed a code that revealed secret information to a foreign power such as France.

Outlandish, yes, Bea thought, but one never knew for sure what depravity hid in the hearts of men.

Determined to resume her investigation at once, perhaps even in the carriage if the duke did not take offense at being ignored, she made her goodbyes to the occupants of the cramped office. To Miss Cornyn, she offered her best wishes on the happy prospect of her upcoming nuptials, for which, she felt certain, the bans would be posted in the coming week. To Mr. Cornyn, she held out her hand to shake, desiring some sort of physical contact with the poor man, who seemed incapable of comprehending the loss of his daughter's virtue. To Mr. Hill, she bid a brusque good day from several feet away. Although his affecting scene with Miss Cornyn had convinced her he wasn't quite the dyed-in-the-wool villain his vicious assault had indicated, she felt more than a tinge of fear in his presence. She could not look at him and fail to recall the way his fingers had squeezed her neck.

Kesgrave, it appeared, suffered from the same defect, for when he approached Mr. Hill to say goodbye, he fisted his right hand and rammed it into the other man's eye. The associate's head swung back, reeling from the force of the punch, as Bea gasped and Miss Cornyn cried out. In anticipation of a second blow, Mr. Hill rounded his shoulder, making himself smaller as he seemed to shrink into his shirt like a turtle vanishing into its shell.

Suddenly, as if struck herself, Bea gasped again as she remembered the turtle she had glanced on Mr. Cornyn's forearm. Now, finally, she understood everything.

"I know who killed Lord Fazeley," she announced loudly, forgetting in her agitation over the truth to use Mr. Wright's appropriately masculine tenor.

'Twas no large matter, however, for nobody heard her over Miss Cornyn's pleas to Kesgrave to stop beating Mr. Hill and Jenkins's staunch defense that his employer was only returning fair for fair.

"If ye don't want yer man to get beaten up, tell yer man to stop beating up helpless wo…uh, Wrights. Defenseless Mr. Wrights and any other stewards in the duke's employ," the groom said, ending his eloquent defense on an awkward note.

"Thank you, Jenkins, for that well-reasoned argument," Kesgrave said with an appreciative nod at his groom. Then he turned to Miss Cornyn, who was cradling Mr. Hill's head against her bosom, an act that provoked a glare from her father. "I must apologize for distressing you with my rough treatment of your beloved," he said gently, "but given that only a few minutes ago he was willing to go to the gallows to expatiate his guilt over unfairly abusing Mr. Wright, I should think a few jabs to the face seems benign in comparison. But I could be wrong. Would he prefer to try the other and report back on his findings?"

Having not committed a capital offense, Mr. Hill stood in no real danger of being subjected to a hangman's noose, and yet the expression on Kesgrave's face, rigid and hard, stated otherwise. With a cock of his head and a word in the right ear, he could arrange the matter as easily as ordering dinner.

For Bea, it was a truly terrifying moment, for it was the instant when she finally understood who the Duke of Kesgrave really was. He was a man endowed by his creator with power and influence few could dream of possessing. She'd thought his authority came from the sycophancy of a beau monde unable to resist the lure of money and status combined in a pleasing form. But in her naïveté she had gotten it backward, for it was very much the other way around: Authority demanded compliance.

Miss Cornyn, thoroughly chastened, did not bother to answer the question, which she knew to be rhetorical. Mr. Hill, however, straightened his shoulders, looked Kesgrave in the eye and apologized for harming Mr. Wright, as if the injury had been done to the duke and not his steward.

Although she took exception to the misplaced apology on principle, Bea had more important matters to discuss. "I know who killed Fazeley," she said again, this time ensuring her voice aligned with her identity.

As she had already made the exact claim with the same conviction earlier in the day, she expected cynicism and doubt from Kesgrave. Instead, he nodded briskly and said, "Of course you do. Please proceed."

Was he mocking her, Bea wondered, or showing an alarming degree of respect for her abilities?

No, not alarming, she told herself, for she had earned his esteem, if indeed that was what he was displaying.

"The mistake we made, your grace, was assuming his murder had something to do with the contents of the book," Bea explained. "But it was far simpler than that. Having been rejected by Mr. Cornyn—and there is no way to describe the wholesale dismissal of his chronicle of everyday life as anything other than personal rejection—Fazeley determined to get revenge on the publisher by reporting his whereabouts to the Navy Office in Somerset House. He is a deserter, you see, and still subject to punishment."

Demonstrating none of the deference they'd exhibited to the duke, the pair of lovers roundly turned on Bea and strenuously objected to her wrongheaded conclusions.

"It's a fiction so preposterous not even Sylvan would countenance it. My father was never in the navy," Miss Cornyn insisted. "He assumed control of this publishing house from my grandfather as soon as he finished his apprenticeship with a printer in Blackfriar. Indeed, he has never even left the confines of London."

"It's true," Mr. Hill said. "He couldn't have been in the navy. He gets frightfully seasick. He can't even look at a picture of the ocean without turning green around the gills. You are looking in the wrong place, Mr. Wright."

Beatrice turned to the publisher, who had uttered no words in his own defense, and asked if he would please roll up his sleeve to display his turtle tattoo. He complied silently while his daughter grumbled that such an action was a waste of time, for she had seen the tattoo upon innumerable occasions in her life and it was hardly remarkable, as many people had such ornamentations.

"It can have nothing to do with your ludicrous and unfair accusation," Miss Cornyn huffed.

"Do you want to explain?" Bea asked.

His face grim, Mr. Cornyn took a deep breath and let out a great sigh. "It means I've crossed the equator."

Miss Cornyn stared at her father, her almond eyes

vacuous and confused. "I don't understand. How could you have crossed the equator if you've never left London?"

Her father looked helplessly at Bea, then Kesgrave, and then turned his back so he was facing the front door. "I was in the navy. It was an argument with my father. A vicious argument. From the day I was born, all he wanted was for me to learn the publishing business and take over the firm. But I wanted something different. I thought I wanted to travel and see what was out there in the world and decide for myself what I wanted to be. So after a particularly brutal row, I ran away and joined the navy. Life in the navy wasn't...I wasn't..." He shook his head as he struggled to find the words to describe the experience. "It wasn't a good match, for the work didn't suit me and I didn't suit the work. I served only two years of a twelve-year commitment. When we pulled into a port in India, I stayed behind. I remained in Madras just long enough to earn my fare home and then boarded a cargo ship to return. Runners are common in the navy. Most men simply stay behind at a port like I did, and the master-at-arms is too busy tracking them down to find us all. An officer called here only once to find me and that was before I returned. I've felt safe here ever since."

"Until Lord Fazeley made his threat," Bea said softly.

The publisher lowered his head. "Yes. I don't know how he figured it out. His writing suggests a shallow man who doesn't notice anything that doesn't directly concern him. And yet his powers of observation were highly developed. I didn't realize he knew until on his way out, when he made a rude gesture and said, 'You know what I call that? The rogue's salute.' And then he left, but I knew where he was going."

"Rogue's salute?" Bea asked as Miss Cornyn began to weep in earnest, which was only to be expected. It had been, by any account, an extremely trying afternoon for the young woman.

"Navy cant," he said, "for the gun fired to signal a court martial."

"And the knife?" she asked.

"Fell in the tussle," Mr. Cornyn explained. "He didn't notice and neither did I until after he had left. Honestly, when I picked it up off the floor, my intention was merely to return it to him. Even as I was running after him, I thought only of giving it back and taking the opportunity to reason with him. I was fully prepared to give the manuscript back without compensation, and I thought returning the dagger would demonstrate my good intentions because it was a very fine weapon and probably worth several thousand pounds. But when I saw him, his burgundy coat in the crowd on the Strand, I thought how simple it would be to make the problem go away. Just a quick, deep stab like they taught us in the navy, and it would all be over." Now tears began to trickle down his face, slowly at first, one then the other, and then in torrents. His daughter walked over and grasped his hand so tightly her fingers turned white. "So I did it and I ran and it seemed like it was all over. Even when the duke's steward inquired about the manuscript, I still thought it was done. I believed your interest was sparked by the gossip and you feared an embarrassing revelation. It never occurred to me, you see, that a duke would be involved in investigating a murder."

Here, Bea felt a perverse urge to apologize, for it was her fault Kesgrave was involved in investigating a murder. If she had shown no interest, he would have shown no interest, and she would not have been able to follow where the information led without his help.

Unable to withstand any more, his daughter lowered her head and pressed it against their clasped fingers. "I'm sorry, Papa. I'm so sorry."

Her guilt at having succumbed to the seductions of the man who would have destroyed her father was all consuming, but the publisher, running his hand over her soft hair, assured her he was grateful to know the truth.

"Truly, my darling, you have no idea how much remorse and shame I have felt at my actions. I gave into a moment of evil impulse and have regretted it ever since. But now, you see, I have nothing to regret," he insisted with a smile devoid of humor. "He was a heartless cad, a blackguard, and he deserved to die for what he did to you. It makes me free in a way I never expected to be again. Please believe that, my darling girl. Please, please believe that and suffer no more guilt." But his pleas only made her sob harder, and he raised her shoulders so he could envelop her in a hug. "Hush, now, my darling, hush. You will be all right. Clarence will take care of you. He has loved you for a long time. I've known it and worried you could never return his regard. But you do and it will be well. All will be well. There, there, now, hush."

Bea watched the father comfort his disconsolate daughter, and an irrational need to apologize rose again in her breast. The sense of responsibility she felt for the scene before her was baffling, for it was not of her making. She was not the one who had raised the jade dagger and driven it into Lord Fazeley's back.

And yet it was entirely of her making, for it was doubtful the authorities would have traced the dagger back to the British Museum and ultimately to the victim himself. Perhaps they would have followed the rumor of a forthcoming manuscript or discovered the drawer full of love letters and assumed the villain had been a woman scorned.

There were many possibilities as to how events might have unfolded but only this moment was certain, and for that she felt awful.

But she believed in order and the sanctity of life and Mr. Cornyn, despite the mistakes he'd made in his early years, did not have the right to decide who lived and who died. For that he must bear responsibility.

Only Bea did not want to be part of the retribution and longed to leave the little office as quickly as possible. Although she had assured the duke earlier that her bruises barely bothered her, now that the urgency of identifying the killer had passed, they pained her quite dreadfully.

Her face stung, her head throbbed, and her heart ached.

With no idea how to extricate herself from the situation, she looked at Kesgrave with what she feared was desperation. Immediately perceiving the problem, perhaps because he felt it just as keenly, he nodded at Jenkins and quietly asked his groom to allow Mr. Cornyn to take as much time as he needed to get his affairs in order before accompanying him to Newgate.

Jenkins gave the plan his prompt approval, adding that he had been about to suggest the very same thing. "The poor miss."

Kesgrave thanked him and turned next to Mr. Hill, who watched the father and daughter comfort each other with misery on his battered face. He murmured something to the young man, who nodded vehemently and sadly before bowing deeply. Then the duke joined Bea by the counter and confirmed with a nod that they may depart.

Bea expected her spirits to improve the moment she stepped outside, but the sense that a heavy cloud hung over her remained. Kesgrave must have felt it too because he didn't say anything right away, instead studying his coach-and-four with a thoughtful expression.

"As Jenkins is not here to drive, the task falls to me," he said, "and I think you would have a more enjoyable experience if you sat up front with me rather than alone in the carriage."

Bea promptly agreed to this arrangement, for the prospect of a solitary coach ride was just as dreary as the duke implied. Furthermore, there was no harm to be done to either of their reputations because she was still dressed as a man—a thoroughly bashed-up man with two black eyes, certainly, but a man nonetheless. She climbed up with Kesgrave's help and settled in for the brief ride back to her aunt's house.

Once Kesgrave had the team in hand and merged with the traffic on Catherine Street, he said, "If I hadn't already extracted a promise from you to stop investigating horrible deaths, I would do so at once. You must not keep exposing yourself to dreadful scenes like that one. It is far too disheartening."

Although Bea agreed with this assessment, as repetitive exposure to such dismal displays would have a wearying effect on even the most cheerful person's temperament, she took exception to his tone, for he sounded far too satisfied with himself. "That cross my path," she said.

"Excuse me?" he said.

"I pledged to cease investigating the horrible deaths that cross my path," she explained, her mood lightening a little as she felt the warmth of the sun on her face. The ache in her head continued unabated, but the one in her heart started to subside. "That was the promise you extracted and the promise by which I will abide."

"I cannot perceive a distinction," he said as he urged his team around a curricle that was stopped in the middle of the road.

"I know, your grace, and for that I'm grateful," she said, before commending him on his skill as a whipster. It was a diversionary tactic, to be sure, but also a sincere compliment, for she had long admired men who could control four high-steppers at once. "Are you a member of the Four Horse Club?"

"I am not, no," he said, "for I find the idea of aping the ways and dress of my coachman to be more insult than homage. I have far too much respect for Jenkins to submit him to that injury. Now do stop trying to distract me and explain what you mean by horrible deaths that *cross your path*. You do not mean that you will *seek out* horrible deaths to investigate."

The outraged horror in his tone made Bea laugh, something she had not thought possible only a few moments before, and she winced when the cut in her lip smarted. "How would I go about that, your grace?"

She posed her denial as a question in order to underscore the utter ridiculousness of his suggestion. At the same time, however, it was a legitimate query, for she had no idea how one would go about finding unusual deaths to investigate. She wondered what method the Bow Street Runners had contrived to stay abreast of public crime and if that technique was available to private citizens.

Recognizing the ambiguity of her response, Kesgrave pressed for a firm disavowal, which Bea evaded by discussing her long-cherished desire to learn how to drive a team of four. For each insistence he made for a straightforward answer, she reminisced about another sedate nag she was forced to endure at Welldale House. There were so many retired hacks to catalog, she didn't have to invent a single one, although she was thoroughly prepared to do so if necessary. She was enjoying the exchange far too much to let it end a moment before they arrived at her home, for it allowed her to forget both the immediate past and the immediate future. For a little while, she was free of Mr. Cornyn's tragic decisions and Mr. Wright's battered face.

Inevitably, the coach stopped in front of Aunt Vera's town house, and Bea insisted on climbing down on her own. The moment of their separation had arrived, and she wanted the break to be as clean as possible. The thought of his treating her with the courtesy due any young woman in his company was intolerable to her, for she longed to be more than just any young woman. That was clear to her now as she contemplated the severing of their bond. With the apprehension of Lord Fazeley's murderer, they had no cause to further their association. Kesgrave was free to set up his nursery with an Incomparable of impeccable breeding, and she was free to return to a life of quiet occupation.

They would meet again, of course, for the season was just getting started and they would frequently be at the same parties and balls. But their interactions would bear no mark of familiarity. They would be sterile and polite and contain none of the informality or intimacy of a sidewalk on the Strand.

That thought made Bea desperately sad.

She'd been so sure she was in no real danger from the

duke, so confident that her feelings were mild and measured and easily resolved. And yet when he'd threatened Mr. Hill with certain execution, when he'd revealed the true extent of his power, it had thrown into stark relief the inadequacies of her situation. This man who had been born to privilege in a way she could barely conceive would never love her.

What of it, she'd thought in brazen defiance.

But as defiant as she was, her heart knew the truth and fluttered wildly in despair.

It was love—pure, simple, disastrous.

'Twas laughable that she could come to this. Nothing in her life of deliberate appeasement and docility had prepared her for such immoderate extremity. Indeed, it still seemed vaguely impossible to her that she had strayed so far from the path of entrenched practicality she had walked for the first six and twenty years of her life.

At least now she had something to mourn properly, she thought mockingly, determined not to wallow in the tragic turn her life had suddenly taken. As was her practice, she would be amused and diverted by the ridiculousness of the situation.

Middling Beatrice Hyde-Clare in love with the high-flying Duke of Kesgrave. It was the apogee of a very good joke.

Kesgrave frowned at her refusal to accept his help but stepped back and allowed her to dismount the carriage on her own. Once they were both firmly on the ground, she held out her hand as a sign of respect and an indication that she considered them equals. She'd expected resistance, but the duke, either recognizing the meaning of the gesture or being far too sensible to argue with a battered woman, took her hand in his own.

Too exhausted from the day's travails to have any self-respect left, Bea allowed herself to relish the pleasure of his firm grip, succumbing momentarily, fleetingly, to the exquisite ache of the hopelessness of her passion.

As absurd as the whole thing was, she took some comfort in knowing how high her standards were. All those clergymen and third sons Aunt Vera had thrown at her head had never stood a stance.

With his hand still clutched in hers, she offered her gratitude with an honest simplicity no one could possibly doubt. "Thank you, Damien. I could not have arrived at the truth without you."

She expected him to respond with amusement—either sincere or mocking—at her daring to use his name, but he regarded her steadily and said with equal gravity. "You're welcome, Beatrice. It was my privilege."

Both observations were fitting tributes, and since they seemed to leave no thought unsaid, Bea withdrew her hand from his grip and turned to walk up the path to her uncle's house. She knew it did not sit well with him to let a young lady subject herself to the harsh criticism of her family without making an effort to mitigate their judgment, and she considered it a sign of his respect that he didn't attempt to intervene.

It was bittersweet, she thought, knowing that he understood so much about her and yet comprehended nothing at all.

Although the consequences of that day's revelations would have to be dealt with in the weeks and perhaps months to come, they lacked the urgency of two blackened eyes and an inappropriate outfit scandalously appropriated from her cousin's closet. Indeed, she was almost grateful for her bruised face because it gave her an ache to focus on that had nothing to do with her heart.

And focus on it she must, Bea thought as she strode up the stone path, for she was about to enter her uncle's house with no ready explanation to account for her unlikely appearance.

Even in her disheartened state, she could not bear the thought of conceding a battle without a fight, and at once her mind began to work on the problem. She was the clever young woman who had solved two murders. Surely, she could come up with a convincing fiction that would justify everything and earn her family's sympathy.

And yet, as she drew closer to the front door, her brain remained stubbornly blank.

Bea didn't panic or slow down her steps, and she resisted the almost overwhelming urge to glance back at the duke, who she knew was still watching, for she had yet to hear his horses pull away. No, she had only one option and that was to keep moving forward—along the path, up the stairs, into the house. It was all she'd had from the moment her dead parents' solicitor had deposited her on this very doorstep twenty years ago.

Calmly, deliberately, she climbed the steps and knocked on the door. Kesgrave's gaze was like an itch on the back of her neck, and she ordered herself to resist its pull.

You're stronger than that, she thought, as the door suddenly opened and Dawson's dulcet greeting was interrupted by his horrified gasp. Clearly, he had not expected to find a battered and bruised stranger standing on the threshold.

And it was then, when she read the horror and confusion on his face as he tried to figure out which stratagem to deploy to dispense with this unsightly invention she presented for his inspection, that she finally knew what to say: Mr. Davies's funeral.

ABOUT THE AUTHOR

Lynn Messina is the author of more than a dozen novels, including the best-selling *Fashionistas*, which has been translated into 16 languages. Her essays have appeared in *Self*, *American Baby* and the Modern Love column in the *New York Times*, and she's a regular contributor to the *Times* Motherlode blog. She lives in New York City with her sons.

Made in the USA
Columbia, SC
14 November 2019